MURDER
IN THE
MOUNTAINS

Jeremy Soldevilla

Christopher
Matthews
Publishing

www.christophermatthewspub.com
Bozeman, Montana

Also by Jeremy Soldevilla

Thief Creek

"The pace was fast and fantastic, the action non-stop..."
— A. Haar

Murder in the Mountains

Copyright © 2013 by Jeremy Soldevilla

Editor: Jeremy Soldevilla
Cover design: Armen Kojoyian
Typeface: Georgia

ISBN 978-1-938985-05-8

Published by
CHRISTOPHER MATTHEWS PUBLISHING
http://christophermatthewspub.com
Bozeman, Montana

Printed in the United States of America

To Melissa
a wonderfully generous and supportive wife.

Acknowledgments

My deepest thanks to The Bozeman Ink Slingers for their support, advice and wisdom in the creation of this book. A tip of the beaver skin cap to the members of the Bridger Mountain Men for inspiration and information. I also owe a debt of gratitude to my father and mother for instilling within me a love of books, writing and the West.

Chapter 1

JENNY FOLLOWED THE COW'S TRACKS in the muddy spring snow until it gave way to the greening pasture.

"Whoa." Her horse stopped its plodding pace and exhaled a cloud of vapor in the brisk mid-morning air.

She'd come as far up the mountain as the old ranger station. This was ridiculous.

"Damn cow," she swore under her breath. The horse's right ear flicked back to catch what she was saying.

Saddle leather creaked as she stood in the stirrups, scanning the landscape for any sign of the runaway bovine.

A chilly mountain breeze whispered through the timber, ruffling the horse's mane and causing Jenny to fasten the top button of her Carhartt jacket.

The horse's ears twitched forward and he lifted his head, his nostrils exploring the air.

At that same moment, Jenny caught a movement out of the corner of her eye. Is that the damn cow finally? She put her hand above her eyes and squinted to get a better look.

Far off, across the pasture, a dark form crouched behind a large pine tree. *That ain't no cow,* she thought. A slight shiver ran through her body, but no breeze was blowing.

The horse whinnied nervously.

Thoughts tumbled through her head. Who the heck is up here this time of year? What's he hiding for? Should I go check him out?

She heard her father's voice in her head. Jenny, mind your own damn business. Stick to your knittin'. If you got a job to do, get 'er done. Your job is to find that heifer and bring her home. Now git.

Jenny reined her horse to the right and moved on, throwing a brief look over her shoulder at the barely hidden man at the tree. Her horse's left ear trained back toward the man, but he dutifully continued in the other direction.

After a few more paces, Jenny turned for a last look up the hillside. She halted the horse and saw the man break from the timber, heading toward the cabin. Even at that distance she realized he was dressed in buckskin and had a large hump of something on his back. Another chill splintered down her spine. The heavy beard and long hair. She had a pretty good idea who that was.

She gently kicked her horse into a trot and headed farther down the pasture.

They had only gone a few more yards when she suddenly stopped short and gasped.

Surrounded by a huge pool of blood lay her black Angus cow. Or, more accurately, what was left of it. An arrow protruded from its chest. Its gut pile lay still steaming next to the body. Half of the cow had been trimmed from the bone. A pair of black and white magpies, perched on the animal's exposed rib cage, tore at the meat and eyed her approach, loath to leave their feast. It wouldn't be long before bears or mountain lions showed up to gorge themselves on the half-finished corpse.

"You bastard!" she screamed back towards the ranger station, her voice echoing up the mountain.

She wheeled her horse around and jammed her heels into its sides, her anger and fear making her kick a little harder than she meant to. The horse, seeming to sense her urgency, picked up his pace and the two charged back down the mountain in the direction they had come from.

∾ ∾ ∾

TWENTY-SEVEN-YEAR-OLD JJ VOLKER peered up from his half-empty cup of cold coffee as did the other cowboys at the counter in the Wilsall Café when the cowbell hanging from the door announced the entrance of Park County Sheriff Colton Stollar. The cook, working in the kitchen, wiped a string of hair from her brow and glanced up from the spattering grease in the fryolater to see who had come in.

A hefty rancher shovelled the last of the cheeseburger into his mouth, dripping a glob of mayonnaise and ketchup onto his coveralls. A scrap of hamburger bun dropped in his lap as he greeted the new arrival, spewing chunks of his lunch into the air, "Afternoon, Sheriff!"

JJ watched Sheriff Stollar stride across the worn wooden floor, past the display of postcards and the humming Wilcoxson's Ice Cream freezer chest. The spotless uniform fit crisply on his six-foot-two frame. His silver badge gleamed like a brand new car's chrome. Craggy good looks, confident bearing and strength emanated from him in electrical waves. With a moustache drooping down the sides of his face, he looked approachable, but underneath the smile lay the aura of a self-assertive man not to be trifled with.

At the lunch counter, the waitress looked up from the coffee cup she was refilling and smiled broadly at the sheriff. She curled a wisp of hair behind her ear and smoothed her apron.

Removing his sunglasses and sliding them into his pocket, Stollar eased himself onto a stool, gave Laurie a wink and smiled back.

"Afternoon, Laurie!".

"Colton." She nodded and threw him a generous wink.

"You're looking gorgeous today. How are those steak fingers?"

"As good as they were when you had 'em yesterday and the day before that, Colton, and just as fresh as you are."

"Well, then I'll have them and a cup of that stuff you call coffee, please."

"You bet." She winked again and headed back to the kitchen, putting a little attitude in her hips.

The sheriff pushed back his Stetson and acknowledged the other lunch customers with a nod. "Hey, Tom. Charles."

"Sheriff." The two cowboys nodded back in unison.

"Howdy, JJ— how's Annie doing?"

At the end of the counter JJ glanced up from the coffee cup he'd gone back to staring into and narrowed his eyes. "About as good as can be expected with a dead sister, I guess."

An audible silence fell over the room and each diner stared down at his own plate of food.

Colton paused for a beat, then said, "Well, tell her I was asking about her."

"Sure, Colton." JJ glanced around the room and mumbled, "Sorry," then went back to staring into his coffee and stirring it idly with his thumb. A brooding helpless anger simmered in him.

Silence hung like a dark cloud until the door of the café burst open and slammed against the wall. Jenny Thompson rushed in and headed for Stollar.

Her no-nonsense entrance was made all the more clamorous by the cadence of long fringe edgings that slapped against her worn leather chinks as she clomped her muddy boots across the plank floor.

Jenny's freckled face was flushed with exertion and damp with specks of mud splattered across her tanned cheeks. "Sheriff!" she said breathlessly. "I seen him! I was chasing one of my cows up off Horseshoe Creek Road near the pass and I seen him running toward the old ranger station. I know it was him, so I rode straight here fast as I could. I figured you'd be eating lunch."

JJ looked up, his eyes narrowing with interest..

"Whoa, Jenny. Slow down." Stollar gestured with his hands. "Who are you talking about?"

"You know well as I do who I'm talking about. He had that long hippie hair, same scraggly long-ass beard, and that stupid fur cap. It was him. I know it was. He killed my damn cow. I think he saw me and was running to try and hide. You get your ass in gear you might be able to catch him."

Everyone stopped eating at once and turned toward the sheriff. Laurie stood motionless in front of him with a plate full of steak fingers and fries in one hand and a plastic ketchup bottle in the other, waiting as expectantly as the rest of the diners.

"Well," he said, speaking aloud to himself. "I won't be able to drive the patrol car up there in all that gumbo. I'll have to go back to Livingston to pick up the four-wheeler."

At this, JJ's fists balled on the counter top. "The hell with that, Colton," he said. "He'll be long gone by the time you get back. Run me up to the ranch and we can grab a couple of horses and chase down that son of a bitch."

Stollar turned toward JJ and appeared to be considering the offer.

"Well?" JJ pressed.

Stollar paused a beat before replying. "You might have a point , JJ. I don't like going up there without backup . . ."

"I'll be your damn backup, Colton," JJ said through gritted teeth.

Stollar looked at him impassively and continued. "I don't like going up there without back up, but you're right, we've had a hell of a time tracking him down, and this is the first sighting of him in months. Alright, JJ, let's go up to your place and I'll borrow one of your horses, but you aren't coming with me. I don't need any company."

JJ glared back into the sheriff's eyes, but didn't argue.

The sheriff's next words nudged the waitress into action again. "Sorry about that, Laurie. I'll have to pass on lunch today. Put 'em away for me and I'll have 'em tomorrow." Stollar grinned and winked at her then threw a five-dollar bill on the counter and tipped his hat forward to sit upright again

"You bet, Colton." Laurie smiled warmly back.

"Let's go, JJ."

Chapter 2

THE NOONDAY SUN WAS HIGH and hot. Puffy white clouds dotted the expansive blue Montana sky like giant sheep as far as the eye could see. In the distance, the snow-tipped tops of the Crazy Mountain range jutted upwards like the spiked spine of a sleeping dragon.

Sheriff Stollar pulled his sunglasses out of his shirt pocket and slipped them on as he crossed the street to his patrol car. He unlocked the door and started to get in, then, re-emerged and looked across the roof at JJ who was already trying to open the locked passenger side door. The brim of his hat shadowed his eyes, but JJ could see the look of concern in them.

"Now, JJ, I appreciate your offer on the horses and for going along with me, but I think it's best you stay home with Annie while I ride out to see what's what. Does that work for you?"

"I guess it will have to, won't it, Colton?" The tightly set lines of JJ's mouth said otherwise.

"I do think its best, John," he repeated, using the name he had called JJ when he was a boy. With a nod he tapped the roof of the car with his knuckles, smiled and got into the driver's seat. He unlocked the other door so JJ could enter.

As they pulled away from the parking area, spitting gravel and dust behind them, JJ clenched his fist and glared up at the mountains. The bastard was up there somewhere. If he could get that son of a bitch alone, he'd tear him apart limb by limb, as he'd done to Annie's little sister, Kaitlin, after he had . . .

"Beautiful day, isn't it?"

Ignoring the sheriff's attempt at casual chatter, JJ pressed his case. "Look, Colton, I don't think you should ride up there alone. That guy is crazy. You know what he did to Kaitie, for chrissake. No telling what could happen. I know what you're thinking, but I ain't gonna do anything stupid. Besides, it's been weeks. No one's been able to find him. It's like he's disappeared. I know the Crazies real well and him real well, and I might have a good chance of finding where he's hid. "

As they turned on to the ranch road, Stollar lifted the radio mic in one hand and looked at JJ. "Listen, son, this is police business. I have to do this by the book. We don't even know for sure that he's our man. I can't let anything happen to you or to him. Whoever did what they did to Kaitlin is a sick bastard. If anything was to go bad up there and something happened to you, how do you think Annie would handle it? She needs you, especially now."

JJ appraised the older man. The sheriff looked his part. JJ knew he was as old as his father, but his strong lean body belied his sixty years. He exuded confidence, strength and brains. If things got ugly up in the Crazies, Colton Stollar would be the right man to take care of it. And yet, JJ wanted his own shot at the sick creep. He deserved it, and neither Colton Stollar nor anyone else was going to deny him that satisfaction. JJ folded his arms and stared out the window, his jaw clenched.

The sheriff pressed the send button on his microphone. "Dispatch, this is Sheriff Stollar. We've had a possible sighting of the Cathcart suspect in the Crazy Mountains outside Wilsall. He was spotted running from the old ranger station up near Ibex. I'm borrowing a horse from the Volker ranch and heading up there."

A brief static crackling pause. "10-4, Colton. You want me to send Rolf up? He's the only one on today. Ben's up in Helena and Sharon's still out with the flu."

"Negative. I can't wait, and it would be a waste for him to try to follow me. I've got my cell with me. If I do bring this guy down I'll call once I'm in range and you can send him up to the Volker place to meet me."

"10-4, Sheriff."

Stollar replaced the mic and pulled into the yard sending two of JJ's dogs into a barking, tail-wagging frenzy. As the two men got out, an old white-muzzled black Labrador Retriever groaned and lifted his chubby body off the front steps of the ranch house and waddled toward the patrol car—his tail wagging the rest of him as he walked.

"I'll saddle up Chief for you, Colton. Won't take me but five minutes." With the decision to accompany the sheriff out of his hands, JJ headed off to the barn.

"You got a rifle scabbard you can throw on that saddle too?" Stollar called.

JJ turned and nodded at the sheriff. He watched him open the trunk and retrieve his 12-gauge shotgun. "You bet," he replied. "No problem." *I hope he gets to use that*, JJ thought.

Chapter 3

BRIDGER JACKSON SLIPPED the big knife out of its sheath and used it to pry up the floorboard in the cabin where he had hidden his cache. Not much to hide. An elk skin medicine bag which held a braid of sweetgrass, two stones—one buffalo-shaped and the other bear-shaped, a pipe made from the tip of a deer antler, a bald eagle's white head feather, a rattlesnake rattle, a beaver's tooth and a few dried herbs. Next to the medicine bag was a tattered Indian blanket roll that held a pair of greasy moccasins, a flint stone and steel, a rusty but serviceable beaver trap, a quarter bottle of whiskey and various types of jerky—deer, elk and antelope. A long strip of rawhide wrapped around the blanket held its contents tight and formed a carrying strap.

Ragged strands of hair got in his line of view as he scrabbled his hand in the hole searching for the other knife. He grunted impatiently and pulled his dirty grey hair into a ponytail, then tore a piece of fringe off his buckskin shirt and tied it back.

Not there.

Rising anxiety grew round the already tense feeling of urgency in his chest. The skinning knife had been handed down to him as a gift to his grandfather from Nez Perce Chief Joseph himself. A beautiful piece of craftsmanship kept razor sharp for over 100 years for gutting animals, fish and occasionally, men. The pang in his gut was more than sadness for the loss. It was panic.

The sparse cabin with no more than a fireplace and table as furnishings didn't take long to explore. The knife was gone.

Waugh. Time's a-wastin', he thought to himself. *That gal's probably most the ways back to Wilsall by now. Gotta make tracks.*

He gathered up the beef he'd managed to trim from the cow and stowed it with the rest of his gear.

Jackson draped the medicine bag around his neck and looped the blanket bundle over his head. He peered out the door of the ranger station, then darted across the muddy field and disappeared into the cover of the timber.

Chapter 4

JJ'S YOUNG WIFE Annie stepped into the yard when she heard the dogs making a ruckus. Her unkempt blond hair, like the haggard expression on her face, sagged dolefully. Although it was midday, she was still dressed in her slippers and pajamas over which she clutched a faded pink floral robe. Shielding her sunken eyes from the sun, she called out, "Hello, Sheriff. What brings you up here today?"

"Hi there, Annie." Stollar glanced toward the barn where JJ had disappeared. "I've got to go up in the Crazies and check something out. JJ was kind enough to lend me old Chief to get up through the mud."

Annie looked through sad, reddened eyes at the sheriff for a moment and said, "Well, you be careful up there. There's no telling who, what . . ." Her voice drifted into a choke. She turned away, biting her lip.

Stollar strode over and put a comforting arm around her. Turning her toward him, he enveloped her petite body in a hug. "Annie, I'm so sorry for your loss," he whispered to the trembling woman. Annie sobbed into his chest.

She turned her tear-damp face up to his. "Do they know anything more? Have they found anyone yet?"

"Not yet, but we're following up on some good leads. These things take time." Annie stared into Stollar's eyes to see if he was hiding the answer there. The sheriff held her gaze but revealed nothing. Annie nodded and turned away. She pulled a wadded tissue from her pocket, blew her nose and walked back into the house. The familiar slap-click of the screen door as it rocked back to the doorframe offered them both a nostalgic sound, but no comfort for what she had lost.

Stollar watched her go. He took a deep breath and sighed heavily. He turned toward JJ, who had come up behind him with the saddled Chief.

The sheriff slid the Remington into the stiff scabbard and checked the cinch before slipping his boot into Chief's stirrup and settling himself into the saddle. The well-oiled leather creaked as it molded to him for the ride. Adjusting the reins, he looked at JJ and said, "She's a good woman, your Annie. Take care of her."

JJ nodded, "Yes sir, I will. I put a couple of bottles of water in the saddle bag there for you."

"Thanks. I'll be back in a couple of hours." Stollar reined Chief toward the mountains, gave him a kick and trotted on his way.

Chapter 5

JJ WATCHED THE SHERIFF ride off until he was a speck in the distance. He launched a stream of spit into the dust at his feet and went into the barn, took a bridle off the peg and carried it over to Spot, a brown and white pinto, younger and spunkier than Chief. After slipping the bridle over Spot's ears, JJ led him out to the fence. The horse's nostrils flared and he stamped his front hoof as JJ threw a blanket and saddle onto his back.

Once he had saddled Spot, JJ crossed the yard and entered the back door of the house. He opened the dish cabinet, but it was empty. All the glasses were piled in the sink with the rest of the dirty dishes. He picked one out of the filthy mess and saw a dead fly lying in the bottom.

"Goddam it, Annie!" He threw the glass across the room where it shattered on the wall. "You ever gonna wash these goddam dishes?"

No answer.

JJ crossed to the living room door. Annie was slumped blank-faced on the sofa watching the wavering light of one of her television stories—some melodramatic soap opera.

"Did you hear me? This place is a damn pig sty. There's dirty dishes all over the kitchen. Pots on the stove. Dirty clothes all over the floor in here. When the hell are you gonna clean it up?"

Without looking away from the television, Annie gave him the finger.

"Son of a bitch!" JJ pounded his fist against the wall. "This is ridiculous. You're not the only one hurting you know. It's time you got off your ass and got on with your life. We can't keep living like this."

Annie used the remote to turn the sound up on the tv. Yelling above it, she said, "If it bothers you that much, why don't you stick around and clean the place instead of always riding off into the mountains?"

"Yeah, you wouldn't want to miss one of your damn shows, would you?" JJ turned and went back into the kitchen.

"Screw it," he said slamming a chair into the table. He cranked the faucet full force and filled the sink with hot water. As the suds bubbled up, he dug a dish out and began scrubbing it with a vengeance.

Damn her, he thought. She would have never let the place go to hell like this before. He slammed the dish into the drying rack and fished out another. She's not the only one who misses Kaitie. He loved Kaitlin as much as Annie did—maybe more, in his own way. After all, he dated Kaitie before he'd even met Annie.

❧   ❧   ❧

SHE WAS SEVENTEEN and he was nineteen. The judges unanimously chose Kaitie Cathcart the Queen of the Wilsall Rodeo that year. Young JJ watched her from the bucking chute as he was getting himself mentally prepared for his own event. She looked cute with her dark brown pigtails flopping up and down under her black hat as she drove her pony on through the barrel race and winning first place. While her girlish cuteness was appealing, he couldn't help noticing how well she filled out her checkered shirt and blue jeans.

A vicious kick and bump against the pen drew his attention back to the matters at hand. The black tornado beneath him named Lightning snorted and stomped rolling his eyes wildly. JJ. re-wrapped the thickly braided reins tight around his gloved hand and placed both heels touching Lightning just above the point of his shoulders. He heard the announcer call out his name.

"Well folks, now we're in for a treat," crackled the voice over the PA system. "Riding Lightning today is a young cowboy from Clyde Park, JJ Volker. He's a toughie, but so is Lightning. The bronc didn't get that name for nothing. Show us what you got, JJ!"

He recalled how he couldn't help sneaking a quick glance at Kaitlin before he pounded his Stetson down on his head and got ready to give the okay for the handler to open the gate. She watched him from behind the corral as she unsaddled her horse. His chest filled with pride and anticipation.

JJ nodded and exploded out of the chute determined to ride Lightning for the whole eight seconds. The bronco, however, couldn't care less about JJ's amorous aspirations. Lightning's white eyes bulged from their sockets and JJ could see his nostrils flaring wide as he tossed his head. He bucked and twisted every time his hooves slammed the ground as if he had landed on a hot griddle. JJ whipped back and forth like a rag doll. The heels of his spurred boots flew in the air and back down into the massive shoulders of the angry bronc. Each time Lightning kicked up with his rear legs, JJ could feel the solid 1200-pound mass of muscle convulse beneath him. In his peripheral vision the crowd and all else was just a blur of wild swirling colors. The only two beings in the world were him and the nightmare he was riding. With one hand jack-knifing above him and the other gripping the handhold, he made it to 5.3 seconds when a sharp twist from Lightning threw him in the air. *Damn it,* he thought as he flew higher than the roof of the grandstand.

The crowd gasped and some stood as he landed with a thud on his back.

At first, he couldn't breathe and remained flat until his breath returned. He was vaguely aware of galloping sounds around him as the pick-up men chased down the bucking black horse to release the flank strap. JJ forced himself to get up, smacked the dust off his jeans with his hat in exaggerated disgust and then raised it to the applauding crowd. As he limped off to the fence, he snuck another peek at Kaitie out of the corner of his eye and was both relieved and disappointed that she seemed not to be paying any attention to him whatsoever.

Later in the afternoon, he sauntered over to her in the parking lot as she was brushing down her horse. "Hey, congratulations, Queenie. Nice job on the barrel racing."

Kaitie turned toward him and flashed a smile. "Why, thanks, Cowboy! You looked pretty good out there yourself until you bumped your head on the sky."

His cheeks flushed red, even through his tan. "Ouch. You saw that, huh? Well, I guess it was Lightning's day. It sure wasn't mine." He reached up, pushed his hat back and scratched his sun-bleached, hay-colored thatch of close-cropped hair. "Here, I bought this for you," he said stretching out his hand and offering her a can of Pepsi. "My name's JJ. I already know yours is Kaitlin."

Taking the can of pop from him, the newly crowned rodeo queen stuck out her other hand and gave him a firm handshake.

"Thank you. Nice to meet you, JJ."

That evening they joined the party of post-rodeo dancers and drinkers filling the tiny Wilsall Main street and two-stepped all night long. Kaitlin was full of energy and JJ spun and dipped her through dance after dance despite a noticeable limp when they'd go to sit down.

They dated throughout the rest of her senior year. The two spent every spare minute together—horseback riding and fishing all summer; hunting in the fall; skiing and country dancing in the winter. There was not anything physical that JJ did that Kaitie couldn't do as well, if not better. And he loved her for it.

In the spring, his mother died of cancer leaving him and his father to tend their ranch alone. Kaitie stopped by every day after school and on the weekends to help with the chores no matter how dirty or how tough they might be. She even tried to cook a meal for them once. However, after her attempt, the three of them agreed that she was much more useful in the barn than in the kitchen.

The night she graduated she and JJ went to dinner in Bozeman. Afterwards, they drove to their favorite spot by the Gallatin River. They got out of his pickup and lay down in the cool grass listening to the water bubbling over the river rocks. She rested her head in the crook of his muscular arm and breathed in the sweet mountain air. A million stars twinkled in the sky.

Turning her head to JJ, Kaitie kissed him on his cheek and sighed. "Are you going to miss me when I go to Missoula next week?"

JJ kicked at a rock with his boot heel. "What do you think?"

"I think you're going to be heartbroken and cry yourself to sleep every night."

JJ didn't respond.

"Well, I'll miss you, JJ Volker. You'd better come up and visit me."

JJ sat up and skipped a rock into the water. "I'm not sure. I'll be busy helping Dad on the ranch, and working at Murdoch's. I don't know how much chance I'll have to get up there."

He pitched another stone, throwing it so hard he missed the river altogether sailing it to the other shore. "I still don't know why you couldn't have stayed in Bozeman and gone to Montana State."

Kaitie tilted her head and gave a dramatic sigh."For the millionth time, they have a really good journalism program in Missoula. You know my dream is to be a reporter. You should be excited for me."

JJ dug a trench in the ground with his boot heel. "I am happy for you, Kait, but I just wish you could have waited till the end of summer to move up there."

Kaitie sat up and put her arms around JJ's broad shoulders. "JJ, look, I know you love working on the ranch with your Dad and riding rodeo. Plus, you're starting your job at Murdoch's. I'm happy for you. I have a job waiting for me in Missoula and I already have some assignments for school I have to do over the summer. We've talked about this. I'm going to be busy with my job and schoolwork and you're going to be busy here. We agreed that when I moved that would be it between us. We both need to focus on our futures. We'll still see each other, just not as much and not in the same way."

JJ pushed his cowboy hat back and rested his forehead against his arms folded on his knees. "But, I love you," he mumbled.

"What?"

"You heard me."

"No I didn't. Your head was buried in your arms."

He tilted his head up to her. The bright moonlight shone off a tear glistening in the corner of his eye. "I said I love you."

Kaitie caught her breath. Her shoulders sagged and she took his face in her hands, rubbing away the tear with her thumb. "Oh, JJ." She kissed him on his cheek. "I love you too. And I always will. This has been the greatest year ever. We've had so much fun. You're like the brother I always wanted. I feel that close to you. Nothing will ever change that."

"I don't mean like that. I mean I really love you."

She gently took his hat off and ran her hand across his bristly haircut. Taking his hands in hers she said, "I know you think you love me. The things we've shared this year are special. I'm sure your emotions are still high from when your mom died.

It's only been a couple of months. But, our dreams and goals are different. I want a career. I want to travel the world. See things. Write about them. I don't want to be married and tied down. You want to be a rancher and help your Dad, and he needs you. He can't work the ranch on his own with his arthritis. You love the ranching and Montana is your life. But, JJ, it's not mine."

A trout leapt out of the river and plopped back in. JJ bowed his head and nodded. Then he looked up with a crooked grin. "Are you sure you're just eighteen?"

She gave him a quizzical look and playfully slapped his arm. "You ate half the cake at my birthday party. You know I am."

"Well you talk more like you just graduated college instead of high school. Come here." He pulled her down on to the grass next to him. "To answer your question, Miss Kaitie Cathcart, Queen of the Rodeo, yes, ma'am, I will miss you."

AS USUAL, a noisy group of friends surrounded Kaitie on Saturday at her farewell barbeque. JJ stood off to the side half-listening to them talking over each other giving her advice on the best places to hang out and things to do in Missoula. After he'd had enough, he crossed the Cathcart's back yard and took his plate to Kaitie's sister, Annie, who was slathering sauce on the grilling chickens.

The fire flared up as she flipped one of the wings. She stepped back wide-eyed bumping into JJ.

"Careful," he said. "You better not drop any of them wings. They're too good to waste."

Annie turned and was face to face with JJ. Her cheeks flushed pink from the heat of the grill, or perhaps it was a blush from finding herself toe to toe with him. She took a step back and blew a stray strand of her soft blond curls out of her face. Her blue eyes sparkled at him.

"Oh, excuse me, JJ," she said shielding her eyes from the strong midday sun shining over his shoulder. "Do you like the chicken?"

"If I didn't like it would I be coming over for my five-hundredth piece?" He smiled at her and held out his plate. "That chicken is fit to eat."

She smiled back and forked the plumpest chicken breast she could find onto his plate. "I'm glad you like it. The sauce is my grandma's recipe and I add a few things to give it some zip."

"You're a real good cook, Annie. Too bad your sister can't even boil water. She cooked dinner for Dad and me once and it was so bad my dog gagged trying to eat it."

Annie laughed and they both looked at Kaitie. "Well, I hope she finds a good cheap place to eat when she's up at the university. If she has to depend on her own cooking, she'll starve. How's your Dad doing, by the way?"

"He's doing pretty good. He misses Mom, but he's doing alright."

"After Kaitie's gone it's going to be quiet around here. Why don't you and your Dad come over for dinner next Sunday? It would be nice to have the company."

JJ smiled broadly. "That would be great. I'm sure Dad would appreciate it. Neither one of us are much better than Kaitie at cooking. Thanks, Annie."

"Good. Come over around four o'clock then."

"Sounds great. We'll be there. I better eat this chicken before it gets cold. I'll go see if I can pry Kaitie away from her fans."

"Okay."

Halfway across the yard JJ glanced back. Annie was still watching him and smiling.

SUNDAY DINNERS WITH ANNIE and her parents became a regular event for JJ and his father. The loss of JJ's mother had left a big hole in both their lives. The Cathcart home was comfortable, and they enjoyed having Annie and her mother dote on them. JJ also liked getting to know Annie.

Both Annie and her sister were attractive young women. Like many of the Montana girls brought up on the ranch, they were tomboys who could keep up with or better their male friends. They could ride hard, drive a hay baler, fix a fence or help birth a calf in the middle of the night. The two sisters bloomed into womanhood with a striking natural beauty and the special strength that comes from weathering the rough Western life.

Aside from their good looks and sweetness, however, the sisters were very different. Kaitie was a spunky, courageous and fun-loving cowgirl. On the weekends she would haul a pickup truck full of whooping friends to local dances and wild parties. Annie, on the other hand, was quiet and gentle, preferring to curl up in pajamas in front of the fire with a good book on a Saturday night.

Although he treasured the rich outdoor life that the awesome resources of Montana provided, JJ found the quiet homebody personality of Annie a comfortable balance that made him happy to be around. His affection for her grew deeper as time went on, and soon they were dating regularly. She made JJ feel he hung the stars whether she was hugging him from behind when he saddled his horse or gently making love to him, her eyes glistening with emotion as she watched his every move.

Over the next three years, Kaitie often came home from school on Sundays for dinner with the family. Her exuberance filled the house with energy and excitement. Annie's reserved presence would be eclipsed by the boisterous enthusiasm of her sister. JJ would feed off Kaitie's energy and the two were constantly challenging each other to horse races or arm wrestling matches that Annie would quietly observe from the sidelines.

For his part, JJ enjoyed roughhousing with Kaitie and was glad to see that she was genuinely happy that he and her sister had become so close, though he had hoped she was a little jealous.

One Sunday he and his father were enjoying their usual meal at the Cathcarts'. Kaitie put down her fork and said, "JJ, you've had that goofy grin on your face all afternoon. In fact, everyone has been acting silly today. Is something going on?"

JJ winked at Annie and everyone at the table chuckled. He said, "You're the investigative reporter wannabe, Kaitie. You figure it out."

Kaitie searched the faces of each person with a puzzled look on her face.

Annie put her left hand on the table, wiggled her fingers and cleared her throat, "Ahem," she said.

Kaitie gasped and covered her mouth with her hand. "Oh, my god! Annie! JJ! Are you . . . ?"

Annie nodded and the table erupted in laughter. Kaitie ran to Annie with tears in her eyes and threw her arms around her.

JJ said, "Yup, I finally hogtied your sister. We wanted to surprise you at dinner. We set a date in June."

Annie hugged her sister and said, "It's just going to be a small wedding. The family and a few friends. I'd like you to be my maid of honor."

ALTHOUGH ANNIE PREFERRED her home life to her husband's "boy fun," as she called it, the two were considered the perfect couple. The first years of their marriage were sweet and comfortable. While she was not the adventurous playmate JJ found in Kaitie, Annie strived to make JJ as happy at home as possible. Not much of a book reader himself, JJ enjoyed hearing Annie tell him about the latest novel she had finished; reading favorite parts to him with all the drama and animation in her voice that the author had intended the reader to feel. While she would occasionally accompany him on horseback rides, she let him enjoy his outside activities on his own or with his friends—fishing, snowmobiling, hunting, camping, skiing—she was generous about giving JJ his freedom. She prepared lunches for him when he had plans for the day— always with a sandwich, a piece of fruit and a homemade cookie. She also made sure to include a brief love note signed with a hand-drawn flower. When he got home, no matter how late it was—and it was always late—she would greet him with a warm hug and a kiss.

As time went on, though, the differences in their personalities began to fray the edges of their marriage. JJ would become frustrated with his wife's lack of interest in the activities he enjoyed and spent increasingly more time out of the house. Annie, sensing a growing distance between them withdrew into herself emotionally. Her inability to participate in his active lifestyle made her feel less adequate and gradually, the romantic passion she had for her husband cooled. Though she still loved him deeply and in her heart she knew he loved her, she could not seem to express that feeling romantically and the two grew further apart.

The day that Sheriff Stollar called them with the terrible news about Kaitlin's murder took a devastating toll upon both JJ and Annie and on their marriage. Annie showed it the worst. She would break into tears for weeks after the funeral. JJ, on the other hand, hid his emotions in a cloud of dark silence. His frustrated rage, however, flared at unexpected moments. He walked through the house slamming doors, or cabinets and every day angry arguments between Annie and him flared up over minor issues. It reached a point where the two of them rarely spoke to one another. She retreated into the living room and the television and he went for long rides in the mountains.

∾   ∾   ∾

AFTER HE FINISHED THE DISHES JJ went into the back bedroom they had converted into an office space and unlocked his gun case. He took out the mahogany presentation box holding the Model 29 Smith and Wesson .44 Magnum pistol that Annie had given him last year for Christmas. He opened the case and took out the gun. It was a beauty with its 24-carat gold plated fiftieth anniversary logo. The handsome blue steel barrel and African wood grips gleamed with an oily newness. Like his hero, Dirty Harry's gun, he thought. It was a real treasure, and he was thrilled when he had received it. He opened the box of hollow point cartridges, loaded the pistol and wrapped it in a cleaning rag he found in the bottom of the gun case. He regretted he didn't have a holster for it, but he had never planned to use it. He tucked the gun in the front of his jeans and let his shirttails cover it up. As quietly as he had opened it, he closed and locked the gun case and headed back through the kitchen.

"Annie," he said, "I'm sorry about before. It's just . . . "He hesitated, waiting for some response from her. If she heard, she didn't seem to care. She kept staring at the television. Always the television; she never picked up a book anymore. He looked at her and thought about kissing her good-bye. He knew it would be a thankless gesture, but he held onto hope. He leaned over and tried to kiss her on her forehead. She frowned and leaned away from him shooing him off as if he were an annoying fly. He sighed and grabbed a bottle of water from the refrigerator and let himself out the back door.

The dogs wagged and bounced around his legs as he made his way to the corral.

"Max, you're staying here," he said to the younger dog. Max's ears and tail wilted. The other, a big yellow Lab named Gopher, settled down but continued to wag his tail. JJ put the pistol and water bottle in the leather saddlebag and mounted Spot in a smooth and practiced move. "C'mon Goph," he called to the older pooch as he turned to head up the trail. Max's ears perked up but he did not advance. "Max—you set. And stay. We'll be back."

Max's ears drooped as he watched Spot, JJ and Gopher trot off northeast of the direction Sheriff Stollar had headed.

Chapter 6

SHERIFF STOLLAR HAD RIDDEN for forty minutes when he reined Chief off the dirt trail and headed up and over the ridge. He reckoned he would come down on the other side where he could approach the cabin unseen. The timber was thick and the ranger cabin had no windows on that side. He doubted there would be anyone in the cabin, but his years of police work had taught him to be cautious, particularly when involved with a psychopath. And clearly, whoever had murdered the Cathcart woman was a psychopath.

He had been in the office standing at the front desk when the dispatch clerk got the frantic call.

"Sheriff's office." The clerk glanced up at Stollar and rolled her eyes dramatically. Stollar grinned back.

"Sir, I'm sorry, I can't understand you. Please calm down and speak more slowly. What did you say you saw?"

Stollar looked up from his paperwork at the change in the tone of the clerk's voice. Her usually ruddy face had drained of color.

"Did you say, 'scalped?'" Her fingers briefly hovered above her keyboard as she adjusted her headset. Stollar came around the desk to view her computer monitor as her fingers resumed clacking information into the database. Before she finished the call, he was pulling on his jacket.

"Rolf," he called across the room. "Grab your jacket and meet me at the chopper. Denise."

The dispatcher kept staring at her computer monitor with a lost look on her face.

"Denise," Stollar repeated. Denise shook her head and turned to the sheriff. "Call the medical examiner and tell him to get up to Ibex to get the body.

The rotors on the helicopter windmilled into action. Deputy Rolf Gustafson made the final pre-flight check and gripped the control stick.

"Where to?"

"Up to the old Ibex ranger station. A rancher called this one in. It's going to be ugly. We've got a scalping and dismemberment."

Gustafson swallowed, but didn't look at Stollar. Lost in their thoughts, neither officer spoke as the chopper crossed the valley and climbed towards Ibex, high in the Crazy Mountains.

Gustafson set down in the meadow in front of the cabin. Although the sun shone brightly, a strong spring wind pummeled the helicopter. Stollar tightened his hat, pulled the collar of his jacket up and hopped to the ground.

Most of the snow in the wide meadow had melted except for small patches protected by the pines. Tiny white heathers and brilliant pink Rocky Mountain laurel sprinkled the bright green mountain grass with their early signs of spring. The carpet of low flowers bowed to Stollar as he crossed the yard and seemed to nod at the streak of blood leading to the cabin porch. Stollar noted that the blood trail led back into the timber.

"Rolf, I'm going in the cabin. Follow that blood and see where it leads."

The deputy gave a quick two-fingered salute and headed back toward the trees.

Stollar pulled on latex gloves as he climbed the steps, steeling himself for what lay beyond the door. A large animal, either a moose or elk, probably spooked by Gustafson, crashed through the underbrush far back in the trees behind him just as he turned the doorknob, making his heart pound and his hand tremble. He had seen plenty of grisly scenes over the years — murders and horrible traffic accidents — but the rancher's description that he had read off Denise's computer indicated that this scene promised to be particularly gory.

The door creaked on rusty hinges as he swung it open. Before his eyes could adjust to the dim light inside he saw the body lying on the table. The sun shone through the window and illuminated the tragic mess splayed across the table like a spotlight on an altar of some demonic sacrifice.

"Jesus," he muttered, closing his eyes and turning away. A lump of gore stuck in his throat and he gagged.

"Colton, come over here." The deputy waved at him from halfway between the trees and the cabin.

Stollar was relieved to delay entering the cabin and walked over to where Gustafson was kneeling over something on the ground.

"What did you see in the cabin?"

Stollar shook his head. "I haven't gone in yet. Looks gruesome. What do you have here?"

"Looks like an Indian tomahawk. There's a knife over there. Both have a lot of evidence on them."

"Right. Get the camera and start taking shots. Tag and bag whatever you find, then join me at the cabin."

Gustafson trudged back to the helicopter.

Stollar waited until his partner finished photographing and bagging the weapons. The two climbed the stairs and entered the cabin. They stepped carefully trying to avoid the blood that was covering much of the floor. The woman's mangled torso lay on the table before them; her arms were on the floor.

"Good lord," said Gustafson, "He cut off her arms and a foot."

Stollar pushed the brim of his hat up and back. "Yeah, I can see that. Scalped her too."

"Jesus."

"Get some pictures, Rolf."

While Gustafson took pictures of the scene, Stollar inspected the body. The arms had been cleanly hacked off, probably with the tomahawk. The marks on the woman's forehead indicated that her scalp had been taken off with a sharp knife — undoubtedly, the knife in the yard next to the tomahawk. The marks on her ankle were less indicative of how her foot had been severed. Stollar searched the floor at the base of the table.

"Rolf, do you see the foot anywhere?"

Gustafson peered around the dim interior. "No, I don't see it, Sheriff. But, look up there." He pointed to the wall. Hanging from a nail was a bloody mass of hair. "There's two of them."

Stollar crossed to the wall and looked at the torn scalp. Hanging next to it was another hairy mass. He lifted the second object and held it out to his deputy. "No, this is a beaver pelt. Not a scalp. Get a picture of the scalp."

In the flash of the camera Stollar noted the Indian blanket on the cot. A blackened pot sat on the woodstove. He looked in it and sniffed. "Whew. Smells like pemmican. Looks like someone's been shacking up here."

"This is all Native American stuff," Gustafson said. "The blanket, the tomahawk, the scalp and all. Figure it's an Indian?"

"Could be. We need to get the weapons fingerprinted and we'll know more."

In the distance he heard the sound of four-wheelers approaching.

"That's probably the M.E. and Forensics. Let's go meet them."

TWO DAYS LATER Rolf Gustafson came into his office and dropped a manila folder on Stollar's desk.

"Wasn't Native American, but close."

Stollar looked up quizzically.

"The Cathcart murder. Guess who?"

Stollar opened the file. "I'll be damned. Bridger Jackson."

He wasn't looking forward to a confrontation with Bridger Jackson. Locals considered Jackson to be a crazy hermit who lived in the wild, ate grubs and was out of his head. Since he never came into town, few people had ever seen him, which added to his mystique. The stories about him were plentiful. They made good campfire tales when you wanted to scare your kids or your friends on a moonlit evening up in the Crazies with shadows and night noises everywhere around you. Even as you told the story, however, you would feel a shivery tingle up the back of your neck, wondering yourself if it might really be true. If a calf or sheep was found dead or someone's money was missing, if a dog never returned home or anything else happened that there seemed to be no other answer for, Jackson was blamed for it.

A few people had seen Jackson over the years: a hunter claimed to have seen him while scouring the high country looking for elk. A young couple picking huckleberries by the lake also had a sighting. Hunters, campers and horseback riders had on occasion seen a woolly fellow that some of the more fanciful folk had suggested was a Montana Yeti. He was described variously as anywhere from six to eight feet tall, depending on who was telling the story. A few claimed he was naked and covered head to toe with hair like an ape. But, the generally accepted view was that he was dressed as a mountain man complete with a large fur cap, leather shirt and leggings and moccasins. His hair was long and stringy, and he sported a full and lengthy beard.

❧   ❧   ❧

IN TRUTH, JACKSON WAS 58 years old, five foot ten inches tall with grey hair worn in either a pony tail or hanging loose. He did indeed dress as a mountain man, for that is what he was. He had been born Bridger Jackson to James Bridger Jackson and his wife Mary. Bridger's grandfather Hezekiah , or Zeke, as he was known had been a trapper and guide in the Rocky Mountains in the 1800's. Zeke became acquainted with the famous Jim Bridger at one of the annual rendezvous when he was a young man. He loved to listen to Jim tell his tall tales around the campfires, each more outrageous than the last. Jim Bridger was well liked amongst frontiersmen, businessmen and Indians alike. His knowledge of the Rockies and how to survive in them was unparalleled. By the end of that first rendezvous, Zeke hooked up with Bridger and stayed in his company for ten years guiding gold miners and hunters through the rough and beautiful mountains of the West. In the late 1800's Jim Bridger's eyes started failing him and he retired to a farm in Kansas City. Zeke carried on trapping beaver, hunting and putting into practice all the many things he had learned by the side of the great and famous mountain man. He stopped guiding people though, as, unlike Jim Bridger, he was not a gregarious fellow and much preferred to be by himself rather than around other people.

One person, however, struck his fancy. At Rendezvous in 1892, Zeke Jackson took a shining to a Cheyenne woman who, like him, preferred to stay away from the crowd of rowdy revelers and Indians who became too wild when they drank their whiskey. Her name was Ame'ha'e, or Flying Woman. Zeke just called her Amy. He met her on the first night of Rendezvous, and by the last night had taken her for his wife.

Almost nine months to the day they had met, they had a son. Zeke named the boy James Bridger in honor of his old friend. When Jim was three years old, Ame'ha'e gave birth to a daughter they named Mary. Zeke and Ame'ha'e brought their children up in their rough cabin near the western Montana-Canadian border. Zeke took his son with him as he traveled the Rockies, teaching him all he knew. When they were home, Ame'ha'e entertained her son with the legends she had heard from the Cheyenne Storytellers in her youth. Jim became well steeped in both mountain man skills and Native American lore. He learned to hunt, fish and trap and to survive in the wilderness.

Because neither Zeke nor Flying Woman believed there was anything their son needed to know that they could not teach him, they never sent him to school. Considering where and how they lived, what they were able to teach him did indeed stand him in much better stead than anything he might have learned from books.

Mary grew up staying close to her mother. She was "different," as Zeke would say— very quiet and withdrawn. Her big brown eyes never focused on anything, but were always looking into another world beyond the view of others. In Zeke's mind, she was just different and he had little time for, or interest in, the child.

One Fall day after Zeke and Jim, who was now twelve years old, had returned with a fresh supply of beaver pelts, Ame'ha'e prevailed on her husband to take the family to a nearby lake for a meal she had prepared for them.

The air was crisp and the mid-October sky hinted of snow in the mountains to the West. The ever-present wind was merely a gentle breeze, and the clouds floated like great glaciers across the vast open sky. Bright yellow leaves from the aspen trees drifted down around the family as they approached the clear azure lake.

Jim and his father went down to the lake's edge to fish. Mary, as usual, sat and stared at the sky and the trees while staying no more than a few feet from her mother. Ame'ha'e unwrapped the pack she had carried and put out the fry bread and deer meat sandwiches she had made. She collected some nearby deadfall and built a small campfire upon which she brewed a pot of coffee.

Down by the lake, Jim was taking a fish off the hook when his father turned sniffing the air. "Coffee's ready. Let's get these trout up to Mama and have a bite." Jim gathered up the four fat brown trout and his pole and scrambled after his father who was striding up to the fire. Ame'ha'e had cut some sticks for them to use to cook the fish, and it wasn't long before she had them cleaned, spitted and roasting.

THE GRIZZLY BEAR SNIFFED the air. He was hungry and busy in his quest to layer on fat for the winter. The roasting fish tickled his senses and he shuffled down toward the beach. All he had eaten were some huckleberries and slugs that he had dug from a rotting tree. He was hungry and grumpy.

Zeke went back down to the edge of the lake to refill his canteen with water when he heard Ame'ha'e scream.

Normally, a grizzly would have given a threatening growl before attacking, but this big bruin was not in a dickering mood. Once he had broken from the cover of the trees, he charged at Ame'ha'e. As he came roaring down the hill, Mary ran toward her father. Jim dropped the fish he was holding and yelled, "Mother!"

He searched frantically for anything he could use as a weapon. He found nothing.

Ame'ha'e screamed as the bear reached her and knocked her off her feet into the campfire. Sparks and burning embers flew into the air as she landed on the flaming wood. Her hair caught fire. She reached up to ward off the bear, but his huge claws ripped across her belly. With another mighty swat, the bear caught her in the shoulder and flung her in the air as Bridger looked on in horror.

Zeke bellowed and waved his arms wildly as he charged toward the bear.

Mary stood and watched without emotion as her mother was mauled, all the while twisting her dark hair in her fingers.

Straddling Ame'ha'e's mangled burning body, the bear turned its head toward Zeke and roared a warning at him. Saliva flew from its mouth. He turned back to his prey and sank his massive teeth into her throat. Her neck snapped as he yanked her up from the ground.

Jim howled with rage and charged toward the monstrous scene.

Zeke yelled, "Jim! No! Stay back! Go to Mary! Now!"

Jim stopped and ran to his sister who was standing in her confused world. Shaking himself, he put his arms around her and buried her face in his chest

Grabbing a burning limb from the fire, Zeke ran toward the bear and swung the flaming branch over his head while roaring his own threat at the beast. As he neared the grizzly, it stood to its full eight foot height snarling and growling with blood and saliva flying from its slobbering maw. With all his enraged strength, Zeke swung the burning bat of wood into the bear's stomach. The bear bellowed and dropped to all fours as Zeke brought the limb around once more hitting him squarely in the face, breaking his jaw and burning his jowls. Roaring in pain and rage, the grizzly turned and lumbered off into the timber. With a heaving chest Zeke stood, his arm still raised holding the branch, and watched the bear bound off.

"Pa!" Jim called out from where he huddled with Mary.

Ignoring his son's call, Zeke turned to the tangled bloody mess that minutes ago had been his beautiful Cheyenne wife. Ame'ha'e's body lay in smoldering tatters. The blood had drained out of her stomach and throat extinguishing the flames on her dress. Her hair was burned off and her face was black from the fire. Zeke vomited as he stumbled to the blanket Ame'ha'e had placed on the ground for them.

"Pa!" Jim yelled again.

Zeke picked up the blanket and placed it over his wife's body. "Stay where you are, Jim! Mind your sister." Zeke turned back to his wife and crumpled down cross-legged next to her body. "My god, Amy. My god. I'm so sorry. I'm so . . ." His voice trailed off as he buried his face in his hands and sobbed.

Jim had never seen his father cry before. With his arm around her, he led Mary to the blanket.

When he reached his father, he sat next to him in the same cross-legged position. He dared not look at the covered body before them; he stared at the ground between his legs. Mary remained standing and gazed vacantly toward the water. A sharp gust of chill wind whipped suddenly through the valley and she shuddered as her hair thrashed around her face.

Chapter 7

SHERIFF STOLLAR NUDGED Chief down the slope and dismounted in front of the cabin. It was one of a series of old Forest Service structures built in the early 1930's for local rangers to use as shelters; now they were rented to campers during the summer and fall seasons. Yellow police tape had been pulled down and scuttled back and forth on the ground as the cool spring wind gently pushed and pulled at the free edges. He shook his head. The new kid from Forensics had probably forgotten to take it down when he left the crime scene.

"Rookie." He grunted to himself.

He walked toward the steps of the cabin looking for signs in the grass. Sure enough, fresh prints led away from the cabin into the trees beyond the clearing. He followed them a few feet before he reached a muddy patch. The prints were smooth, leaving no treadmarks from boots or shoes. Most likely moccasin prints—most likely belonging to Jackson. Not many other people would traipse around these mountains in the fresh springtime mud with moccasins on. Bridger Jackson would.

In all his years as a law officer, he had never come across Jackson personally. Of course, he had heard the stories, but most of them were far-fetched and a lot more fiction than fact, he surmised. For that matter, there were darn few facts available about the man. He was arrested once some years back. A rancher over in Big Timber had accused Jackson of shooting one of his cows. He claimed he had seen Jackson shoot the cow but had run him off with his own shotgun before Jackson could get to it. The Sweetgrass County sheriff tracked him down and arrested him. He had not resisted.

They took a mug shot of him, fingerprinted and questioned him. He didn't say much other than denying he had anything to do with the incident. They kept him in jail for all of two hours. They had not been able to locate a rifle or any other evidence that he had shot the cow. All they had was the rancher's charge that he was positive he had seen Jackson shoot the cow before running off.

It was fewer than two hours after they had jailed Jackson that another rancher came into the police station dragging fourteen-year-old Sonny Tomlinson by his shirt collar, and deposited him unceremoniously on the waiting room bench. The rancher leaned across the counter and addressed the officer in charge.

"Dan, I caught this little peckerwood riding around on his dirt bike and shooting at my cows. Fortunately for him, he missed, cause I woulda shot him myself if he had killed one. I came up on him in my truck and caught him as he was trying to start up his bike to take off. I don't know what you want to do with him, but if you want me to take care of him I'll be more'n happy to." He squinted at the boy who returned his glare with his middle finger.

"Hmmm. That's okay, Brian. Let Nancy take your statement and you can go. We'll take it from here."

The rancher turned toward the teenager and gave him a stern look. "Son, if I ever catch you on my property again . . . Well, let's just say I better not."

He leaned in closer to the police officer and lowered his voice so the boy would not hear. "Dan, I tell you that kid is no good. He's Chip Tomlinson's boy. Probably gets it from his no-good father. You ought to have a talk with his old man."

"Thanks, Brian. We'll have a talk with him. Nancy, will you take Mr. Casey's statement?" He walked around the counter to Sonny and said, "Come on, son, let's have a little chat."

It didn't take long for Sonny to confess to joyriding and shooting his rifle. He also admitted to killing the cow at the MacPherson ranch. After the confession, they released Jackson and had the deputy drive him to the trailhead in the mountains from where they had taken him.

Stollar had reviewed Jackson's file. He had looked at the mug shot of the scruffy man who could have stepped out of a history book from the chapter on the late 1800s. His dirty grey hair was in a long braid reaching his waist. His face was a craggy landscape of gullies and ridges running north to south. Bushy eyebrows hung over deep-set, dark and haunted eyes. His nose was that of a Native American, large and flat with a crooked hint of a past break. Covering most of the lower portion of his face was a matted tangle of beard. He had been dressed in greasy buckskins with fringe hanging here and there on his shirt and leggings.

Other than the MacPherson misidentification incident, nothing concrete appeared on his rap sheet. Some notes indicated that he had been accused of various crimes and misdemeanors over the years —theft, breaking and entering, drug distribution, vagrancy and drunkenness. He had neither gone to jail nor been convicted on any of these charges because they had all been unsubstantiated. Generally, with the more serious accusations it turned out that Jackson was the first one accused, but each time the real perpetrator turned out to be someone else. He was an easy target given his odd behavior, mountain man lifestyle and the legends that surrounded him.

The Kaitie Cathcart case, however, did seem to point in his direction. They had found Jackson's steel tomahawk covered with blood and gore from where he had chopped off the woman's limbs. The most disturbing evidence was the bone handled skinning knife that he used to scalp her. The fingerprints were Jackson's and the blood, skin and hair samples were the Cathcart woman's.

There was also the bear trap that had snapped her foot off. Stollar shuddered to think about it. It was a huge #16 grizzly trap—forty-two and a half inches long and weighing almost fifty pounds. After searching the area around the cabin last week, he and Gustafson had located her foot in the center of the bear trap in the woods. Although Jackson's prints were not found on the trap, he was known to trap beaver and otter. Trapping bear, however, was illegal and he had never been convicted of poaching. Nevertheless, he might have been the one who had set out the bear trap.

Stollar entered the cabin. The body and other items had been removed. The floor had been cleaned. Upon closer observation, however, he spotted fresh mud tracks leading to a spot near the back of the room. Following the tracks, he noticed one of the planks in the floor was slightly askew and he knelt down and inspected it. It was loose and he pried it up. He unclipped the flashlight from his belt and shined it into the shallow hole. It was empty save for a sprig of sage. The pungent herb was used in many Native American cleansing and healing rituals, but did not grow in the immediate area, so it was unlikely that this branch had blown into the cabin on its own. Indentations in the dry dirt indicated that other items had lain in the hole recently.   Perhaps Jackson had returned to the cabin to retrieve the items from this cache hole and that was when he'd been spotted this morning by the cowgirl.

Stollar stood and tugged on his mustache. Why would Jackson have murdered the woman? That was one of the questions that nagged at him. It was not rape. At least, they had found no evidence that she had been raped. Where would Jackson have run into Kaitie? It's not as if he was the kind to be hanging around the bars that she frequented, or even the kind to be seen anywhere near a town where she might be. This was a brutal and seemingly senseless killing. What might have motivated Jackson to do it?

He'd heard the theory that the victim may have been hiking in the forest and unwittingly stepped on the grizzly trap, which snapped her foot off at the ankle. Jackson came across her when checking his traps and hauled her body back to the cabin. Fearing he'd be caught for poaching, his plan might have been to chop her up and hide her body parts. A stretch, but a plausible theory. However, if he had not intentionally killed Kaitie, why wouldn't Jackson report the accident to the police? Did he think that they wouldn't believe him? Likely, he supposed, but maybe it was that he was as crazy as everyone thought and this act was some result of his aberrant mind gone wild. No matter. Until he could be interviewed, Jackson was the primary suspect and had to be brought in for questioning.

After taking one more look around the cabin, the sheriff turned and headed out the door. Once outside, he took a deep breath of the fresh air. He mounted Chief and followed the footprints through the grass and into the trees.

Chapter 8

JACKSON CLIMBED HIGHER into the mountains toward the well-hidden cave that he had made his home. As much as possible he avoided the snow piles that still lingered in the high altitude rocks and fields. By nature and training, he was careful about leaving tracks. Under the circumstances, he knew he needed to disappear as much as possible. He wished he had had time to cover his tracks at the cabin, but with all the deep four-wheeler ruts from the police inspectors in the mud and spring grass around the cabin, he was confident that his prints would be hard to identify. They would be hunting for him, that's for sure, he thought. That cowgirl who spied him up in the pasture this morning took off on her horse like a bat out of hell. Probably headed into Clyde Park or Wilsall to do her duty. He guessed the sheriff was already on his trail. If he did not want to be found, they wouldn't find him. He knew these mountains better than anyone alive. And, he knew how to take care of himself. His father had made sure of that. From the time he was able to walk, Bridger's father had taken him with him on his hunting trips. He learned how to trap, track game and humans, shoot, skin, fish and survive in the wilderness in temperatures as low as 50 degrees below zero. He had likely spent more time with his father outdoors than in.

His favorite childhood memories were those of listening to his father's experiences in the Rockies, as well as tales of his grandfather Zeke's adventures as a mountain man in the heyday of the mountain men. The days when you could roam for hundreds of miles through Wyoming, Colorado, Idaho and Montana and never see another human if you didn't want to—living off the land and never having to answer to anybody but the Great Spirit.

As if to remind him of the potency of the Spirit, a strong wind came up and roared like a freight train through the tops of the pine trees, nearly throwing Jackson off balance as he climbed a craggy rock. The wind blew past him and moved farther down the slope. He stopped to rest. He dug into his pack for a hunk of jerky and ripped off a piece between his teeth; the salty meat renewed his energy.

He thought about his father and mother and how he had reached this point. Maybe if they had brought him up as other children were he would not be as anti-social. Had they let him go to public school instead of keeping him hidden on the reservation he might now be working as an outfitter, a mechanic or even a businessman. He chuckled at the thought. No, he was happy holding on to his heritage and roaming the high mountains of the West living as his forebears had.

He did, however, feel lonely sometimes. The disconnection between his parents, himself and the rest of the world had made him an independent person, but one who felt that something was missing in his life. His parents had been disconnected from each other. His mother clearly had some mental problem. She never spoke, but only grunted to express herself from time to time. Her dark black hair, dark skin, black eyes and quiet ways bespoke her Native American heritage. The way she stared into the distance as though searching for some long lost loved thing that would appear on the horizon someday confused Bridger. As time went on, he came to accept that that was the way she was. He also accepted that she did not acknowledge his existence. Never offering a hug, a kiss or even an encouraging smile. However, she showed none of these signs of affection with his father either. She lived in her own world and that was the way it was.

His father, Jim Jackson, on the other hand, did try to show his wife affection. He hugged her each time they came home from one of their trips. He cooked and cared for the three of them. He would speak to her as if she was listening even though she would be staring into space or at the mountains beyond. Once, when Bridger was eight years old, he asked his father why his mother never spoke. After several moments of thoughtful silence, Jim told his son of a horrific event involving a grizzly bear that he and Bridger's mother had witnessed when they were both young. In the attack, his mother had seen her mother torn apart by the bear. And ever since she had spoken not a word.

"So, you've known Mama since she was a little girl?"

Bridger noted but did not understand his father's long silent pause that followed his question.

"Yes, that's right. Now c'mon, there's chores to be done." And, that was as much history about his mother as Bridger ever learned.

Chapter 9

AS A RESULT OF THE TRAGIC grizzly bear incident, Zeke and his two children suffered considerable mental breakdowns. While young Mary had never spoken more than a few grunts, now she was totally silent and more distant than ever. Jim had difficulty sleeping from the nightmares that haunted him every night. He missed his mother and the love she had given him that neither his father nor his sister could ever show.

As time went on, Zeke rarely spoke to his children. The solitary mountain life he had chosen to live with his family far from society, which had once been such a pleasure, began to eat away at him. Without his beloved Amy to share it and bring him the comforts of a warm wife on a harsh winter's night his heart had frozen in a glacier of loneliness. His human warmth and ability to love and care had been mauled and destroyed by the grizzly bear just as had Ame'ha'e. The misery he felt because of her death turned to cold bitterness in his heart and his anger manifested itself through vicious cruelty to his son.

The only times he addressed Jim were to bark orders or to yell insults at him as he beat him whenever the boy did something wrong—which was about everything he did. As Zeke grew more bitter, the beatings grew harsher. What had started as slaps across the back of Jim's head turned to lashings with leather whips, belts, bridles or whatever item was handy enough for Zeke to use against his son.

His treatment of Mary was of a different sort of cruelty. Although Mary was silent and lost in a world of her own, she had inherited her mother's good looks. Black eyes, shiny black hair, a strong Indian nose and high cheekbones. As she came into womanhood, her body filled out firmly and full. As a younger girl, her father had little use for her since she neither spoke nor could be counted on to help with chores. His frustration with her lack of usefulness was tempered by a tiny ember of affection that smoldered deep within him when he looked at the poor girl, so confused with what life had dealt her. As she matured he was reminded of his dead wife more each day.

Zeke started molesting his daughter when she was twelve years old. He would send Jim out on long errands — collecting wood, checking traps, whatever would keep him away for a few hours. With his son gone, he would force Mary to engage in sex with him. "Force" is too strong a word, for she was merely a passive participant in the events. Zeke would have his way with her— his mixed emotions of anger, loneliness and self-loathing turned to sexual savagery on the hapless girl who had neither the strength nor presence of mind to ward him off.

Returning from fishing one grey autumn day, Jim dragged his gnarled walking stick through the dry dead leaves. The naked branches above him swayed back and forth in the chill wind. The four cutthroat trout hanging from his stringer were still river-cold. He shivered as their wet bodies slapped against his legs. Dirty clouds of smoke curled up from the chimney as he approached home.

He pushed open the cabin door. In the dim, smoky interior, a grunting hump rose under the bed covers, moving and pushing. Pinned by the heaving mound, Mary turned her head and looked at him with dead eyes. He stood watching, still holding the trout twisting gape-mouthed on their line. The humping stopped and the covers slid to the floor. His father rose naked from the tangle of blankets. Jim stared from his father to his sister's nude body. She was almost fifteen and he hadn't seen her without any clothes since she was a baby. He had never seen any woman naked. His breathing stopped and he couldn't tear his eyes from her smooth white body, her budding breasts, her soft patch of hair. He felt himself stirring in his crotch.

"Mary?" he said.

Zeke stood, sweating and still erect, and bellowed at him, "Get the hell out of here!"

Snapping out of his stupor, Jim dropped his fish, turned and stumbled out the door. He had only gone a few feet when he fell to his knees and vomited. He was on all fours when his father, still naked, charged out into the yard wielding an oak axe handle and began beating him with it.

"I was teaching her a lesson," he spat out between flailings, his face crimson with rage and embarrassment. "She . . . she . . . ," he stammered and kept beating Jim until the boy whipped around, grabbed the axe handle and tore it out of his father's grip. Jim scrambled to his feet brandishing the piece of oak with both hands above his head. The two men glared at each other their chests heaving in unison with fury, exhaustion and pain.

"Boy, you put that down right now or so help me . . . " Jim could see the fear in his father's eyes.

He had never challenged his father before. He realized for the first time that he could actually take his old man— pay him back for all the beatings he had suffered. His father looked pathetic and small standing naked before him.

"You can't do this anymore," Jim screamed. With tears burning his eyes he swung the axe handle back to deliver a blow to his father's head. Zeke ducked and threw up an arm to ward off the attack. As he held the weapon in mid-strike, Jim caught sight of his sister standing in the doorway staring expressionlessly at the two of them. He looked back at his father still frozen in his defensive posture and dropped the axe handle in the dirt. He spat at his father's feet, turned his back and walked away across the yard. He had only gone a few feet when he heard a strange wailing cry coming from his sister.

As he turned to look at her he felt a violent crack across the side of his face. His ears rang and his face was on fire. His father stood behind him with the axe handle ready to swing again. Before Zeke could deliver a second blow, Jim caught the old man's wrist and twisted it with all his young strength causing his father to drop the handle and howl with pain. Still gripping his father's wrist, Jim forced him to his knees and in the same move, grabbed the axe handle from the ground and began to smash it any place and every place on the naked man's body. Every time Zeke tried to struggle to his feet, Jim cracked the handle down on him until he was face down in the dirt in his own blood and sweat. Jim kept beating him with increasing savagery until all the strength and fury drained out of him. With heaving breaths Jim straddled the lifeless body of his father and began to sob. He stood crying in wracking spasms, his falling tears leaving droplets in the dust on his father's mangled back. As his weeping subsided and turned to shuddering breaths, Jim looked up at the cabin and saw Mary still standing in the doorway, naked and twisting a strand of her long black hair staring vacantly back at him.

❧   ❧   ❧

BRIDGER KNEW NOTHING of this story. Nor did he know how his father had disposed of Zeke's body or how he ran off with his sister Mary and ended up living with the Blackfeet tribe in northern Montana. But that is where the two ended up. He also did not know that Zeke had got Mary pregnant and that Jim was passing his sister off as his wife.

The Blackfeet knew Zeke from past rendezvous gatherings. They had met Jim Jackson as a young boy who accompanied his father at those events. When he arrived at their reservation with his pregnant wife they took them in and let them live in a far northeastern part of the reservation. Although the woman was silent and crazy, the young man was interested in learning the ways of the Blackfeet, and they taught him many things.

Within months after arriving at the reservation Mary gave birth to a boy that Jim named Bridger. He brought the boy up on the reservation and the three of them lived there for the next eight years.

Bridger grew up playing with the Blackfeet boys, learning their games and their skills. They taught him their customs and their beliefs. He gained a deep respect for the natural world and the spirits that inhabit it. He would listen to the tales of the storytellers and watch the Bear Shaman perform his fascinating magic healing rites. He also learned to mistrust white men and to have faith only in himself and his Native American brothers.

His mother, Mary, remained silent and became increasingly disturbed in her actions. She would wander off and go missing for two or three days at a time. Bridger or his father would track her down and bring her back. While Bridger had become an excellent tracker, she had an innate skill at disappearing and leaving almost no trace of where she had gone. More than once he found her filthy and disheveled in a cave or a fall of timber covered in blood and with the carcasses of marmots, rabbits or other small mammals scattered at her feet, the flesh gnawed off their bones.

While his father and he were treated as tribe members, the Blackfeet were uncomfortable with the *matsaki,* or crazy Cheyenne woman, in their midst. Jim knew he and his family would have to leave the reservation. Father, son and mother traveled south to the high mountains of the Crazies where they built a small cabin and lived off the land.

One day in Bridger's fifteenth year, Mary disappeared and did not return to the cabin. After waiting all day, his father said, "I've got to go find your mother. I want you to stay here in case she comes back before I do."

With that, Bridger's father headed off to the north and never returned. Nor did his mother. Bridger waited for his parents to come back for two days. On the third day, he went in search of them. He followed his father's trail for several miles, but lost the track at the Musselshell River bank. It was spring and the runoff was heavy. The river churned violently, overflowing its banks. He would never learn his parents' fate. His assumption was that his father, at least, had likely drowned in the turbulent river. What had happened to his mother would forever remain an unsolved mystery. He hoped that she had found peace in the other world she appeared to live in.

With nowhere else to go, Bridger returned to the Blackfeet reservation where he was welcomed by the tribe. He remained there for several years learning more of the Native American ways. As he came into his early twenties, he left the reservation and returned to the Crazy Mountains to live by himself. He much preferred to keep his own company, living and surviving with the skills he had learned from his father and his Native American brothers. The modern world offered him nothing. He found comfort living his solitary life far from the stresses and confusion of society.

Chapter 10

THE THREE OF THEM HAD been up this familiar trail many times, and JJ let the reins hang loose while Spot plodded rhythmically along with Gopher trotting just ahead of him. The day was warm and the comforting scent of the sagebrush relaxed JJ as he rocked in the saddle. His mind drifted to thoughts of Annie. Stollar was right. She was a good woman and JJ knew it. He regretted having lost his temper with her. She had always been good to him and he loved her for it. She was always bubbly and cheerful. Even when he was in the doldrums she could bring a smile to his face with some gentle teasing or words of comfort— whatever the moment called for.

JJ shivered as a sudden breeze blew across the plain followed by the shadow of a huge cloud bank that blocked the sun. A reminder that as close as spring was, there was still a touch of winter to deal with. He buttoned his jacket and hunched forward in the saddle.

Yes, Annie was a good woman. Better than he deserved. True, she didn't have the exuberance and energy that her sister Kaitie had. She didn't like to join him in the things he loved to do, but she allowed him a lot of freedom and rarely questioned where he was going or what he was doing like he'd seen other men's wives do. She trusted him. JJ sighed deeply. She trusted him.

A pang of shame came over him as he recalled his betrayal of Annie with her sister. It had only been that one time, and he blamed it on the drinking. He had also tried to excuse himself because he told himself that he was a man of passion and needed an outlet for that passion that Annie was unwilling or unable to give. But he knew now that he was just trying to rationalize his frailty.

What would life have been like if I had married Kaitie? he asked himself. She was beautiful, brave and wild, and the ache he felt for her had never let him be. She was the opposite of her sister. She loved adventure and taking risks. She could outride and outdrink anyone he knew. Even him. She wanted to take the whole world by storm and nothing was going to stop her. Annie, on the other hand, was careful. Always cautious. She was content having her world encompassed by the wire fences of their ranch. She understood his need for excitement, but she also sensed, better than he himself, his need for a comfortable safe place to come home to. He sighed again. Annie grounded him. She had been the right choice for him. His head knew it, but his heart was always torn between the two sisters.

Kaitie had been so vibrant and full of life. He would never forget the last day he'd seen her. It was just two weeks before she was killed. The day was glorious—one of those end of winter days when the sun unexpectedly warms into the upper fifties and teases you into thinking spring is almost here, reminding you why you put up with the long Montana winter.

Annie had just poured him a cup of coffee and was shuffling around the kitchen in her fluffy slippers and bathrobe. Kaitie came down the stairs one slow step at a time and entered the kitchen with puffy eyes and bed head.

"Well, good morning, Sunshine!" JJ smiled at her.

"Mmmm. Morning, everyone." Kaitie mumbled. She yawned deeply and stretched her arms above her head towards the ceiling, lifting the t-shirt she'd slept in above her waist and exposing her bikini panties. JJ unconsciously and unavoidably raised an eyebrow and grinned. She shook her head and fluffed her hair with her hands getting the sleep snarls out of it.

Even fresh from bed she was gorgeous, JJ thought. Her tangle of hair begged to be caressed. With the sun shining behind her through the kitchen window, he could see every curve of her delicious body silhouetted through her t-shirt. Legs that never ended. Even the chipped red polish on every other toe somehow added to her sexiness. JJ watched every step she took as she scuffed to the table.

"I'm sure you want this," Annie said as she placed a large mug of steaming coffee in front of her sister.

"Oh, yes, sweetie. Thanks. I slept like a rock, but I think that was because someone must have hit me in the head with one."

"I believe that if you recall, it was Captain Morgan who sailed in and socked you with a rock last night," JJ said.

"Ugh. Don't remind me. As I recall, you and the Captain were pretty chummy yourselves last night."

"Okay, but I will remind you, you promised to go for a ride with me today."

Kaitie squinted at the window, "I remember. It's a beautiful day for it. Do you want to come, Annie?"

JJ looked at his wife with a cynical smirk. "She won't go."

Annie shook her head. "You know I don't like riding that much. Besides, I've got laundry to do and I told our neighbor I'd help her make some cookies for her daughter's Future Farmers of America dinner. You two go ahead. A day like today shouldn't be wasted"

"She's right," said JJ. "Let's get crackin, Miss Cathcart. Daylight's burning. Get some pants and boots on and let's go."

Kaitie yawned and waved him down with one hand. "Hold your water there, cowboy. Let me grab a piece of toast and I'll get dressed." She leaned across the table and took a slice of toast off his plate allowing him a generous glimpse down the front of her t-shirt. He could feel Annie's eyes burning into the back of his head.

"Hey! That's mine," he called after her.

Kaitie crammed the entire piece of toast into her mouth, squinched her eyes at him and holding the corners of her shirt she curtsied, turned and dashed up the stairs two at a time.

"She's something." JJ laughed.

Annie slapped him playfully with the dishtowel. "Yes, she is. And you'd better stop ogling her something, Mister."

"Hey, she's the one dancing around in a t-shirt."

"Never mind. You just behave yourself."

JJ looked at Annie's stained and faded cotton nightgown with the torn hem hanging shapelessly on her. "It wouldn't hurt you to wear just a t-shirt now and then."

"What, and freeze my butt off in this drafty old ranch house? No thank you."

"Well, if that was all you were wearing, I'd warm you up."

"You just be quiet now and hand me your plate."

He gave her his plate. He got up and strode to the window. By the time he turned around Annie had cleaned and dried his dish and cup and was just finishing wiping off the table. *There's no one can clean a kitchen faster than she can,* he thought.

"Ready!" Sleepy Kaitie had gone up the stairs and beautiful Kaitie the cowgirl glided down. Her glistening hair was tied in two pigtails peeking out from under a black Stetson hat. She wore a tight-fitting red plaid shirt with pearl buttons tucked into a snug pair of Wrangler jeans cinched up with a belt bearing the same silver rodeo queen buckle she had won in Wilsall years ago. On her feet were a pair of Justin Square Toes. She adjusted her hat in the wall mirror in the living room.

"You look ready to ride, Missy." JJ grinned and ducked as Annie swung the dishcloth at his head.

"Well, what are you waiting for, JJ? Daylight's burning." Kaitie turned and flounced out the front door waving to Annie as she left.

THE EARLY SPRING DAY was glorious. Brilliant blue and white Alpine flowers shimmered on their gracile stems like tiny stars in the sunnier spots along the trail. The horses had worked off their morning friskiness and had settled into a relaxing walk. The sun that was warming the two riders was melting the dwindling patches of snow. Damp patches trickled into little rivulets, which became sparkling waterfalls of diamonds tumbling out of the rocks and on down the mountain.

Kaitie breathed in deeply, "Doesn't it smell wonderful? I love this time of the year."

"It is nice," JJ agreed. "Clears the head. That was fun last night, though. I'm glad you came down for the weekend. Annie and I haven't gone dancing or even out anywhere since that last time you stayed with us."

"That was fun. I love dancing with you. Always have."

JJ nodded and they let the peacefulness surround them again.

Without looking at her JJ asked Kaitie, " Do you go out a lot up in Missoula? Got a boyfriend yet?"

"No, no boyfriends. I go out every now and then, but I'm pretty busy with my writing."

"How's that going? Are you still freelancing?"

"Still freelancing. It's hard though. I haven't sold anything for awhile. I've got an idea for an article I'm starting on now. I got an advance on it from a sporting magazine. So, I guess I won't starve for a few more weeks."

"A sporting magazine? Is it Sports Illustrated? You gonna write about the swimsuit models, or are you gonna be one? I'd buy that issue!" J turned and grinned at her.

Kaitie rolled her eyes at him."Shutup, JJ. It's got nothing to do with swimsuit models and it's Field and Stream, not Sports Illustrated. I'm not going to tell you what it's about. I don't like to talk about my writing before I'm done with it. But I will tell you the research is getting interesting."

"Aw, c'mon, you can tell me. Okay, here's the deal. I'll race you up to the cabin at Ibex. If I win, you tell me what the story's about."

"Well, you aren't going to win, so what do I get when I win?"

"That's not going to happen, but if some miracle occurs and you do beat me, I'll buy you a beer at the café when we get back. Deal?"

"Two beers and it's a deal. Hyah!" Kaitie jammed her bootheels into her horse and bolted forward slapping it's rump.

JJ's horse, surprised by the sudden burst of activity, took a step back. JJ kicked him and they took off after Kaitie.

The two horses thundered up the road, their riders bent low over their necks. They took the switchbacks with ease. As they came to a flat plain, JJ began to gain on Kaitie. His horse was a nose away from her flank. Kaitie kicked hard and bolted away from JJ, making the turn on to the narrow trail heading up to Ibex cabin. As she neared the cabin, Kaitie slowed her horse down fearing he might break an ankle galloping through the spongy spring soil.

JJ came up behind her and reined his horse in as well. Both horses and riders were panting.

"I could use those beers right about now," said Kaitie wiping her forehead with her sleeve. She swung out of her saddle and dropped to the ground.

"I'd say that was a bit of a jump start there," said JJ dismounting. "I'm afraid you'll have to settle for bottled water for now." He handed her a bottle from his saddle pack and grabbed one for himself.

They walked the horses down to a stream and let them drink, then walked back up to the steps of the cabin, sat and opened their bottles. They each took a long drink. Kaitie put her bottle down and leaned back on her elbows, her hat falling from her head. She closed her eyes, turned her face up to the sun, shook her hair out and laughed.

JJ turned close to her and looked at her happy face. His heart was pounding, but not from the exertion of the horse race. She was so beautiful. Her laugh, her hair, her skin, her lips. They were irresistible. He could feel himself drawn into the aura of her.

Kaitie opened her eyes and looked at him. His face was inches from hers.

"Kait, you are so beautiful," he whispered. "I still love you."

Kaitie blinked and looked deeply into his eyes that were now so close to hers.

"I love you too, JJ, but . . . "

Their lips met and their love for each other awakened, took hold and pulled them passionately against each other. JJ crushed Kaitie to his chest clutching her strong back. He wanted the kiss to go on forever. His hand floated along the soft cotton of her shirt and moved toward her breast. Before he could go any further Kaitie caught his hand and pulled back from him.

Her breath was coming fast and she looked intently at him. "JJ, we can't do this anymore."

JJ sagged back against the step. "I can't help it, Kait. I still love you. That time up at your place in Missoula . . . ."

"That time in Missoula was a mistake. We were both drunk and I was lonely and weak. It was sweet, but it shouldn't have happened."

"I was lonely too."

"You were only up there for the weekend. You'd been with Annie just the day before. What do you mean you were lonely?"

"I love Annie. I do. But she's not like you. You're full of life and energy and passion. Annie, she's a good woman and she takes good care of me, but I come home and we have dinner and she'll go read a book and then go to bed with or without me. It doesn't matter to her. I don't remember the last time we made love. She doesn't seem to care, and I'm not sure I care anymore. But when I'm with you, it's like it was when we were younger. I feel on fire around you. I can't explain it any better than that."

"It's called lust, JJ."

"It ain't just lust, Kait. I've loved you since that first night we danced in Wilsall. Remember?"

Kaitie looked down at her boots and nodded.

"You light me up," he continued. "You're a beautiful woman, but it's not just about your looks. It's your excitement about things around you. Hell, it's just who you are." JJ gently turned her chin up and looked deeply in her eyes. "Kait. I love you, plain as that. Always have, always will."

Kaitie looked at him a moment longer, sadness and empathy showing in her dark eyes, then turned away and stared at her feet. The two sat in silence for a few moments.

Without looking up, Kaitie said, "JJ, I know you love me, and it makes me feel good to know that you do. I love you too, but it's like I told you that night by the river. Do you remember that night, just before I left for school? "

It was JJ's turn to nod.

"I need to focus on myself and my career. I don't mean to sound selfish, but that's what I want to do. You need someone . . . No, you need Annie. She's good for you. I know she isn't Miss Outdoors or Miss Party Girl, but she loves you and she's always there for you. There's not a lot of women who would give you all the freedom she gives you."

JJ hung his head and sighed. "I know. I know. I'm a lucky man. I'm sorry for coming on to you like that and I won't do it again. But one thing, Kait, know that I'm always going to love you too."

"The same goes for me, JJ. Till the day I die."

THOSE WORDS OF HERS came back to him now like a boulder on his chest.

The death of her sister had killed a part of Annie as well. Ever since she had learned the savagery of Kaitlin's death Annie had been inconsolable. She wept for days up to and following the funeral. She wouldn't speak to anyone, not even JJ. He tried to comfort her, but she showed no sign of being relieved of the smallest amount of her anguish. Her generally happy disposition had vanished along with any communication between the two.

Eventually, JJ stopped even trying to reach her. She sat in front of the television all day and went to bed early without him. He would go to work, do his chores, live his separate life and at the end of the day, he'd crawl exhausted into their cold, emotionally separate bed staring at the ceiling and failing to sleep. He wanted to connect with her, both figuratively and literally. To hold her and be held. He needed her to know how much she meant to him. How he realized the love he had for her and that she had for him was what mattered most. He wanted to come clean about the time he cheated on her with Kaitie and his realization that it was Annie and no one else whom he needed most.

Now that this crazy Bridger Jackson had surfaced as a clear suspect, he dared to hope that once he was brought to justice Kaitlin's death might be put behind them and at last, he would be able to win back his wife.

He arrived at the ranger cabin not long after Stollar had gone. As they neared the cabin, Gopher's fur raised a flag of warning along his spine and he emitted a low threatening growl. JJ dismounted and approached the cabin. A blood smear on the porch pointed like a hideous arrow to the doorway and Gopher sniffed at it as JJ climbed the stairs. *This must be where he took her*, he thought. His hand shook as he turned the doorknob. The rusty hinges creaked as the door swung slowly open and a stifling close smell wafted out as if a tortured spirit was escaping into the fresh air outside. JJ felt light-headed and steadied himself against the doorjamb, a mixture of dread and nausea pushing at the back of his throat.

The afternoon sun had heated the cabin like an oven. The ranger station was typical of those built in the 1930's—a sparse room with a small wood stove in one corner and a cot in the other. Tiny motes of dust floated through the dim shaft of sunlight filtering through the window. In the middle of the room stood a rough-hewn table with a bench on one side of it. JJ took a deep breath and approached it slowly, hesitantly but irrevocably. Dried blood and fresh blade marks in the table testified to the vicious butchering that had taken place here. A dizzying interfusion of revulsion and anguish swept over JJ. He shut his eyes. His mind swirled and grasped at visions that refused to allow him to see his sweet sister-in-law in this monstrous room. A happy, smiling Kaitie danced a vigorous two-step in his head as she had that first night they met after the Wilsall Rodeo. A beautiful, giggling Kaitie leapt up to catch her sister's bouquet thrown at the wedding reception. A joyful, laughing Kaitie raced her horse across the golden valley, her hat and long brown hair bouncing wildly against her back as she turned to catch sight of him racing after her.

Opening his eyes, he prayed that the gruesome death table with its hacked and stained top would have magically disappeared. However, no; there it stood having taken the deadly chopping blows of the butchering axe, absorbing the lifeblood and terrified screams of Kaitie as she was battered to death on this table where many before her had innocently dined. JJ choked and gagged, nearly vomiting.

With tears welling in his eyes he clenched his fists in anger and screamed to the rafters overhead, "You son of a bitch!" He kicked the heavy wooden table to the floor, and charged from the cabin. Once outside, he sat on the top step, put his head in his hands and wept. "I'll get him, Kaitie. I swear I'll get him."

Chapter 11

THE BIG HORN SHEEP STOOD regally with its white-tipped muzzle in the high mountain air, munching a mouthful of grass; its massive horns curled a silhouette around its face. The rich brown fur on its sturdy body and the distinctly outlined white of its butt looked almost unreal in its perfection.

It was only 50 yards in front of him and a real beauty. He had been tracking it all day, and now it was in his sights. The sheep would easily bring him $20,000.00 or more from the Asian businessman he dealt with. He beaded in on the trophy sheep and squeezed the trigger. The shot exploded from the rifle echoing off the mountains. The big animal jolted, then dropped to its knees and fell on its side at the edge of a steep precipice.

"Sweet," the shooter said aloud with a leer on his face. He scrambled up the rocks to claim his prize. The ram was huge, at least 270 pounds, he reckoned. He was big and awesome, even with his tongue hanging out. The hunter pulled his knife out and set about gutting the beast.

෯   ෯   ෯

SHERIFF STOLLAR HEARD the gunshot far off to the northwest of his position. He had been working his way up the mountain following Jackson's trail as best he could. It wasn't easy – especially on the rocky ground at this elevation. In fact, he was afraid he had lost the trail when he heard the crack of the rifle. He figured that the trail had been heading more toward the east, and it had been fresh. Jackson would have had to cut back across the ridge and move fast to have gotten to wherever that gunshot came from. In addition, why would he be shooting? It was not hunting season, and he knew Bridger was smart enough not to be poaching in the off-season. Besides, poaching fines were stiff these days— in Montana you could get fined tens of thousands of dollars and face up to several years in prison—Jackson preferred to keep a low profile, and wouldn't bring attention to himself by poaching.

Stollar dismounted and surveyed the ground. He pushed his hat back and rubbed his chin. He looked to his left and then to his right. Behind him, Chief blew out a deep huff and pawed at the ground.

Rubbing the horse's nose, Stollar said, "Well, Chief," looks like we've lost Jackson's trail. Might as well see who's shooting up the place. What do you think?

In response, Chief shook his head, jangling his bit, and let go with a heavy stream of piss.

"I'll take that as you couldn't care less, huh? Okay, let's get moving." He pulled himself up on the big horse and turned him toward the west. He gave him a kick and Chief took off at a quick trot.

∾   ∾   ∾

JJ INSPECTED THE TRACKS on the ground in front of the cabin. There were fresh boot prints and horse sign from the sheriff and Chief. He could also make out moccasin prints that the sheriff's tracks were following.

He called Gopher to his side and kneeling down, tapped the clearest moccasin print commanding, "Gopher. Find it!" The dog responded and went into tracking mode intently sniffing the ground, wagging his tail and heading into the timber. JJ didn't know if he'd get the chance to use it, but he checked his pistol, shoved it into his belt, swung up on Spot and followed the tracking dog up the mountain. With any luck he'd find Jackson before the sheriff would.

∾   ∾   ∾

FROM HIS HIDING SPOT, high in the rocks, Jackson watched as the sheriff dismounted and then re-mounted his horse. He also heard the rifle shot, and was relieved to see that it had attracted the officer's attention, pulling him off the trail and toward the west. He watched until the sheriff disappeared over the ridge, then rose to his feet and headed up the mountain toward his cave.

Chapter 12

IF THE SHERIFF'S HORSE hadn't whinnied as he made his way up the ridge, the hunter, intent on skinning the ram, wouldn't have known he was coming until it would have been too late. It was already too late to hide the carcass. He grabbed his knife and his rifle and scrambled down the rocky slope to the trees below. He rolled behind a big fir and turned in time to see the sheriff riding toward his pilfered sheep.

"Damn it," he cursed. There went twenty, maybe even thirty thousand dollars worth of effort. Chip Tomlinson had made a lot of money selling his poached wildlife to wealthy executives from around the world—Asians, Arabs, Californians, Texans and New Yorkers all with big wallets, big mansions and even bigger egos, wanting to prove how rich and macho they were by having huge wild game trophies hanging in their dens. Some would fly out to Montana to go on illegal hunting trips with Tomlinson, and others would pay top dollar to have him do the killing and shipping for them. He had made a comfortable living for himself since he started his illicit business. He averaged well over two hundred thousand dollars a year, tax-free. So far, he had managed to avoid being caught. There was way too much at stake if he did get caught, so he was careful, very careful. A poacher over in the Elkhorns who was convicted for killing a trophy bighorn had to pay $30,000 to the State, he lost his license to hunt for life, and he did some serious jail time to boot. Tomlinson could easily get up to five years in prison or more for poaching if they ever came across his workshop. However, they would not. He had hidden it well, and nobody, not even his wife, knew it existed.

That damn reporter had found out about it though. But that had been his own stupid fault. She was a hot little number. Kaitie, that was her real name, though she had told him it was Karen. She had come on to him at the Mint Bar over in Big Timber by playing up to him, acting all drunk and horny. He was drunk himself. He had been switching between Moose Drool beers and shots of Jack Daniels all afternoon and into the evening in celebration of the end of another illegal hunting trip. This one for a mountain lion with two dudes from Connecticut who had paid him mucho dinero— mucho. So he was feeling good—and horny.

He remembered Red, the bartender, had poured him a shot of Jack and said, "Compliments of that little lady down the bar, Chip," and nodded in Kaitie's direction.

He gave Tomlinson a wink and walked away. Tomlinson focused his bleary eyes on the woman. Nice! She was wearing a low-cut black tank top under a plaid cowgirl shirt. He couldn't take his eyes off the luscious globes beckoning to him. Her jeans fit tautly over her legs and sweet butt as she leaned toward the bar giving him a wave and a smile. Her brunette hair was carefully brushed, framing a gorgeous face— big brown eyes and full lips painted dark red. He raised his shot glass in thanks and with a little effort, he worked himself off his bar stool and made his unsteady way to the one next to hers.

As he sat, she gave him a friendly smile. "Hey, cowboy!" she said in greeting.

"Thanks for the drink, sweetheart," he slurred, leering at her, trying unsuccessfully to remind himself not to stare too long at her breasts.

From the adjacent room the four-piece band, the Bar-Three Wranglers, was cranking out a decent cover of Toby Keith's I Love This Bar. *An appropriate tune,* thought Tomlinson. He loved this bar. It was a typical Montana drinking hole where one could still smoke cigarettes. Tattered and faded dollar bills, some with drunken scrawlings on them, covered the smoke-stained acoustical tiles of the low ceiling. Bras of all colors, sizes and styles dangled from the antlers on various skulls mounted on the walls. NASCAR and beer posters with hot chicks in Daisy Duke shorts hung everywhere. Thursday night cowboys in Carharrt jeans cinched with big buckled belts clicked pool balls across worn green felt tabletops, and the bar was getting crowded.

"Enjoy," she said above the noise and clinked her shot glass against his.

"I will," he smiled back at her and downed his drink. He wiped the stubble on his chin with the heel of his hand. "Much obliged, Miss . . .?

Kaitie placed her empty glass on the bar and said, "Karen."

"Well, pleased to meet you, Karen. I'm Chip. Where you from?"

"California"

"California, huh? What brings you to Montana?"

"A little bit of vacation and a little bit of business. My father asked me to come and find out about hunting spots and outfitters for him and his business partners. They heard there was some great trophy hunting in Montana and wanted to plan a trip. I noticed your camo hat and jacket and thought you might be able to give me some advice."

Tomlinson pushed the bill of his cap back and flashed her his best stud smile. "Honey, you bought the right man a drink. I am probably the best outfitter in the Rockies. I can get your daddy mountain lion, bear, pronghorn, buffalo — you name it."

He reached into his shirt pocket, fished out a business card and leaning close into her, he slid it into her tank top with a wink, his fingers gently brushing her breast. "Here's one of my cards. Have him give me a call and I'll hook him up."

She leaned back, extracted the business card from her bra, and examined it, giving him the opportunity to examine her.

"Well, thanks, Chip. I'll pass this on to him. He and his friends will be coming out this summer so he'll probably give you a call soon."

"Hunting season doesn't start until the fall, though."

She looked at him and smiled with those beautiful red lips."Well, that's what I thought," she said. She leaned in closer to him and lowered her silky voice. "But Daddy seemed to think there were private places that you could go to out of season. He said it cost more, but believe me, money is definitely no object for him and his friends. Would you happen to know any places like that?"

Tomlinson looked her in the eye with a grin and lowering his voice, said, "I may be able to help him out, honey. Have him give me a call, and we'll talk turkey." He slipped an arm around her waist. "Now, how about you? You hunting for anything? I can help you with that too. You want another drink?" He snorted as he laughed.

She returned his lascivious grin with one of her own. "Not tonight, cowboy. Thanks. I've got to get up early tomorrow so I need to get my beauty sleep. But, I'll tell you what, on Saturday, if you will show me one of the places you'd take my daddy's group, I'll treat you to dinner and maybe another Jack or two."

He paused and turned the empty shot glass in his beefy hands before answering. "Sure. You bet, Kathy. I'll show you some of the prettiest country you'll ever see. How 'bout I pick you up around two o'clock on Saturday?"

"The name's Karen. Sounds good. Why don't I meet you here for lunch?"

"You got it, Karen."

"See you Saturday then, Chip. Bye now."

She slid languorously off the stool and sauntered her way out the door. Leaning with one elbow against the bar, Tomlinson pulled the brim of his cap back down and watched her move. "Like two puppies fighting in a potato sack," he murmured aloud. Red smiled and poured him another shot.

Chapter 13

IT TOOK A MOMENT FOR KATIE'S eyes to adjust after walking in from the bright midday sunlight into the darkened bar on Saturday. The room was lit solely by some buzzing neon signs and what little light filtered through the dusty fly-specked window. Tomlinson was sitting at the bar with two empty beer bottles in front of him and a half-filled one in his hand. The bartender sat chunking quarters into one of the video poker machines on the wall opposite the bar with a cigarette dangling out of his mouth. Unlike Thursday night, there were only two other patrons sitting at the far end of the bar, no pool players, no band. The place had the leftover smell of stale cigarettes, stale beer and stale lives that permeates a seedy bar during the daytime hours.

"I was beginning to think you weren't going to show up."

He was squinting from the sunlight struggling its way through the dim barroom. With the benefit of the hazy daylight, Kaitie was able to make a clearer assessment of him than the other night. His puffy red eyes and days old stubble made it hard to determine his age, but he looked to be in his late thirties or early forties. He had the hardened look of a serious and potentially dangerous drinker. The dirty baseball cap he was wearing sat back and slightly askew on his head revealing the beginnings of a receding hairline.

Kaitie smiled back. "Wouldn't have missed it. I got moving a little late this morning. Sorry."

"You want a drink?"

"No, thanks. But, do they have anything to eat? I'm starved."

"The only thing I'd recommend are the burgers. How's that sound?"

"Fine by me."

Tomlinson swiveled in the direction of the bartender. "Jimmy, get off your lazy ass and get us two cheeseburgers, will ya?"

Jimmy grumbled, mashed his cigarette butt into the ashtray and shuffled slowly through the swinging half-doors into the kitchen.

Kaitie watched him go then turned to Chip and said, "I thought you couldn't smoke in the bars in Montana anymore."

Chip smirked. "Yeah, the fuckers in Helena passed that law about two years ago. Jimmy don't give a shit though. As long as there's only a few regulars in here he'll light up and so will they."

"So, are we going to check out the old hunting grounds? Daddy's excited I found you."

"Well, I am the best around," he boasted. "You tell your old man I can get him whatever he wants whenever he wants it. But tell him not to mention it to anyone else until we talk."

"Oh? Why not?" she asked.

"I only deal with an exclusive clientele that I know personally."

Kaitie looked at him with a sly grin. "And I'll bet you know where to get some fine trophies even in the off-season, and you don't want everybody knowing it."

Tomlinson did not respond. He chugged down the last of his beer, deposited the empty bottle with a thump next to the other two and wiped his mouth on his sleeve.

"You sure you don't want something to drink?"

"Maybe some coffee."

Tomlinson yelled toward the kitchen, "Jimmy! Bring us two coffees on your way back." Tomlinson squinted at Kaitie as if sizing her up. "So, you say your father knows that hunting in the summer ain't exactly legal, right?"

Kaitie nodded. "Yes, he knows. But, one of the fellows in the group is an old friend who will be visiting from back East celebrating his sixty-fifth birthday. He's got cancer or something and Dad promised he'd take him hunting if he's up to it. The only chance he can get away is in June. Is that okay?"

The bartender, with a fresh cigarette in his mouth, slid two plates of greasy cheeseburgers accessorized with a limp pickle spear and a handful of chips across the bar in front of them.

"Coffee's comin up."

Kaitie picked at her chips and watched Tomlinson take a big bite out of his hamburger, grease dribbling down his chin.

"It's okay," he mumbled with a mouthful of meat and bread, "I can take care of him and his party, but I'll have to charge them extra for the risk."

"That's fine. Dad said for you to give me a price and he'll pay whatever it is. It doesn't matter how much." She took a small bite of her hamburger, put the remainder down and pushed the plate back across the bar. "Guess I wasn't so hungry after all."

"You gonna eat that pickle?"

"No, you can have it."

Tomlinson stuffed the rest of his hamburger into his mouth and followed it with Kaitie's pickle.

"You done?" he asked.

Kaitie nodded. Tomlinson slapped some bills on the bar, put his arm around Kaitie and said, "Let's go, young lady." He shepherded her out to his truck. She climbed in the passenger side and slid over to the middle of the seat.

"This is so exciting!" she gushed. "Riding into the country with a real outlaw!" She dropped her hand to his thigh and gave it a squeeze.

"Hold on there, gal," he said clearly buzzed and with a grin that said he was pleased with himself. "Who said I was an outlaw?"

"Oh, I'm sorry," she replied with a teasing false apology. "Should I have said 'entrepreneurial business man?' I mean if you're hunting big game out of season, that's kinda dangerous, isn't it?"

"Well, it ain't for the faint of heart," he said. "You've got to know what you're doing, where to do it and how to keep others from knowing you're doing it. And while we're on the subject . . . " his tone got suddenly serious, "you need to know there are some big risks in the stuff I'm involved in and what I tell you and show you ain't for public consumption."

Kaitie flashed a big innocent grin at him and made a slow exaggerated X across her chest. "Cross my heart and hope to die." She watched Tomlinson follow her fingers letting his eyes rest on the bulge of her breast as her blouse pulled more open.

"I won't say anything to anyone. I'm fascinated by all this. And I've gotta tell you, it gets me kind of hot being with you. I want to hear about everything." As she spoke, she ran her hand up and down his leg, kicking his activity center into high gear.

He gave her a wink and stepped on the gas.

⁂   ⁂   ⁂

AS THE TRUCK PICKED UP SPEED Tomlinson smiled. It was turning into a good day. *The hell with showing her the hunting spots,* he thought, I'm taking her to the shop. His number one rule was never to let anyone know about his work place. It was where he kept his kills and where he skinned and mounted them. It was also where he kept all his files and records. If anybody in law enforcement ever uncovered all the information and incriminating evidence in that place the fines he would have to pay and the years he would spend in jail would be astronomical.

Then again, he had another rule. Never pass up a good lay. And this woman was obviously hot for him. She was young and real good looking, not the kind he could normally attract. However, he thought he looked pretty good, and the women always seemed to like the bad boys. Let her think I'm an outlaw, he figured. And, once she sees my workshop, she'll be even hotter.

"Before I show you some hunting spots, how about I show you where I work on the animals I kill?"

"Oooo, I'd love that," she cooed sliding her hand farther up his leg.

He hurried down the highway and turned off onto a gravel road heading into the mountain. They bounced along the washboard trail until it came to a stop at a weather beaten pasture fence with "No trespassing" signs posted every few feet. Tomlinson got out of the truck, unlocked the gate and drove through, relocking the gate behind him. The road had ended and ahead lay only green pasture. The truck bounced and rattled its way across the field, over big rocks and across a creek, finally coming to a stop at another fence.

Tomlinson shut off the engine and turned to Kaitie as she turned to him. He put his hand behind her head and brought her mouth to his with all the passion that had been building up in him since she had first touched his leg. They kissed and pawed at each other for a few minutes and he began to undo her blouse.

Kaitie pulled back and held him off, and said huskily, "Hey, I thought you said we were going to see your workshop. Do you have a bed or a sofa in there by any chance?"

"You bet," he said with a grin and a wink. "Let me show you where I do my stuff."

They got out of the truck and Kaitie followed Tomlinson along a game trail that wound through the pine trees. A crisp wind whispered through the treetops and Kaitie shivered and pulled her jacket collar around her neck.

Shortly, they came to a small log cabin. Hammered into the door and wall were a number of signs warning "No trespassing — violators WILL be shot." A large padlock on the door and only one small window would have made breaking in impossible.

Tomlinson pulled his key ring out and unlocked the lock, slipping it from the heavy hasp. He carefully opened the door; a choking draft of air filled with dust, animal fur, heat and the stench of death rushed out and enveloped them. Kaitie couldn't hold back a gag.

"Stay here a moment," he said.

She was happy to remain out in the fresh mountain air as long as possible rather than enter the dark and foul smelling building. She watched Tomlinson bend down and carefully release a well-hidden trip wire from a small hook inside the doorway.

"My homeland security device," he said. "Anyone breaking in here would trip this wire and KA-BOOM!" His big grin revealed gaps where teeth were missing. Kaitie hoped her smile hid her revulsion.

He led her into the cabin and pointed to the other end of the trip wire that led to a device that wrapped around a large bundle of dynamite fixed to a five-gallon can of gasoline.

"They'd blow their ass to kingdom come," he chuckled. "Can't be too careful."

Kaitie eyed the bundle of TNT and gulped. "I guess they would," she said. "Looks like enough explosive to blow them farther than that!"

"Yeah, well, like I said—you can't be too careful. Let's get some light on the subject," Tomlinson said, and lit a kerosene lamp illuminating the dank workshop and adding its oily smell to the mixture of fetid odors of death, blood, rotten meat and embalming chemicals.

The room itself was oppressive and close, like a tomb. As her eyes became accustomed to the dim interior, Kaitie saw that this was where Tomlinson did his taxidermy. A number of animal heads — deer, elk, pronghorns, beaver and even a buffalo— hung everywhere. They were mounted on the walls, piled on the floor and stacked on wooden shelves. A long worktable stood against one wall stained with dried blood and speckled with desiccated chunks of meat. The wood was worn and splintered from axe and knife hackings. Dead flies and some still living and buzzing lazily covered the table and the floor beneath it. Cans of formaldehyde, body putty and various bottles of other chemicals sat atop the workbench. Hanging from nails above it was a collection of saws, knives and assorted tools used to rip through the flesh and bones of all types of animals large and small.

A huge grizzly bear skin was stretched and nailed against the opposite wall. The head of the grizzly lolled backwards from the neck as flies climbed in and out of the eyeless sockets. What remained of the bear's tongue hung from its massive maw and provided even more dining for the busy black flies and the maggots they were developing from. An acidic lump rose in Kaitie's throat and she was afraid she would throw up. She managed to hold it down nevertheless, and pointed to the bear.

"Where did you get him?" she asked.

"Shot him over in the Absorkees a couple days ago. Fellow in Arizona's gonna pay me $9,500 once I get him mounted."

"He must have just come out of hibernation, huh?"

"That's right. I would have liked to have him fattened up a bit more, but the Arizona guy wanted this thing soon so he could display it this summer in his resort in New Mexico. He has this fancy place with over 70 rooms and the house features all kinds of bear crap. I can't remember the name of it." Tomlinson walked over to a dusty desk in one corner of the room, picked up a ledger, and thumbed through it. "Yeah, it's called the Bear Creek Resort. You and your dad ought to go sometime. Looks swanky. "

Kaitie eyed the journal with interest as Tomlinson threw it back down. He opened a drawer and pulled out a bottle of Jack Daniels.

"How about a snort, sweetheart?" He offered the bottle to her.

"Sure," she replied as she took it and downed a stinging mouthful. She hoped the drink would deaden her senses enough to stand the ghastly cabin and its contents.

Sweeping his hand grandly around the room, Tomlinson said, "Well, what do you think of my workshop? Got some nice trophies in here. Like I said, I can get your dad anything he wants, just about whenever he wants it. Why don't you come over and sit here with me?" Tomlinson said as he dropped down on to a filthy cot parked underneath the drying bearskin.

Kaitie choked back another wave of nausea as the stench, the whiskey, the greasy hamburger and the revolting horror of what surrounded her mingled with her feeling of disgust at the thought of having sex with this man. She took another long haul off the Jack Daniels and steeled herself for what she was about to do. It helped. She put on a sexy smile for Tomlinson and sauntered over to the bed holding the whiskey bottle out for him.

He took one more pull on the bottle and drew her down to him on the cot. Kaitie let Tomlinson lay her down and closed her eyes as he brushed back her hair. Her body tensed as he leaned into her and kissed her neck. The bristles on his unshaven face scratched her skin. His breathing quickened and his alcoholic stench wafted up into her nostrils. She held her breath. She felt his wet lips on hers and nearly gagged as he slid his fat tongue into her mouth.

God, what am I doing? she thought to herself. She opened her eyes. His were closed as he moaned above her. The feeling of his tongue filling her mouth repulsed her. The animal heads in the room seemed to be watching the two of them in mute wonder. She looked past Tomlinson's sweaty face and gazed up at the dangling bear head above them. A wiggling maggot slipped from one crusty eye socket and dropped onto Tomlinson's back.

Sweat broke out on her forehead. At once she felt cold and hot at the same time and a dizzying wave of nausea rolled up from her stomach. She could hold back no longer. An eruption of vomit from deep within her gut tore up through her throat and filled both her mouth and his, covering the two of them in a bath of disgorgement.

"Holy shit!" he sputtered as he leapt off her, spitting puke from his mouth and wiping it from his face.

"Oh my God, Chip! I am so sorry," Kaitie cried, wiping her chin with her sleeve. "I am so embarrassed."

Tomlinson grabbed a stained towel from the workbench and wiped his face and shirt with it. "Here," he said, and threw the filthy rag at her.

With her head spinning and her stomach churning, Kaitie ran to the door in time to launch another stomach full of gore onto the ground. As she leaned against the outside of the cabin, head down, Kaitie repeated, "I am so sorry, Chip. I think I had better go home. I'm sorry."

"Yeah, I guess you'd better."

Kaitie sat in the grass letting the soothing mountain air wash over her as Tomlinson closed up the cabin. After resetting the trip wire, he shut the door and replaced the sturdy padlock.

On the ride back Kaitie pretended to fall asleep. Not a word passed between the two of them until Tomlinson dropped her off at her car and they said goodbye. As she stuck the key in the ignition, he leaned in her window and asked, "You sure you're okay?"

"I'll be fine. I'm just not used to drinking whisky this early in the day I guess. Let me make it up to you. I still owe you dinner. How about tonight? We could go out, or we can grab a pizza and have it in my room at the motel. There are a couple of good movies on the TV we could watch. It might be fun. What do you think?"

Tomlinson thought for a moment. "Yeah, pizza and a movie and you—sounds good to me. I like pepperoni. I'll bring some beers."

"7:00 okay?" she raised a curious eyebrow then wrote down the name of the motel for him, "See you tonight." She pulled out and headed down the road. Glancing in the rear view mirror, she saw Tomlinson inspecting the wet stains on his shirt, and smiled to herself.

Chapter 14

ONCE SHE GOT BACK TO THE MOTEL Kaitie went to the bathroom and turned on the shower. She undressed and climbed into the tub humming happily to herself. The refreshing hot water splashed down on her, washing away the putrescent memory of Tomlinson's cabin.

As she lathered the shampoo in her hair she thought about her plan. Things were moving almost too easily for her. She had not anticipated that he would take her right to his taxidermy shop. On top of that, he had tipped her off to where he kept his record book. When she started the research for her article on poaching, she thought it would turn out to be an expository piece. While gathering information from some of the seedier locals at the bars in and around Big Timber she had heard Chip Tomlinson's name a couple of times. Nothing concrete, but suspicions that he might be able to give her some information about the things she needed for her article. Getting this lead to a major poacher could turn her article into a top selling exposé. Although Field and Stream magazine had hired her to do this piece, there might even be more here if she could get the names of some major businessmen from Tomlinson's records. It could be the break she had hoped for since journalism school.

Her plan was a little cheesy, and more than a little dangerous. Nevertheless, if that is what it took to move her into the big league, so be it. She knew that sleazeball would want to sleep with her tonight, but if her plan worked, she would get lucky and be able to avoid that. She was glad she had brought the Ambien with her. She hadn't sold a story in months and as a result had not been sleeping well. Her doctor had given her a prescription for the sleeping pills and they never failed to knock her out for the night. One tiny tablet and she would sleep like the dead until morning. She thought three might do the trick for Chip.

After washing her hair, Kaitie got out of the shower and dried off. She wrapped the towel around her and got the pills from her purse. Taking the bottle and the glass from the sink, she crossed the room and tapped out three Ambien on the desktop. She pressed down on the tablets with the glass crushing them into a fine powder. Using a credit card, she swept the powder onto a piece of notepaper that she folded and slipped into the pocket of her jeans. She put on a plaid shirt buttoning only the bottom three buttons and pulled on her pants. She posed and smiled at herself in the mirror and decided she was ready for Tomlinson.

KATIE LOOKED AT THE CLOCK on the nightstand. 7:00 came and went. So did 7:30. She paced the floor checking the clock every five minutes. It was almost 8:00 when there was a knock at her door. Opening it, she saw Tomlinson standing there holding two six packs of beer. One pack was missing two bottles already.

"Sorry I'm a little late, darlin'. I got delayed at home."

Yeah, she thought, *probably the wife gave him a hard time about going out, especially bathed in that cheap cologne.*

"No problem," she smiled at him. "Come on in. I'm starving. I'll call for the pizza now. Pepperoni, right?

"Sure. Sounds good." He stepped into the room and put the beers in the mini-bar, extracting two bottles for himself and Kaitie. He twisted them open and blew out a windy burp. With a snap of his fingers he shot the caps into the wastebasket.

Crossing the room to the phone Kaitie felt his eyes taking in her tight jeans. She hoped her plan worked. The thought of kissing him again was repulsive. But, a girl's got to make a living, she joked to herself. She ordered the pizza and Tomlinson picked up the television guide card absently looking at the different movies that were available.

While they waited for the pizza delivery, they drank their beers and picked out a movie. They sat back down on the couch and Tomlinson put his arm around her pulling her close.

"I'm looking forward to this," he said with a grin.

"Me too!" As she replied, he turned her face toward him and kissed her hard on the mouth. Resisting the strong urge to pull away, Kaitie let him kiss her and even managed to respond with a little manufactured passion before she put a hand on his chest and gently pushed him back.

"Wait a minute, big boy," she smiled at him. "How about some Jack with that?"

"Why not?" he said, letting out another deep beer belch and a sigh. "You got ice?"

"You bet. I'll just be a second." She went into the bathroom, took the two tumblers off the shelf, dropped a couple of ice cubes in them and fished the packet of powdered sleeping pills out of her pocket. She shook the powder in Tomlinson's glass and filled it halfway with Jack Daniels, giving it a good stir with her finger. As the drink absorbed the sleeping powder, Kaitie poured herself a small shot. Some of the crystals of powder were still visible as they swirled in the brown liquid, but she knew she could keep his attention focused on her. She pulled her blouse open a bit more, picked up the glasses and sauntered out to the couch. As she had anticipated, his eyes stayed focused on her breasts as she walked toward him, until he finally looked up in her eyes.

"Down the hatch," she said, offering him his glass and holding his gaze with her eyes. He took it without looking down and gulped it with a thirstiness that had nothing to do with his drink. Kaitie poured him another Jack, but declined his offer to have one with him.

"I think I'll stick to the beer until later," she said. "I don't want to fall asleep during . . . the movie, you know."

"Yeah. The movie," he grinned, throwing back his drink.

Snuggling closer to him Kaitie said, "So, tell me some more about your business."

"Not much to tell. I have been hunting since I was five years old. I know pretty much every inch of the Crazies, the Absorkees, the Tobacco Roots and most of the other mountains around here. I have trapped in most of the waters in Western Montana and Idaho and am one of the best shots around. I know the best places to find elk, deer, bear, pronghorn—you name it. I've got clients who come from every corner of the world looking for that big trophy for their den. You wouldn't believe what they pay me," he bragged. "You also wouldn't believe some of the big shots who I take out."

"Oh? Like who?" Kaitie asked filling his glass with more whiskey.

"Well, that's confidential, sweetheart. But the names in my record book would make your head spin. Especially if you knew what they were hunting and when."

"Wow. Sounds exciting. And a little dangerous. Aren't you afraid of getting caught?"

Tomlinson smiled at her as he filled his own empty glass. "Not me, babe. I am real careful. Besides, my record book is my insurance policy. I've gotten into some close calls with the law over the years. I won't deny it. But, knowing the guys I know, I've got a lot of strings I've been able to pull to get me out of jams."

Tomlinson regaled Kaitie with other stories about his prowess and adventures until the pizza delivery arrived and the Jack Daniels had diminished to less than a third of a bottle.

Kaitie opened the box of pizza and laid some slices out on the napkins she had placed on the coffee table.

"I've got to pee," Tomlinson slurred thickly and got to his feet, but only with the help of the sofa arm. "Whoa!" he said as he lost his balance and fell sideways into the desk.

Kaitie turned and looked back at him. "You okay?

"Yeah, got up a little too spoody. I mean speedy." Using the desk as leverage, Tomlinson shakily launched himself toward the bathroom and leaned against the door jamb, holding on to catch his balance. From the doorway, he reached across to the sink like a mountain climber getting a good grip before his next precarious move. Holding on to the sink he let go of the doorjamb, and placed his foot to take his next step. Kaitie saw him take a misstep and fall crashing down with his face against the base of the toilet.

"Oh, crap," he mumbled and closed his eyes.

"Chip! Are you alright?" Kaitie called running to the bathroom. She almost felt sorry for the guy, lying there in a lump with his face squashed against the toilet.

Tomlinson tried to pull himself up by grasping the toilet bowl and attempting to get his leg under him, but slid back down to the floor. Squinting at her with one bloodshot eye, he slurred, "Oh, man. I'm sorry, baby. Lemme get up and take my whiz. I'll be right out."

Kaitie helped him to his feet and steadied him over the commode, then left and closed the bathroom door.

Kaitie eyed him with genuine concern as he exited the bathroom. His face was ashen, his pants were only half-zipped and there was piss all over the front of them. His eyes were unfocused and he weaved back and forth as if he would fall down any moment. Maybe she had dosed him too much, she worried.

"Come on. Let's get you on the bed. You don't look too well," she said as she went to support him and steer him toward the bed.

"Good idea," he half grinned as Kaitie slipped an arm around him and the two of them lurched gracelessly across the room. He fell back on the pillow and she lifted his legs on to the bed.

"Here," she said, "let's get those pants off." Kaitie removed his shoes, undid his pants and worked the soggy things off him. She pulled the covers up and tucked him in.

"Thanksh, honey," Tomlinson slurred with closed eyes

"Get some sleep, Chip," Kaitie said and she quietly walked out of the room closing the door behind her carrying the pee-soaked trousers. Once outside the room she felt in the pants pocket for his keys. There they were. She smiled as she checked and found the key she had seen him use for the cabin.

Everything was working as planned. Now, to see if she remembered how to get to the cabin. After checking to make sure Tomlinson was sound asleep, Kaitie slipped out of the motel room and drove west on I-90 to the turn-off at the ranch road sign.

ALTHOUGH IT WAS LATE, the moon and the stars in the big sky of Montana made it easy to see the road as she bounced along. Farther into the mountains the trees began to get thicker and the road became almost invisible. She began to think she might be lost when she came upon the pasture with the fence and no trespassing signs. Fumbling with Tomlinson's key ring Kaitie found the key to unlock the gate, opened it and drove through. Her car splashed across the silvery moonlit creek sending two mule deer bounding into the timber.

Her heart began to race with excitement. She knew she was on to a big story, but she was also conscious that she was playing a particularly dangerous game. She chewed on her thumbnail. The sooner she could get the information she was looking for, the sooner she could get back and get Tomlinson out of her room. For now, though, her adrenalin was pumping at the prospect of what she was about to do.

After parking her car, she made her way through the trees and across the moon-splashed yard. The cabin beckoned to her like a treasure chest waiting to be unlocked.

After unlocking the door and opening it slightly Kaitie knelt down and gingerly unhooked the trip wire on Tomlinson's security device. She held her breath and her hands shook as she anticipated a huge explosion. When the wire dropped free without any blast she let out a sigh of relief.

Kaitie coughed and covered her nose and mouth as the door swung open and the foul air made its escape. She clicked on her flashlight and crossed the floor to the desk where she had seen Tomlinson leave his journal. It was the most valuable prize she could get tonight. She picked it up and began to leaf through it. Each page had several columns: dates, client names, addresses and other contact information. The next columns itemized the game animal supplied, where it was poached, who shot it and how much the buyer paid for the excursion or trophy.

The prices paid were staggering. In some cases, tens of thousands of dollars were made on one hunting trip. The animals included everything from bison to wolves, mountain lions to golden and bald eagles. Kaitie wondered why anyone would pay that much to own the remains of an animal.

Scanning the column of addresses, she noticed clients from every corner of the world—Asia, the Middle East, Europe and South America. None of the names of those foreigners held any meaning for her, but some of their titles indicated that they were princes, presidents and military officers. The American names and titles, however, made her gasp. Here were a well-known senator, a governor, numerous actors and a long list of high-ranking judges, politicians and top corporate executives. Small wonder that Tomlinson had evaded capture and prosecution for so long with a little black book filled with the names of clients like these. As she noted VIP after VIP, Kaitie's story began to develop into an even more major project in her mind. This was inflammatory stuff and much bigger than a mere exposé of poachers.

She pulled her camera out of her purse and took photos of each of the pages in the journal. After photographing the book, Kaitie took shots of the various dismembered and mounted animals in the workshop. When she focused on the hanging trophies the hair on her neck prickled. She felt as though they were snarling at her and ready to pounce. A further search of the cabin turned up nothing relevant and the urgent voice in her head insisted she leave this place as soon as possible. After one last look around, Kaitie let herself out of the cabin, carefully resetting the trip wire.

The mix of excitement and fear she had experienced when approaching the cabin was nothing in comparison to the heart-pounding rush she felt as she bounced her way along the ranch road to the highway and back to town. She smiled broadly. Her original plan to do an article on poaching in Montana had seemed marketable. There were plenty of hunting and conservation publications who would pay her for a well-written article on the topic. However, the names she had captured from the journal with her camera were huge. This story would make international news once it got out. It would be the story of a lifetime for her. It might even win her a Pulitzer Prize. By the time Kaitie reached the motel, she had already begun formulating the article in her head.

She parked and quietly let herself into the room. Tomlinson's bear-like snoring told her that he was still deep asleep. He would be out for several more hours. She was too excited to sleep, and the thought of crawling into bed with that man and worse, waking up next to him in the morning, was too much for her to even consider lying down. No, she needed to get out of here. No point in hanging around. Kaitie quickly gathered up her things and loaded her overnight bag, laptop and purse into her car. She returned to the room and scribbled a note to Tomlinson:

Dear Chip,

I hope you're feeling better. I tried to wake you but you were sound asleep. I have an early flight back to California so have to leave. I'll have Daddy get in touch with you.

Kisses,

Karen

She put the note in the motel envelope and stuck it hanging halfway out of the bathroom mirror where Tomlinson would see it when he got up. She let herself out of the room and went down to the lobby to pay the sleepy night desk clerk. It was 3:00 in the morning when she turned her car back on to I-90 and headed home to Missoula.

Chapter 15

TOMLINSON OPENED HIS BLOODSHOT EYES. The red numerals on the digital alarm clock read 8:14. He rubbed his throbbing temples and squinted around the room trying to place where he was. He turned over and saw that the spot next to him was unslept in. He threw the covers back and made his way unsteadily to the bathroom where he saw the note on the mirror.

"Damn it," he mumbled aloud after reading it. "Shouldn't have had that much to drink."

He stumbled into the other room and found his pants draped over the chair. He pulled them on and buckled his belt. He patted his rear pocket to make sure his wallet was there and then patted the front one to check for his keys. No keys. He felt his other pocket with the same result.

"Damn it." He searched the floors and all the furniture. He picked up the pizza box hoping they might be hiding under it, but there were no keys.

"Damn it!" he pitched the pizza box across the room. Tomlinson went to the window and saw his truck was still there, but where were those damn keys? He was sure he'd put them in his pants when he got out of the truck last night. That chick wouldn't have taken them, would she? He went down to the parking lot and checked inside his truck through the window. No keys. He pounded on the truck's hood.

He went back to the room and did another thorough search. Nothing. The keys were clearly gone. She must have taken them, but why? He scratched the morning stubble on his chin. Was she pissed off and screwing with him? He had been a perfect gentleman, and as far as he could recall, he hadn't taken advantage of her last night. Maybe that's why she was pissed. Maybe she had left them at the front desk for some reason. Tomlinson went down to the motel office and found the desk clerk sleeping in a chair in the back office.

"Hey, kid," he called. The young man opened his eyes and came out yawning.

"Good morning, sir."

"Morning. I was in room 281 last night. My wife checked out earlier this morning. Brunette. About my height."

"Oh, yeah," the boy answered rubbing his eyes and stifling another yawn. "She checked out real early— about 3:00." He looked at the invoice on his desk. "You mean Mrs. Cathcart, right?"

"Cathcart. Yeah right. Karen Cathcart."

The clerk glanced down at the invoice again.

"No, she signed 'Kaitie Cathcart.'" He showed Tomlinson the signed credit card receipt attached to the invoice.

Tomlinson hid his surprise, took the invoice and looked more closely at it. It was made out to a Kaitie Cathcart at 2757 Cottonwood Street in Missoula.

"Oh yeah," he replied, handing the bill back to the clerk. Her real name is Karen, but she goes by Kaitie for her professional work. Anyway, did she happen to leave some car keys with you when she left?"

"No, she sure didn't."

"Hmmm. Well, I'll go take another look around the room. Can I still use the phone in there?"

"I shut it down after she paid her bill. Sorry. I didn't know you were still in the room. Is it a local call?"

Tomlinson nodded.

"I'll turn it back on for you then, if it's just the one call. Will you be vacating your room soon?"

"Yeah, right after I make the call. Thanks, pal."

Something weird is going on here, Tomlinson thought as he headed back to the room. His inner alarm was starting a slow build up. *Okay*, he thought, *I can see why she'd use a false name. Chicks do that all the time. But what's up with that Missoula address? She said she was from California. Is she a cop?* Christ, he had shown her his workshop and told her enough about himself to cause some real problems. This was not good.

When he got back to the room the first thing he did was write down Kaitie Cathcart's address—2757 Cottonwood Street, Missoula. He picked up the phone and called his wife.

"Hey, Nancy."

He was not in the mood to hear the irritation in her voice. "Where are you? You didn't call or . . . ."

"Yeah, yeah. Look, I ran into an old buddy last night and we got into it pretty heavy. I was too loaded to drive so he took me to the Elkhorn Motel out near Big Timber and dumped me here to sleep it off. I lost my keys somewhere and can't drive my truck. There's a spare set in the kitchen drawer. Can you bring them over to me so I can get out of this place?"

"An old buddy, huh?" she snapped. "You think I'm stupid? Don't start this shit again. You said last time . . . "

"Nancy, just shut up and bring me my keys."

"Son of a bitch," she said and slammed down the phone.

Tomlinson tucked the piece of paper with Kaitie's address on it in his pocket and went down to wait for his wife by the truck.

"That bitch," he growled, covering both Kaitie and Nancy.

℞   ℞   ℞

ON THE WAY TO MISSOULA Tomlinson massaged his forehead. The overcast sky matched the grey fuzziness in his brain. The dull ache in his head was compounded by his confusion as to what was going on. The chick had given him a fake name and apparently a fake story about coming from California. He pounded his fist against the steering wheel in anger at her and at himself. It wasn't like him to get suckered. He was smart and he was careful. He was always the one who was one step ahead of everyone else. He had to be. It was why he had escaped to Montana and how he had been able to hide out here for the past fourteen years.

He liked it in Montana. It suited him. He loved to hunt, there was plenty of game and his poaching business made him a lot of money. A whole lot of money. In addition, the state was so big and under-populated it was easy to keep out of the sight of law enforcement. No wonder Ted Kaczynski, the Unabomber, was successful at avoiding capture for so long by holing up in the mountains out here. In fact, he recalled, it was hearing about the crazy Unabomber that gave him the idea of going to Montana in the first place.

He had hated Nebraska. What was to like? His life there had been crap. After slapping his mother and him around nearly every day for the first ten years of his life, Tomlinson's alcoholic father ended up in prison for battering some farmer to death in a bar fight. His mother, no slouch in the drinking department herself, was killed in a drunk driving incident when he was eleven. By then he'd been drinking and doing drugs himself. The court turned him over to his grandparents— a couple of dotty old codgers living in a run-down trailer home on a wasted piece of farmland. They hated him, hated each other and hated life. Like his parents, they were big drinkers with nasty tempers. His grandfather used to beat him with a belt until a growth spurt at thirteen provided him with the strength and nerve to start hitting back. He spent the next four years in and out of jail for various minor crimes—mostly drunken assault and battery.

At eighteen, he got his girlfriend pregnant. She gave birth to a son the day his grandmother died of cirrhosis of the liver. His grandfather refused Tomlinson's demands to let his girlfriend and son move into the trailer. Nor would he let him have any of the proceeds from the paltry life insurance policy from his grandmother's death. They got into a shouting match that escalated into a pathetic punching bout between him and the old man. It was with a mixture of self-righteousness, rage and rum that Tomlinson pulled the shotgun from under his bed and blew his grandfather's head off his neck. He came up with the plan to hideout in Montana that day.

The road sign said "Missoula 40 Miles." Light raindrops splattered on his windshield as he pushed the old pickup to eighty. No sooner did he turn on the wipers than the sprinkling turned into a torrential downpour hammering the truck and rendering the wipers useless. Slowing down some, Tomlinson squinted through the brief glimpses of the highway that the tick-tocking windshield wipers would afford him. As quickly as it had started, the deluge subsided into a steady light spring rain shower. Tomlinson resumed his speed and settled back into thinking about his departure from Nebraska fourteen years ago.

After pocketing his grandmother's insurance money and what little he rifled from his grandfather's wallet, Tomlinson stepped over the old man's mangled body and headed to town where he picked up Nancy and their newborn son and headed northwest.

He had been lucky enough to meet an outfitter in a bar in central Montana. The outfitter was badly in need of some help and was happy to pay him under the table that first hunting season. He even let him and his young family move into the old trailer on his property. Tomlinson found he loved learning the outfitting business as well as becoming familiar with many of the best hunting sites around. He also appreciated the huge tips he made from the wealthy hunters that traveled to Montana each season.

Within two years he had made enough to afford a small trailer, and he began to develop his own clients. Some of the wealthier ones would get him to take them out in the off-season. His reputation for confidentiality, skills as an outfitter and willingness to push beyond the law spread via word of mouth. Soon he developed an exclusive well-paying clientele and the money rolled in. Not only was he making a good living off the hunting, but also he discovered that selling big game organs, skins and mountings to buyers around the world was where the best dollars were. He taught himself taxidermy, and to avoid the prying eyes of the Fish, Wildlife and Parks officers, he built himself a workshop tucked into a well-hidden canyon deep in the Crazy Mountains. Now he was making hundreds of thousands of dollars.

It was a great living and he was careful to keep it that way. For the first time in years, he was worried. Falling for a piece of ass, he had lowered his guard and broken his cardinal rule about keeping his business secret. Worse, he had shown the bitch his workshop. Hell, she had said she was from California. He had figured it couldn't hurt to take her there if it meant getting some action. But now his warning bells were going off. This chick in Missoula had lied to him about her name; lied to him about where she lived and had probably lied to him about the whole "Daddy wants to go hunting" bullshit. The more he thought about it the more he was sure she had to be a cop—either an FWP game warden or worse, a state cop. She had to be.

"Damn it!" He slammed his fist against the steering wheel again.

He would have to get the truth out of her, and if the truth was she was a cop, he'd have to get rid of her. If it were only to arrest him for the poaching, that would be bad enough. However, she might be a fed looking into his grandfather's murder case. Even if she wasn't, that old piece of business would likely turn up in an investigation. He had managed to stay hidden all these years and he wasn't going to let the murder of his grandfather catch up to him now.

The rain stopped and Tomlinson turned off the wipers. A few more miles and he would be in Missoula. He needed a plan.

Chapter 16

KAITIE WAS EXHAUSTED by the time she arrived at her place in Missoula. She couldn't wait to take a hot bath and go to bed. First, she needed to check and make sure that she had captured the pages of the journal and the pictures of the cabin on her camera. She set up her laptop on the desk in the corner of her one room apartment. As it booted up she reached into her purse for her camera. A sudden sinking feeling filled the pit of her stomach when she felt the key ring in her purse. With shaking hands, she pulled out the foreign keys.

"Oh my God!" she gasped aloud. In her hurry to leave the motel, she had forgotten to replace Tomlinson's keys. A wave of panic flooded through her body. The idea of seeing him again was too nerve-wracking and dangerous. Until she had her article written and he was in prison, seeing Chip Tomlinson was not an option. But when he found his keys were gone he'd know it had been her that had taken them. She paced the room clenching the keys in her hand.

The bar, she thought. She would drop them off at the Mint Bar where they had met. She knew Tomlinson hung out there, and the bartender would return his keys to him.

Sighing a breath of relief, Kaitie ran some bath water. While the tub filled, she attached her camera to the computer and downloaded the pictures. She printed off a couple sheets to make sure the photos of the pages were of sufficient quality to read. As the printer processed the photos, she plugged in her backup thumb drive and, although exhausted, she dutifully typed some notes into her daily journal. Before shutting down, she backed up the files to her thumb drive as always to be on the safe side. Throwing the drive into the drawer, she shut down the computer. She took her bath, crawled into bed and shut off the light. For almost an hour, her brain worked on angles for the article in her head. *I'll never sleep,* she thought. Somewhere into the fourth revision of the opening sentence, she drifted off.

KAITIE WAS STILL DEEP asleep that morning when she woke to a loud insistent knocking on her door. The bedroom was cold and she shivered as she slipped on her robe. Her brow wrinkled in concern as she crossed to the door. Leaving the security latch locked, Kaitie opened the door a few inches. She was unable to suppress a slight gasp when she saw Chip Tomlinson standing outside.

A tight smile spread across his face as he took in her shocked look. "Well, good morning, Karen. Or, should I say 'Kaitie?' Did you miss your plane?"

Stay calm, she thought, her fingers tightening on the doorknob. Stay calm.

"Oh my gosh! Hi!" Kaitie said. "Uh, yeah, I came back here to my apartment to get my things and was so tired I fell asleep. How did you . . . ?"

He interrupted her with a sneer in his voice. "I believe you have something of mine. May I come in?"

"Oh. Of course. I'm sorry. Still not awake yet." A shudder of fear went through her as Kaitie unlatched the door with trembling fingers and Tomlinson strode in.

"You got my keys?" he demanded more than asked.

"Oh. Yes. I am so sorry. They fell out of your pants when I undressed you last night. I picked them up and I must have thrown them in my purse without thinking. Force of habit, I guess." She managed a withering smile. "Let me get them for you. I was going to take them back to . . . "

"So, Karen . . . err, Kaitie, let me ask you something." Tomlinson wandered around the apartment picking up and inspecting little items as he went. "I thought you said you live in California."

A slight flush of red began to creep up her neck from her chest. She hated that telltale sign of nerves, but could never manage to control it. She kept her head down as she searched through her purse for the keys. "I do. Most of the year I live out there. But, Daddy got me this apartment when I went to college and I sometimes stay here when I've had enough of the Coast. Here are your keys. Sorry"

He snatched the keys from her. "Nice place you have here. So, what were you doing in the Elkhorn Motel if you've got this apartment here in Missoula?"

She looked at him shyly. "Well, to be honest, I knew I wanted to sleep with you the minute I saw you, so I gave you a fake name and rented the room at the Elkhorn as a precaution and so we wouldn't have to drive all the way back to Missoula. You know, just to be on the safe side. I'm sorry for the subterfuge, but a gal's gotta protect herself." She forced a nervous smile.

Without looking at Kaitie, Tomlinson mulled this over and grunted a noncommittal, "Hmmm." as he continued to snoop around the apartment. She could tell he was smoldering and no sexy come-ons were going to influence him this time.

Kaitie's heart was pounding and her mind was racing. She ran her fingers through her hair. The last thing she wanted was to see this boorish pig again, and now here he was in her apartment. He knew where she lived and he knew her real name. She tried to maintain a calm facade but inside she was screaming for help at the top of her lungs.

Trying to sound nonchalant she asked, "How'd you find me?"

"The kid at the motel desk gave me all your info."

"But they aren't supposed to . . ."

"The kid is probably eighteen years old and works the night shift. You think he gives a shit about policies?"

Kaitie shook her head no. Tomlinson continued to walk around the apartment checking out different things along the way. Kaitie realized with horror that the printouts she'd made from the camera were sitting in the printer. She nervously watched as he strolled closer to her desk.

"So are you still flying back to California to see Daddy or was that bullshit too?" Tomlinson was smiling as he said it, but Kaitie did not like the undertone in his voice.

"Um, yes. I have to go back." She dug her fingernails into the palms of her hands knowing he was hovering over the incriminating journal printouts.

Tomlinson picked up a porcelain moose statue sitting next to the printer that she used as a paperweight. Kaitie caught her breath. He began to flip and catch it as he spoke,. "So, when is your flight then?"

"Please be careful with that," she reached out quickly trying to divert his attention. "My grandma gave it to me." No sooner had she spoken, than

Tomlinson missed his catch and the moose fell to the floor breaking into pieces. "Oh, no, Chip!" she gasped, torn with the sorrow of losing her keepsake but relieved at the same time that his focus had been drawn away from the printer tray's contents.

With feigned concern, Tomlinson apologized and began picking up the larger shards, looking for a place to put them. Kaitie bent and picked up the remaining pieces, laying them on her kitchen table and told Tomlinson, "Just leave them over here. Maybe I can fix it later."

Tomlinson carefully laid the antlers and legs on the table and repeated, "I'm sorry about that, but yeah, I think you can glue that back together. Now, when did you say your flight to California is?"

"I'll have to make a new reservation. I guess I'll try to get out by tomorrow morning."

"Oh yeah?" he said. "That's great, because I never did get to show you where I would take your father hunting. I could run you up there right now. It won't take more than a half hour or so. You've got to see it. It's beautiful."

Anything to get him out of here, she thought. "That would be wonderful. I'll need to get back this afternoon, though, so can we go now?"

"Sounds like a plan, Kar . . . Kaitie. Get dressed and we'll go."

To keep his attention focused away from the desk, Kaitie said, "Can you grab my pants from the chair over there? I just need to get my shirt from the bathroom and we can go."

While Tomlinson fetched her jeans, Kaitie darted into the bathroom and quickly pulled on her shirt, buttoning it up as she walked over and took the pants.

"Sorry we didn't get to finish things last night," Tomlinson said with an admiring grin as he watched her dress.

"Me too," she lied, fumbling her belt buckle with nervous fingers. Eager to get him out of her apartment but still fearful of his mood, she picked up her purse and headed resolutely to the door. "OK, all set. Let's go, Chip!"

"You bet." With a smirk, Tomlinson squeezed by Kaitie at the door and they left the apartment.

∾   ∾   ∾

AS THEY DROVE WEST along I-90 Kaitie felt her pulse rate picking up. She had hoped never to see Tomlinson again, and now he had found her in a lie and was driving her to who knew where. His attempts at idle chatter did not make her any more comfortable.

"I never asked. What is it you do for a living?" The undertone behind his words frightened her.

With her mind nervously focused on her situation, Kaitie didn't think to make something up and automatically answered, "I write. Nothing much. Articles and stuff mostly."

"A writer, huh? What kinds of articles?"

Kaitie realized her mistake too late. She should have come up with something else. Feigning indifference she said, "Oh, just girl stuff. Dating advice, beauty tips, nothing very interesting, I'm afraid."

"I see. So, in your dating advice articles do you advise women to pick up men in cowboy bars?"

She looked at him. "No. I advise them to get to know a man first—over coffee or lunch."

"So, why did you buy me a drink at The Mint the other night? Am I a research project?"

Kaitie turned her gaze out the window to the craggy mountains in the distance jutting up and scraping the sky. They looked ominous.

"No. You had an interesting face, and I hoped to get to know you better. That's why I didn't sleep with you that first night and suggested lunch the next day. Plus," she added with a smile, "I'll admit I was a little tipsy."

Tomlinson looked directly into her eyes and asked bluntly, "You aren't a cop are you?"

Trying to remain calm, Kaitie forced a slight laugh which she hoped did not expose her nervousness and answered, "No, of course not. What made you ask that?"

"Had to ask. I told you a lot of things about me and my business that I don't usually share with anyone. Like I said before, I can't take any chances."

"I understand. Don't worry about me. I'm harmless." Kaitie felt her wildly thumping heart would explode from her chest at any moment. "So, where are we going?"

Tomlinson turned off the interstate and headed toward the tiny ranch town of Clyde Park, not far from where her sister and friends lived. Her anxiety jumped another level and she prayed they would not run into anyone she knew. That would be next to impossible to avoid if they stopped in the town.

Sounding artificially convivial, Tomlinson told Kaitie, "I'm going to show you one of my favorite hunting spots. If your dad is looking for elk, deer or bear this is one of the prime places I could take him."

To Kaitie's relief, Tomlinson drove straight through Clyde Park without stopping. On the other side of town, he turned up a gravel road toward the mountains.

"These are called the Crazy Mountains," he said.

She looked out at the mountains rising over eleven thousand feet from the valley they'd been driving through. She acted as if she was seeing them for the first time, though she had grown up in their shadow and had spent her childhood hiking, biking and riding through them.

"Wow! They are awesome," she said. "Why are they called the Crazy Mountains?"

"There are a couple of stories about that. The geological reason is that the rock is up-thrusted lava and looks different from the other mountains nearby. The Indians thought the mountains were haunted and called them the "Mad Mountains" because of their rugged peaks and howling winds. Myself, I'm particular to the legend that a pioneer woman went crazy after her family was killed by Indians and she took refuge up here in the Crazies somewhere. It's easy to get lost up in there if you don't know what you're doing."

"I'll bet it is." Kaitie glanced at Tomlinson out of the corner of her eye. His chattiness and change of mood seemed genuine. While she prayed this was so, she still could not lose the sense of the dangerous situation she was in. She resolved to play along with him. She rolled her eyes looking back at the spiky mountains knowing she had no other choice anyway.

They bounced along the gravel road as it became rougher and rockier, twisting its way higher into the heart of the foreboding mountains. Storm clouds darkened the sky threatening rain or snow. At last, the road ended at a clearing in which sat a small cabin. Kaitie knew this to be one of the old ranger station cabins. She and her sister had played in it many times as young girls.

"It's a National Forest Service cabin," said Tomlinson pointing at the structure. "They sometimes rent these out to campers during the summer. This one is pretty run-down though. A crazy old coot sometimes shacks up here in the winter. Lives like a mountain man. Dresses like one. Lives off what he catches and occasionally still sells pelts. He keeps to himself mostly. I seen him a coupla times. There's lots of game up here, which is why he hangs out in these parts. It's also where I do a lot of my hunting."

Tomlinson shut the engine off in his truck and turned to Kaitie with a look that filled her with dread. She shivered with a damp coldness that was only partially due to the crisp mountain air. There was no humor in his face, only a deadly serious glare. Her stomach, heart and head churned in a turmoil of anxiety.

"So, tell me what were you doing up at my cabin? And don't give me any bullshit."

Kaitie stammered, "Wha . . . ? What do you mean? What are you talking . . . ?"

Tomlinson swung his hand up and slapped her hard across the face making her eyes tear. She could feel an angry welt forming on her cheek. A small trickle of blood from her swollen and broken lip slid down her chin.

"I said no bullshit!" he roared at her. He grabbed her by the hair and pulled her head back so hard that it cracked against the cab's rear window.

Bringing his face within inches of hers, he hissed, "Are you a fucking cop? If you're a cop, so help me, I'll . . . ."

"No! I'm not a cop. For chrissake let me go!"

He jerked back on her hair once again. "Not until you tell me what you were doing up there. Now talk."

Her panicked mind working frantically, words began to spill out of Kaitie without any thought behind them, "I'm sorry. But, you passed out and I couldn't sleep. I was bored, and when I took your pants off and the keys fell out on the floor I got this crazy idea of going back up to your workshop to look at the stuff you had up there. It was stupid and rude, I know, but I was curious. I really am sorry."

"You're lying and I know you're lying." Another painful jerk on her hair. "Once I realized you had taken my keys I got an extra set from home and drove up to the cabin to see if you had gone up there. Your boot tracks were all over the place. When I went inside, I found my records book on the right hand side of my desk. I never put the book there. I am very careful about that book, and I always keep it at the upper left hand corner of my desk. I was sure you'd been snooping in it. When I went to your apartment, I saw you had made copies of the pages. They were sitting in your printer tray on your desk."

Kaitie's eyes widened as her anxiety turned to full-bore panic. She felt the rising heat of

Tomlinson's anger as his threatening face leaned in closer to hers. "Now I want to know, what the hell were you doing with my record book?"

Kaitie's breath was coming heavily. "Nothing. I . . ."

Tomlinson backhanded Kaitie again. "Don't lie!"

Kaitie sobbed, "Okay. Okay. I'm a writer. I'm doing an article on hunting in the Rockies and your story is an interesting one. I was trying to do research and . . ."

Glaring at her with increasing impatience Tomlinson cut her off and snarled, "And what the hell were you copying my record book for?"

Her mind was racing. She had to escape. As she stammered, Kaitie inched her hand to the truck's door handle praying it was not locked.

"I . . . I . . . thought some of those people might add some flavor to my article and I was going to see if I could get an interview with one of them."

Tomlinson appeared to mull this over. "You're not a cop?"

Mercifully, Tomlinson relaxed his grip on her hair. Holding back the damnable tears she felt would burst forth any moment, she pleaded, "No. I swear to you. I'm just looking for a story. I won't even write about you. I won't even write the story."

"A story for who? About what?" Tomlinson's anger was welling up in his voice again, but at least he had let go of her hair.

"I don't remember. Some sports magazine. I have the name in my purse here." She picked her purse up off the truck floor and began rummaging in it. Her fingers felt the canister of bear spray that she carried with her at all times in case she went backcountry hiking. With her heart pounding like a sledgehammer, she snapped the cap on the cylinder and whipped it out spraying Tomlinson directly in his eyes.

He screamed in agony and Kaitie frantically yanked up on the door handle. She fell to the ground, but scrambled up and headed into the timber as fast as she could go.

The effects of the pepper spray were immediate and overwhelming. Tomlinson's eyes and face burned as if he had been scorched by a flamethrower. His inflamed throat swelled, causing him to cough and gasp desperately for air. His larynx was paralyzed and he could no longer scream. All he could do was writhe in excruciating pain on the front seat of his truck. Eventually he managed to grope for the door handle and stumble into the open air. His skin and eyes still burned and he continued to gulp for air, but he stumbled after Kaitie in the direction of the noises she was making as she charged through the trees.

KATIE FOUND A GAME TRAIL and ran as hard as she could looking back to see if Tomlinson was gaining on her. He was still well behind her stumbling clumsily and rubbing his eyes, but headed in her direction. Tomlinson tried to holler, but all that came out was a raspy croak. She could tell he was gaining on her. She turned off the game trail and charged into the thick of the trees. She looked back to see where he was and stepped on a pile of loose pine branches. She felt the branches spring under her foot, followed by a loud metallic snap and immense pressure on her ankle. She took another step and fell face down on the rocks. She looked at her ankle in disbelief and despite Tomlinson's relentless pursuit, Kaitie screamed.

Blood was pouring on the ground and her foot was gone. It had been severed from her leg and was lying in the center of a massive bear trap now exposed from under the pine branches where it had lain. The horror of what was happening washed over her at the same time the agony shot like a bolt of lightning up her leg. She let out a wrenching cry of terror.

Despite her panic and pain, Kaitie realized she had to stanch the bleeding or die from loss of blood. Frantically, she ripped a strip off her blouse and bound it tightly around her bloody stump. Weeping and with adrenaline, pain and fear pumping like a jack-hammer through every vein in her body, Kaitie crawled up the steep slope above her, praying to locate a place to hide. She dragged herself across the ground, climbing ever higher. She reached up and grabbed a rock that jutted out above her and tried to pull herself up to the next level. But, the rock gave way and she tumbled down the slope rolling through dry brush and shale until she bumped into a soft tree which stopped her dead. She rolled over to get her bearings and realized that she had not rolled into a tree at all, but had crashed into Chip Tomlinson's legs.

"Well, hello there," Tomlinson said with a cruel grin. He was squinting and trying to keep his eyes opened. His face was bright red from the pepper spray. He was obviously still in great pain, but smiling at her.

In desperation, Kaitie pleaded "Please. Oh, God, Chip, my foot. Please help me."

He looked down at the bloody bandage around her ankle feigning concern. "Ouch. That's not good. We had better get you to a hospital or you're going to bleed to death. Then you'll never be able to write your article, will you?"

"Please," Kaitie begged, choking on her tears. "I feel like I'm going to faint. Please help me."

"Okay. I'll help you, but first . . . " Tomlinson pressed his boot down on her bloody ankle. Kaitie cried out. With his foot applying constant pressure Tomlinson continued, "First, tell me the truth. What was that article about?"

Katie cried, "Oh my God, I don't know. I hadn't even started writing it."

Tomlinson pressed down harder and Kaitie screamed.

"Okay. Truth. I was going to write about the poaching business. But, I swear I wasn't going to use your name. I swear I won't even write the article now. Just please get me to a doctor."

Tomlinson lifted his foot. "That's much better. See how honesty pays off? Now let's get you taken care of."

He reached down and helped her to stand up on her one good leg, but the effort and pain of standing and the loss of blood was more than she could bear and she fainted.

❧   ❧   ❧

TOMLINSON TRIED CARRYING Kaitie's limp body in his arms, but found that too tiring and shifted her to his shoulder. Blood ran down over the front of his shirt. Although the going was awkward and the slope was steep, he managed to make his way down the mountain. When he reached the bear trap that encircled Kaitie's severed foot. He dropped her from his shoulder, wiped the rivers of tears flowing from his seared eyes with the heels of his hands and sat to rest and think.

In spite of his discomfort from the bear spray, he chuckled to himself about the trap. How ironic! It was only last week that he had been looking for it. He had forgotten exactly where he had set it late last fall and needed to retrieve it before a game warden came across it. It was a stroke of good luck that he had found it. Well, he chuckled again, Kaitie had found it. He had set it close to this cabin because he knew that bear would be down in this area come spring. Trapping bear was strictly illegal, and if a game warden had come across it, it would mean that the FWP folks would be trying to find out who had put it there. He should thank Kaitie for finding it. Plus, her stepping in it was unexpectedly helping with his plan to get rid of her.

While he was relieved that she was not a cop, the fact that she was a reporter convinced him he needed to proceed with his plan. Although under the circumstances she may have been telling him the truth, he could not be sure that she had not already submitted her story to whatever magazine or newspaper she was working for. If her article got published, it would mean the end of his life. Even if they only convicted him of poaching, the fines would wipe him out financially and he would likely spend the next ten years or more in jail. Worse, if a poaching investigation led to discovering he had murdered his grandfather back in Nebraska, at best he would get life, at worst, the chair. He needed reassurance. He needed to get back into her apartment and see if she had left any evidence there—a notebook, anything on her computer. If he could get on to her computer he might be able to find out what she had submitted, if anything. Her keys were in her purse back in the truck.

Lying next to him, Kaitie moaned softly. He looked at her and the anger welled up in him. The bitch had come close to ruining his life. She had nearly blinded him. She had come on to him just to use him for her story. He had exposed his business to her and she intended to betray him with that information. He knew he could not let her live. He did not want to let her live. She was losing blood at such a great rate she would soon die on her own. All he would have to do is wait. But, the more he thought about how she had nearly destroyed him, the more he was intent on following through with his plan.

It was a good plan. When he had been searching for the bear trap last week he had hiked past the ranger cabin and had noticed a wisp of smoke coming from the chimney. It was too early in the year for anyone to be allowed to stay there. Curious about who would be up here this time of year, Tomlinson had cautiously approached. As he climbed the steps, he noticed that the padlock normally in place had been torn from the door. He moved to the window and peered into the hazy interior. Although it was hard to see, there didn't appear to be anyone inside. He rapped on the door and receiving no answer, let himself in.

The fire in the woodstove had burnt down to some lazily smoking embers. The room smelled of wood smoke, sage and man, dirty man. Someone had been living in the cabin for some time. An old

Indian blanket lay crumpled on the bed. A hatchet, no, a tomahawk was lying on the wooden table. He picked it up and examined it. Eagle feathers were tied to the top and a leather thong was wrapped around the handle. The blade was well-honed and extremely sharp. A half-burnt sage smudge stick lay next to the tomahawk. He knew the Indians used these in their cleansing ceremonies. On top of the woodstove was a pot of some foul-smelling soup of some kind. Tomlinson's first thought was that an Indian had been staying here. However, it was rare that Indians spent much time in this part of the Crazies.

He continued to survey the room. As he passed the window, something moving through the woods caught his eye. Stepping closer, he watched as a bearded man dressed in buckskin made his way down the game trail heading toward the cabin.

Before the man could come around to the front of the cabin, Tomlinson let himself out the door and hurried to a stand of trees some ways off. He watched in amazement as a figure from 100 years ago headed up into the cabin. It was a mountain man! He was dressed in fringed buckskin with a large fur cap on his head. Over his shoulder were slung two rabbits and a squirrel.

It dawned on him. This was probably where that mountain man, Bridger Jackson, had wintered. He had never run into the weirdo, but like everyone else, he had heard the tales. So, he really did exist!

"I'll be damned," he muttered under his breath. Rather than risk a confrontation with him, Tomlinson gave up the search for his trap and headed back down the mountain.

This morning as he had neared Missoula he hit upon a plan that would both rid him of Kaitie and set up the mountain man as the killer. He could not have known she would find his trap for him, but now, he would leave it where it was and let the sheriff's department tie it to the mountain man along with her murder. It was time to get on with the plan.

Tomlinson slung Kaitie's unconscious body over his shoulder and headed down toward the cabin. As he broke into the clearing just beyond the timber, he laid Kaitie on the ground.

He crossed the clearing to the cabin and called out, "Hello! Anybody in there?"

No answer. *Good*, he thought. He went back to Kaitie, picked her up under the arms and dragged her to the cabin. The blood-soaked shirt bandage pulled off her ankle and a steady stream of blood trailed behind her. She regained consciousness and gave out a weak cry with as much breath as she had in her.

"Shut up," Tomlinson barked at her. He hurried his pace and dragged her backwards up the steps. The cabin door was unlocked and he took her inside and lifted her onto the table in the middle of the room.

Scanning the cabin's interior, he was relieved to see that Jackson had not moved out. He was especially pleased to see that the mountain man had conveniently left his tomahawk on the bed. Tomlinson picked it up and walked back to Kaitie.

Tomlinson bent over her and brought his face close to hers. There was not much life left in her. He needed to act fast. He shook her and she barely opened her eyes and looked at him.

"You bastard," she hissed hoarsely through clenched teeth.

He held the tomahawk in his right hand.

"Call me what you want, Kaitie, but you were the lying bitch who got yourself into this. Now I want to know the truth. Have you sent the article or any pictures in to any magazine yet?"

She said nothing, but glared defiantly back into his eyes. He raised the tomahawk.

"Tell me," he yelled," or I'll chop off something else besides your foot."

She managed a weak smile. In a barely audible whisper, so quiet he had to bend to her mouth to hear her, she said, "For me to know and you to find . . ."

"DAMN YOU!" he bellowed, and with a mighty swing, he brought the tomahawk down on her shoulder. The sharp blade cut through the bone and her arm spraying blood across the table. Kaitie's arm fell to the floor as she tried to scream. But, there was not enough strength left in her. In a fit of rage Tomlinson once again raised the hatchet and brought it down on her other arm. This time she did not even attempt to scream.

At first Tomlinson thought she had passed out again. Bending down he listened and realized she was no longer breathing. He looked around the room and at the gruesome scene in front of him. Blood was everywhere. He had used the mountain man's tomahawk to kill Kaitie, but he wanted something more to clearly point the crime at Jackson. As he scanned the darkened room, his eyes fell upon the skinning knife. That's it, he thought! The bugger is supposed to be part Indian. Let's make this look good.

Slicing the girl's scalp off was the hard part. Even for him. He had skinned plenty of animals in his time, but scalping a person seemed to require a bit more finesse. It was important that it look authentic, not a hack job. He gripped a hank of brown hair in his fist and with a smooth slice of the razor sharp knife ripped the trophy from the now exposed skull.

Good job, he thought proudly, wiping the work sweat from his forehead with the back of his shirtsleeve. Tomlinson hung the dripping scalp on an empty nail next to a beaver pelt. *No point getting rid of the body,* he thought. *Let the mountain man or the police worry about it.* He wiped the tomahawk and the knife handles clean of his prints and threw them out into the yard to the side of the cabin.

With a last look around, Tomlinson left the cabin and made his way to his truck. He picked up Kaitie's purse from the floor and dug through it until he found her keys. His clothes were drenched with blood. He would have to change before he went to Missoula. He started the truck and headed for home, hoping that Nancy would be out. He didn't want to have to deal with her.

Chapter 17

AS TOMLINSON TURNED THE CORNER of his street, he was relieved to see Nancy's car was not in the driveway. He went in the house and headed directly to the bathroom. He was looking forward to a hot shower and turned the faucets on full blast. He stripped out of his blood-soaked clothes, dropped them in a pile on the floor and stepped into the steaming spray. The cleansing wash of the shower was refreshing and he hummed a nameless tune as his adrenaline leveled off. He did not hear his wife come in the house until there was a sharp rapping at the bathroom door.

Damn it, he thought. I don't need her crap.

"What do you want?" he called out above the noise of the shower.

"I want to talk to you."

"Can it wait till later? I'm kind of busy today."

"No, it can't wait. I'm coming in." He heard her open the bathroom door and pulled the shower curtain aside, shampoo suds stinging his eyes.

She gasped at the bloody clothes on the floor. "What did you do, gut a whale?"

"Something I was working on at the shop," he said shutting off the shower. "Hand me that towel." She threw him a towel and he dried himself off as she gathered up the clothes on the floor.

"You need to wash those today," he said pointing to the pile on the floor.

She raised her eyebrow at him. "Yeah, I'll get right on it." She lifted the clothes hamper and threw in the messy bundle slamming the lid down.

Tomlinson watched her display with amusement. It was so easy to get her riled up. Rubbing his hair with the towel he said, "So what is it you want to talk about? Hurry it up. I gotta get going."

Nancy put her hands on her hips. "You've got to get going? You can't talk to me for five minutes? Where are you going that is so important? Off to see your girl friend from last night?"

"Yeah, that's where I'm going. Off to see my girl friend. It's none of your friggin business where I'm going. Now get out of my way. I've got to get dressed." He pushed by her causing her to hit her elbow on the door handle.

"Ow. Watch it, asshole," she said rubbing her arm and following him into the bedroom.

Sorting through the closet, he said, "So, what is it that's so important? You know where my blue shirt is?"

"Goddamn it! No, I don't know where your goddamn blue shirt is! Will you listen to me?"

"Do I have a choice? Ah, here it is." He pulled out the blue shirt and put it on. He could see Nancy was steaming mad. The sooner he could get out of there the better.

"I've had it with you, Charles. I'm finished."

"What are you talking about?"

"I'm talking about you treat me like crap. You screw around with any whore you pick up in a bar, and you are always in a bar because you're a drunk. You never spend any time with me or your son. Sonny's always getting into trouble and I'm the one who has to deal with it. You expect me to do everything around here while you're off on a bender or doing some girl in a motel. Last night was the last straw. I've had it. I'm fed up. I'm not doing this anymore."

"Yeah. Okay, don't do it anymore. Have you seen my belt?"

Nancy stormed across the room and snatched a belt from under a pile of shoes dumped in the corner. Her face was red and tears of anger flushed down her cheeks. She came at him swinging the belt and slapped him with it, screaming.

"Here's your friggin belt! I'm done! I met with a lawyer this morning and I want a divorce. That's what I wanted to talk to you about. I want you out." She burst into tears and sat on the edge of the bed weeping into her hands.

Tomlinson was stunned. He and Nancy fought plenty of times, but she had never gone to a lawyer before. They had been through a lot of crap over the years, starting with her running away with him after he had killed his grandfather, but she always ended up sticking by him. He knew he wasn't the model husband, but divorce? Maybe she was serious this time. He sat next to her on the bed and tried to put his arm around her, but she shrugged it away.

"Leave me alone," she wept.

He softened his tone, "Look, Nancy, I'm sorry. You don't need to do this. I really do have to go, but we can talk about this tonight. Okay?"

"I don't care. I don't care anymore. Go do whatever it is you have to do."

With nothing more to say, Tomlinson slipped on his shoes and left the house headed to Missoula.

❧ ❧ ❧

TOMLINSON ARRIVED AT KAITIE'S apartment and let himself in. If she had submitted anything to her magazine, he was sure she would have done it via her computer. Being careful not to leave any fingerprints, he went to her desk and booted up her computer. As the machine began to whir into its start-up process, Tomlinson scanned the top of her desk. Sitting in the printer tray were the copies of the pictures Kaitie had taken. Leafing through them, he saw they were mostly of his journal entries, but there were also several of the insides of his cabin as well. Each photo increased his anger even more at the woman for duping him and at himself for allowing her to do so. He shook his head and smirked recalling with satisfaction the justifiable brutality he had inflicted on her at the cabin.

Her fancy camera lay next to the machine still plugged into the computer from when she had uploaded the pictures. He picked it up and admired its high quality. *A nice souvenir*, he thought to himself, and placed it on top of the photos he was going to take with him. He sat and turned his attention to the computer. Although he was no expert, he knew how to check her email and document files, and searched through them satisfying himself that she had not sent or stored anything that would implicate him in any crimes. Evidently, she had not submitted anything to any publications yet—at least not via the computer. With a sigh of relief, he shut off the machine, carefully wiped down all the items he had come into contact with, gathered up the photos and the camera and left the apartment.

Chapter 18

CROUCHED IN HIS SMALL HIDING SPOT behind the fir tree, Tomlinson saw the sheriff ride his horse up the ridge where the half-gutted ram lay on the blood-damp ground. He watched him dismount slowly, draw his shotgun out of the scabbard and inspect the kill. The body would still be warm to the touch and the blood would not even have begun to coagulate. It would be clear to the sheriff that the sheep had just been shot and that whoever had killed it had to be nearby.

Tomlinson hunkered down lower behind the tree as the sheriff released the safety on the shotgun and cautiously began to follow his trail down toward the timber. The going was difficult because of the steep terrain and the sheriff had to hold his gun in one hand while using the other to steady himself as he worked his way down the mountain.

At one point, he stopped, surveyed the landscape and called out, "Alright, I know you're down there. Come on out and let's talk."

Tomlinson took a deep breath. What the hell was the sheriff doing up here? This couldn't be about the sheep—he had just shot it. Despite the cold, Tomlinson felt rivulets of sweat streaming down the plane of his rigid back muscles and pool at the band of his jockey shorts. There was no way the lawman could have figured out about his role in the reporter's death, no way. He closed his eyes and pushed his head back hard against the rough bark of the tree. Think! He admonished himself. Think! You must have missed something. He had left enough evidence pointing at the crazy mountain man to keep himself or anyone else out of suspicion. But, maybe Kaitie had reported him to the sheriff. Damn it. He had not even thought of that, he had been too focused on whether or not she had submitted a story about him.

The sheriff continued on and reached a point along the mountain face where he stopped and looked around. Tomlinson could see he had come to a spot where there were no more footholds. He would have to climb down to a small outcropping of rock about six feet below where he now stood. This would require that he use both hands to climb He would have to put down his gun. It would not be easy. Once he landed on the outcropping, he would have to make his way along a slim path toward the fir trees. But, if he missed the outcropping, there was a treacherous drop of two hundred feet.

Tomlinson watched from his spot behind the tree and saw the sheriff kneel and lie down on his belly. Holding the tip of the gun barrel, he lowered the shotgun gently to the ledge below. As the sheriff was letting his rifle down an opportunity began to develop in Tomlinson's mind. If the sheriff missed the outcropping or fell off it, he would never survive the drop. This would likely be his only chance before the officer would reach the trees and arrest him.

After depositing the shotgun on the ledge below him, the sheriff turned toward the face of the mountain. Placing his boot in a small crevice and holding on to an overhanging branch with one hand and the rocky ledge with the other, he began to lower himself to the outcropping.

Tomlinson saw his chance. He squinted through his riflescope, and beaded in on the sheriff's right hand. As he was midway into his descent, Tomlinson slowly squeezed the trigger and fired a shot at the rock the sheriff was gripping. There was a loud crack from the rifle and almost simultaneously, the bullet shattered the rock from the lawman's grip. The sheriff turned in surprise and with his other hand reached up to grab at anything, but there was nothing but air. His body arched backwards into empty space. The toe of his boot barely scratched the edge of the outcropping. It was the last bit of earth the sheriff touched before he landed in a broken heap moments later two hundred feet below.

Tomlinson looked at the sheriff's crumpled body far below him. He took off his hunting cap and wiped the sweat from his brow.

"Nice shooting," he congratulated himself.

He climbed back up the ridge to the ram, and as if nothing had interrupted him, finished the gutting job he had started.

Chapter 19

THANKS TO HIS MANY YEARS of hunting, JJ Volker was an excellent tracker. A broken branch, an upturned rock or a discarded cigarette—the slightest clue told him a story. His sharp eyes and experience enabled him to track any living creature through any terrain. At the same time, however, he knew Bridger was adept at hiding any trail that might lead to him.

It was ironic that the man JJ was tracking was the same one who had long ago taught him many of the skills he was now using. When JJ was a boy, his father had a sideline as a hunting guide. He would take men into the mountains for elk and deer when the biting winds and snow of late fall would blow closed the door on ranch work until the spring thaw. Having spent his whole life hunting and fishing throughout the Crazy Mountains, JJ's father knew them well and passed his teachings down to his son. He also introduced him to his friend, Bridger Jackson. His father often told him no finer hunter or tracker existed than Bridger, and JJ was sure it was true. He was in awe of the exotic mountain man and eagerly absorbed everything his father's unusual friend taught him.

As did many boys raised in the West, his father grew up with a strong interest in the mountain man mystique. As he got older, Bill Volker attended the mountain man rendezvous in Wyoming each summer. These weekend rendezvous attracted history buffs and enthusiasts from around the country and around the world—men and women who enjoyed dressing in the fashion of the mountain men or Native Americans of yore in clothes they had made themselves out of traditional materials. Collections of antiques and handcrafted reproductions were displayed and bragged about, shooting contests were held and true and tall tales were told and retold around campfires. Bubbling pots of various hearty concoctions of soups and stews filled the night air with delicious smells and contributed to a warm camaraderie.

These events drew young Bridger's interest partially because he enjoyed the companionship of the men and women who respected and reveled in the life of his forebears. However, he also yearned for clues to the whereabouts or the fates of his father and mother and he hoped that perhaps he might learn something of them through this close-knit community of devotees and hardcore outdoorsmen.

He never did discover anymore about his parents. He did, however, befriend a Montanan named Bill Volker. Volker was the same age as he and lived on a ranch in the tiny town of Clyde Park, not far from where he made his home in the Crazy Mountains. Other than the people he would meet once a year at the rendezvous, Bill was the only friend he had or cared to have. Because of their riflery skills, the two men often competed against each other in the shooting competitions swapping first and second place between each other. Their friendly rivalry and mutual respect for one another brought the two together naturally. Bridger appreciated that Bill accepted his choice to live in the style he wanted to live in without any apparent judgment. When they would return to Montana after the rendezvous, Bill and Bridger would occasionally hunt together, the one sharing his wealth of knowledge of the natural world, the other sharing his companionship.

After his son, JJ, was born, Bill had little time for going to rendezvous and eventually stopped going altogether. As a result, he and Bridger crossed paths less frequently, and as will happen even with the best of friends, they stopped seeing each other at all. JJ became the focus of Bill's life and he enjoyed the time he spent raising his son— fishing, hunting, playing ball or working together on the ranch.

One fall weekend when JJ was ten years old, his father took him hunting far up in the Crazy Mountains. The two covered about twenty miles slogging up and down slopes through trees and snow and saw only one elk that charged away before they could get a shot. Though exhausted, JJ was determined to keep up with his father and manfully trudged along, adjusting the heft of his backpack as he went.

He was relieved when at last they arrived at their campsite for the evening. Dropping his pack, he rubbed his shoulders and with a heavy sigh, sat down on a large boulder near the empty fire pit.

"You hungry?" his father asked.

"Starving."

"We can eat as soon as you get a fire going. It's not going to start itself, you know."

With an exaggerated groan, JJ lifted himself off his rock and dragged in a healthy pile of firewood. Within a few minutes, he had built a good fire the way his father had taught him.

His father put a pot of chili on the fire and passed JJ a bag of potato chips.

"Are you disappointed we didn't get a shot off today?"

JJ stuffed a handful of chips in his mouth. "Not really. A little, I guess. But, this is the part I like. We got any marshmallows?"

His father smiled, "Of course, but you can have those after we eat dinner. You gonna eat all those chips or can I have some?"

AFTER THEY ATE, they cleaned their dishes in the river. JJ had appointed himself fire tender and kept it well-stoked with wood as the darkness and chill of the night settled in around them. The few early evening stars that had appeared in the sky soon led the way for a brilliant blanket of millions of twinkling lights. The vast Milky Way snaked its way through the sea of constellations above their heads. While his father smoked his pipe, JJ sat silently staring at the stars while the sapwood popped and the creatures of the night spoke to the wind. Not far off an elk bugled, coyotes yipped back and forth and a screech owl pierced the evening with its shrieking call. When a nearby wolf howled at the moon, JJ jumped, wide-eyed and looked at his father in wonder. His father returned his wide-eyed look and then smiled comfortingly back at him. It felt like he and his dad were the only people on earth and the animals were sharing their wild world with them.

He lay back on the ground, hands clasped behind his head, eyelids drooping and drifting serenely towards sleep when a deep voice behind his father growled out, "Wagh!" JJ yelped and leapt to his feet, heart pounding, trying to identify what kind of creature made that sound.

A gravelly voice called out, "Hello, the camp!"

Emerging from the trees behind his father, a wooly bearded man in buckskin clothing wearing a big fur cap shuffled into the firelight. He looked to be about ten feet tall. JJ's eyes were wide as saucers, and in his shock, he stepped back and tripped over a log, falling backward into their tent, collapsing it around him in a tangled heap of canvas, rope and poles.

To his amazement, his father and the huge man clasped each other on the shoulders and burst out laughing at him. Relieved that he and his father were not about to die at the hands of a half beast / half human creature, JJ managed an embarrassed chuckle as he tried to untangle himself from the crumpled tent.

Still laughing, the big man strode over and reached out a hand to help him up. "Ho, Hoss. Grab a hold and I'll pull ye up."

JJ looked up at the hairy stranger with the glint in his eye then over at his father for reassurance. His father was still laughing so hard tears were running down his cheeks. With some slight trepidation, JJ stretched out his hand and let the man draw him to his feet.

Once he was standing, the big man stepped back, and JJ realized with some relief that he was not really ten feet tall, but actually normal height, about the same as his dad. His clothes, and particularly his fur cap fashioned from the skin of a coyote, made him appear larger than he was.

JJ squeaked out a meek, "Thank you."

The man doffed his coyote cap and offered a generous smile. "Howdy, son. Didn't mean to scare you." Returning the cap to his head, he turned to JJ's father and said, "Is this your young'un, Bill?"

Wiping the tears from his eyes, but still with a big smile on his face, Bill nodded, "That's my boy. Name is JJ. You about scared him half to death."

"Wagh! From the way you leapt up there yourself, I'd say I put a good fear into you as well, Ol' Coon. You might want to check your britches."

JJ stared in awe at the two men as his father replied, "Well, I can't say I was expecting any company, leastwise you of all people." The two men clasped hands with warm affection. "It's great to see you, Bridger! JJ, this is an old friend of mine, Mr. Jackson."

"Hello."

Mr. Jackson extended his hand. "Call me Bridger, son. That's my moniker."

JJ put his small hand in Bridger's big paw and smiled shyly back at him, not quite sure what to make of the exotically dressed man. JJ's father brought Bridger a cup of coffee and gestured for him to join them. As they settled in, he placed another log on the fire sending a plume of sparks dancing towards the stars.

Bridger took off his cap, cupped his coffee mug in his hands and stretched his feet out toward the fire. JJ noticed his hair was tied in a long braid.

"I seen your fire from higher up and got kinda curious. I made my way down here and at first I thought my eyes was a-foolin me. Then I told myself, why, that's ol' Bill, and sure enough, here you set. It's been many moons, ain't it?"

"That it has, Bridger. Are you still living up here on your own?"

"You're mighty well told I am. Ain't no prettier place and ain't no better company. Present company excepted." He nodded towards the two Volker men.

The two men talked with a warm familiarity catching each other up on what had been happening in their lives since they had last hunted together.

Fascinated by the unusual visitor, JJ inspected him as the reflection of the flames lit up his bushy face. His beard was a tangle of curly hairs with pieces of food or vegetation trapped throughout. His black hair hung in a long braid tied with a leather thong. A large white-tipped feather was stuck in the thong. JJ recognized it as an eagle feather. His shirt was made of buckskin and fringed at the sleeves, shoulders and chest. Bright colored beads adorned some of the fringes. Around his neck were a small pouch and a larger leather bag that hung to his waist. His pants were made of a heavy wool cloth held up with a rough leather belt. A large bone-handled knife stuck out of a fringed leather sheath attached to the belt. On his feet, he wore a pair of moccasins.

JJ tried to follow the conversation between his father and Bridger whose rough voice and unusual phrases were entertaining and amusing. The lateness of the hour and the long day of tramping through the mountains combined with the comforting warmth of the fire gradually took their toll on him. Curling up on the ground, he fell asleep dreaming of mountain men as the two old friends communed through the night.

JJ AWOKE TO FIND himself bundled warmly in his sleeping bag inside the tent. His father was breaking kindling sticks into the fire pit. There was no sign of Bridger Jackson.

"Rise and shine, JJ," his father called.

"Mornin, Dad. Where's Mr. Jackson?

"He'll be back. He went back to where he lives to get his gun. He's going to show us where we can find plenty of elk."

"Good. I like him."

"Me too."

❧   ❧   ❧

IN SPITE OF his current feelings about Bridger, JJ recalled fondly that first time he had met him. On their way home from that hunting trip his father told him how he and Bridger met and about his friend's passionate commitment to a rugged lifestyle that he had inherited from his father and his father's father before him. On subsequent hunting trips over the next couple of years, JJ and his father would occasionally get additional surprise visits from the mountain man. Each time was a thrill for JJ who looked up to his father's independent and eccentric friend. An expert hunter and tracker, Bridger taught the boy many of the skills that had been passed on to him by his father and his Native American brethren.

As the years passed, JJ's father suffered with severe arthritis and had to give up hunting. Although JJ continued to hunt, he never again met up with Bridger. He would occasionally hear the references to him that the locals would make accusing the "crazy mountain man" of random events and misdeeds. JJ paid little heed to these comments ascribing them to overactive imaginations and small minds. That is, until Kaitie's killing. At first there were the usual unsubstantiated accusations that the mountain man must be the killer, which JJ discounted. It was not long before rumors emerged that the evidence in the case pointed strongly at Bridger.

It had been several years since JJ had seen him. The affable mountain man that JJ knew from his youth would not have committed such a heinous crime. As more stories circulated about the implements used and the scalping that had taken place, JJ found it harder to defend his former friend and mentor, not only to his accusers but eventually to himself as well. As much as he did not want to believe the theories, for all he knew,

Bridger may have gone crazy living up in the mountains like a hermit. He may indeed have snapped.

For whatever reasons, JJ had to admit that he might be the killer. The doubts and the anger tortured him. As time went on, the image of Jackson in JJ's mind grew more evil and more guilty. Whoever had taken Kaitie's life had also robbed him of Annie's affection. And, even if it was Bridger, he would pay.

The sheriff's office seemed to be making no headway in finding the killer. If it was Bridger, chances were they might never capture him. He could hide out as he had for years in the vastness of the Crazy Mountains, or for that matter, could have escaped over the border to Canada. The more time that elapsed, the more conflicted and angry JJ became. He had to know if Bridger was the killer, and he knew he could be the only person who might have a chance of locating and confronting the elusive mountain man.

He wondered if he did find Bridger, then what? He now had too many doubts about Bridger's innocence. No matter who had so savagely murdered Kaitie, he wanted that person to suffer as she did. Former friend or not, if the mountain man had gone crazy and was the one who had killed his sister-in-law, he would suffer for it. He didn't have the answer, but he knew he had to take some action to bring closure to this miserable situation, and in the process, he hoped to help Annie move on and to repair the relationship they had once had.

JJ followed Bridger's trail higher into the mountain. He was heading for the rockier, steeper slope where there would be less chance of someone being able to follow him. He had been right. JJ reached a point where he had to dismount Spot. The shale and steep grade were too much for a horse and rider. He tied Spot to an aspen tree. Gopher wagged his tail and pranced around JJ's legs as he secured his horse. He took the dog canteen off the saddle and offered some water to Gopher.

"It's going to be up to you now, Gopher." The Lab did not look up but wagged his tail at JJ's voice as he lapped the water. JJ took a few gulps from his own water bottle, capped it and hung it from his belt. He did the same with the dog canteen, and knelt down to the faint moccasin track in the dry and rocky dirt. Pointing to the footprint, he commanded his dog, "Gopher, track."

The dog immediately went to work, his mobile tail wagging as he sniffed at the footprint. After circling the area a few times, he picked up the trail and headed up the rocky slope with JJ following behind. The hot Montana sun beat down on them as they made their way up the shards of loose rock, higher up the mountain. At some points, the shale was so unstable JJ would slide back down a foot or so and would have to scramble on all fours to make any progress. He slid down yet again when he heard a rifle crack off to the west. He stood at alert trying to pinpoint where the shot had come from. Gopher kept sniffing and heading in the opposite direction continuing up toward the ridge. JJ decided to trust Gopher and followed him up the slope.

Chapter 20

JACKSON ALSO HEARD the second gunshot from his hiding spot near the ridge. His curiosity aroused, he crawled out of his dusty cave to investigate. As he entered the sunlight, he heard the sounds of rocks sliding below him. Someone or something was making its way up the slope. Peering down from the edge of the cave's entrance, he saw a man and a dog tracking his trail. He ducked back into the cave and waited.

He had spent many seasons in this cave, and except for the times when he occasionally stayed in one of the old ranger cabins in the deep winter, this was his home. As a domicile, it was relatively perfect. The small entrance kept bears out and minimized the cold air and snow that might enter the interior. After a short crawl, one came upon a small four-foot square alcove, almost a foyer. Beyond this area, a large cavern opened up; the ceilings of which rose to thirty feet or more. It was easy to have a warm cooking fire in this space, as the smoke would drift to the upper reaches of the cavern and dissipate into the fissures within the rocky surface.

Jackson preferred the solitude and security that the cave provided him. He had few possessions, and more than enough room to hold those he had. His bed was a simple one, but both comfortable and aromatic. It consisted of a shallow trench filled with fir and sage branches over which lay a thick buffalo skin. He had also provided himself with a wilderness home security and food gathering system. Placed strategically around the outside perimeter of the cave were several well-hidden traps of varying sizes and capabilities. There were smaller snare traps for catching squirrel or rabbit. Larger traps were set for catching bigger game. Most lethal was his bow trap, which consisted of a strong bow lashed to two stakes driven securely into the ground. A large animal tripping the release cord would be pierced with an arrow at an elevation that would kill or at least chase off a bear should one come too close to the cave. Although Bridger would have preferred not to use such a dangerous trap, an ugly incident with a bear trying to gain entrance into his cave last season had made him take this precautionary step.

Pacing in his cave, Bridger worried about the man heading up the mountain. *He must be a police officer,* he thought. Probably a deputy of the sheriff he had seen tracking him earlier. He was sure it related to the death of the woman in the ranger cabin. Of course, the law was targeting him as the murder suspect. He couldn't blame them. He had found her mangled body as they had in the old ranger station. They were his weapons they would have come across in their investigation. He had stayed in the cabin many times over the winter when he was too tired to make it back to his cave. The last time he had stayed there, he had kept his most important possessions, in particular, his medicine bag, hidden under a plank in the cabin as he went to bathe in the creek. Unfortunately, and uncharacteristically, he had carelessly left some of his items out in the cabin. The damaging pieces of evidence would reveal he had stayed there. The general tendency of the community to blame him for most things that happened in and around the Crazies would not help either.

When he had returned to the cabin that day and discovered the dead woman's butchered body he didn't know what to do. As experienced with death and killing as Bridger was, the horrific scene that confronted him was frightening. He had known that he should report it to the sheriff's office, but he also knew that they would end up charging, and most likely, convicting him of the murder. Most troublesome was that he could not locate his tomahawk or his skinning knife. He searched for them with a growing concern that they may have been the instruments used to destroy the poor woman. As he looked in vain for his tools, he heard the staccato thrumming of a helicopter approaching from the valley. His strong sense of survival and lack of trust in the legal establishment convinced him to leave the scene as quickly as possible. With no time to search further, Bridger left the cabin and headed into the timber and the long trail to his cave.

He stayed away from the cabin for a few days, but the absence of his medicine bag as well as the few other things he had left behind weighed on him. He decided he needed to take a chance and go back. He made his way down the mountain and through the timber until he reached the field around the old ranger cabin. Yellow crime scene tape surrounded the perimeter. It seemed like bad luck to go beyond the tape, and he had no desire to revisit the grisly scene inside, but he had to retrieve his things.

The police had padlocked the only door. However, Bridger knew how to enter from the back where a loose foundation stone allowed him to crawl inside underneath the cabin floor. From there he loosened one of the floorboards and squeezed up into the cabin itself. In the haze of the interior, Bridger saw that the body was gone, but the blood remained caked on the table and floor. Black flies buzzed everywhere. He used the knife on his belt to pry up one of the floorboards where he had a hiding place for his most precious possessions. With a sigh of relief, he retrieved his medicine bag and slipped it over his head. He put the other items in his cache into his old Indian blanket, rolled it up and secured the bundle with the leather carrying strap and looped that over his shoulder as well.

He searched anxiously for his tomahawk and skinning knife, but could not find them. Satisfied there was nothing more of his in the cabin, Bridger slipped back down through the floorboard and squeezed through the small opening in the foundation. He replaced the rock and headed across the field into the protective forest.

As he slipped into the trees, he heard a dog barking. Looking over his shoulder Bridger noticed a girl on a horse riding up to the cabin with a small black dog beside her. In the distance, he heard her yelling at the dog to be quiet as she watched him disappear into the timber. He began to run, making sure to keep his tracks well disguised.

With a last look back, he saw that the girl was not following him, but had wheeled her horse around and was returning the way she had come. With some relief he pushed on up through the timber toward the safety of his cave.

Chapter 21

JJ FOLLOWED GOPHER as they made their way higher up the rocky slope. The dog wagged his tail more vigorously and moved more quickly the higher they went. JJ fell behind, his breathing labored from the strenuous hike and the altitude. He stopped to rest, allowing the cooling breeze to chill the dampness on his skin. Scanning the mountain ahead, he saw a number of small caves were worn out of the cliff face. The ridge was not far away which meant that Jackson must be nearby. He whistled softly to Gopher, calling him back and drew his pistol. Taking a deep breath, he cocked the gun and moved forward.

JJ felt a slight tug on his boot. As he looked down, he heard the twang of the bowstring and screamed as an arrow sliced into his thigh. The impact knocked him off his feet. There was a loud explosion as his gun fired and flew from his hand when he hit the ground. Shaking, JJ looked at his leg. A long wooden arrow protruded from both sides of his thigh. It had embedded itself nearly up to the fletching. Looking up the trail, he saw where a bow trap had been hidden in a copse of juniper bushes. A sudden gust of wind blew up with a rush from below driving stinging sand and dust into his eyes. From somewhere close he could hear Gopher barking and whining. Clouds darkened the sky and the world swirled out of focus as he tried to grasp what was happening to him. Waves of consciousness washed over and away from him.

He was trembling. Cold. His teeth chattered and his body shook. Sweat streamed down his face, burning his eyes and blurring his vision. His heart slammed against his chest and his lungs pumped shallowly trying to draw in the thin air to keep him from fainting. Every inch of his skin was damp and clammy. His leg was twitching uncontrollably. In disbelief, he stared at the arrow shaft that had punctured his thigh whipping back and forth with each jerk of his leg. He gripped his thigh with both hands trying to stop the painful shaking. It was no use. His leg was operating on its own sending agonizing pulses throughout his body. His heart rate was slowing and the waves of consciousness were occurring less frequently. That arrow had to come out. *Focus*, he thought. *I've got to focus.*

With shaking hands, he gripped the feathered end of the shaft. Panting heavily, and with his eyes squeezed shut, he gritted his teeth and tried to snap it off. Blood burbled around the entry point while he worked at the arrow. His arms quivered with exertion, but the wood would not even bend.

"Oh, god!" he cried. His eyes rolled up in his head and he fell back against the rock wall. A rough wetness rubbing his cheek and eyes brought him back to a fuzzy consciousness. Gopher was licking his face and whining.

Got to move, he thought. JJ struggled to stand. He tried to take a step but his leg collapsed under him. He was not sure whether the arrow had severed a tendon. He had to get down the mountain, but even the thought of trying to get up again was mentally exhausting. His hands turned blue and he panted rapidly. His head was swimming. With great determination, he turned over, trying to shake off the dizziness. Kneeling on his good leg, he again attempted to stand. He was halfway up when his wounded leg gave out on him as the excruciating pain blazed up his body. He felt his body convulsing and his mind sliding away from him. His eyes rolled up in his head and blackness blanketed him.

∾ ∾ ∾

FROM HIS CAVE Bridger heard the scream followed by a gunshot. Grabbing his rifle, he left his cave and headed to the trap site. As he approached, he saw a man with the arrow from his bow trap sticking out of his leg struggling to stand and then collapsing to the ground. A dog paced back and forth whining anxiously and poking the body with his nose.

Bridger knelt down and watched the man and his dog from a safe distance. When he saw that the man threatened no risk to him, Bridger cautiously approached, releasing the safety on his rifle and keeping it ready.

The dog turned and lowered his head, growling as he neared. Standing protectively next to his master, the dog barked at him, his hackles bristling. Bridger knelt down, reached out his hand, and spoke soothingly.

"Good boy. Take it easy. I don't mean you no harm. Shush now."

Though the fur on his back remained up, the Lab stopped barking, lowered his head and cautiously sniffed at the outstretched fingers. Apparently accepting Bridger, the dog cautiously turned to the fallen man and lay down next to him whimpering softly.

Bridger moved to the unconscious man who was shivering and sweating profusely. His leg was twitching and blood was seeping into his pants. A fancy pistol lay next to him, and Bridger picked it up. He was relieved that it was not a police revolver and stuck it in his belt. He drew his knife and grabbing the cloth at the thigh, he cut into the pants leg and stripped it off. He inspected the wound. While there was significant bleeding, the arrow was helping to minimize the flow. However, the more the man trembled the more the entry hole opened and closed keeping the blood from clotting. Bridger cut a wide strip of cloth from the pants leg and placed it on the ground. Gripping the long end of the arrow with both hands, he tried to break it, but the willow held strong. Using his knife, he sawed the shaft in two and pulled each half from the man's leg. As he pulled the arrow out the man groaned in his unconsciousness. Blood, no longer dammed up, spilled freely from the wound. Taking a small container of pine resin from his medicine bag, he spread the sticky substance over the bleeding holes and wrapped the strip of cloth tightly around the leg.

Bridger knelt down and sliding his arms under the wounded man, lifted him. Still cradling the man he knelt, picked up his rifle and turned back on the trail toward his cave.

The dog padded behind.

A PUNGENT SCENT OF HERBS and smoke insinuated itself into JJ's emerging consciousness. He was warm and comfortable except that both his head and leg were throbbing. A sharp stab of pain brought him to semi-wakefulness and he groaned. From outside the fog in his head he heard a gruff voice.

"I don't want no trouble from you. Not that I s'pect you got much trouble in you. "

JJ groaned again and peered through half opened eyes. "Bridger?" he croaked.

Even through the haze, JJ could see that Jackson was taken aback that he called him by his name. Jackson squinted at him and shook his head, clearly confused.

"That's me. Who are you?"

Wincing, JJ turned and struggled to lie on his side. "It's JJ. JJ Volker."

A broad smile of recognition spread across Jackson's weathered face. "JJ! Well, I'll be damned! It is you. What are you doing way up here?"

JJ didn't smile back. It wasn't because of the pain in his leg. He glared into Jackson's eyes. Was this the bastard that had killed Kaitie and ruined his own life?

"I been looking for you," he said with a set jaw.

"Wagh! Well, you done found me, sure enough, ol hoss! Ain't this is a shining day!"

Despite his anger, seeing Bridger's familiar smiling face and hearing his antiquated patois brought back memories of his youth and good times spent with his father's dear friend. A small seed of doubt about the man's guilt planted itself in JJ's brain and put down roots. He looked down and away from the sparkling eyes. He didn't want to dull his bitterness or weaken his resolve.

Bridger bubbled on, "I'm sorry about that bow trap. I've had troubles with critters up here and use it to keep 'em away from my place. I'm glad it didn't harm you no worse. Now that you're up, I'll take a gander at that leg of yours."

JJ lay on his back and surveyed his surroundings. He was in a high ceilinged cavern with walls soaring at least thirty feet above his head. A campfire burned low in the middle of the "room" glowing and smoking lazily. A cast-iron kettle and pot were rigged above the fire pit. The bed he was lying in consisted of what appeared to be a buffalo blanket spread over something soft and springy. It smelled like pine boughs. Another blanket covered him. Various pieces of handmade furniture and other items indicated that this was an established home for the mountain man, not merely an abandoned animal den.

Through the smoky half-light, JJ watched as Bridger stoked the fire and placed a couple of sticks of wood and sagebrush under the kettle sending a fragrant rush of smoke and flames up and around the kitchen scene. From a leather bag near the fire, he took a smaller pouch containing a mixture of herbs and bark and measured several palms-full into the boiling kettle.

Bridger busied himself gathering cloth bandages and various other items. These he brought to the bedside and returned to the kettle for a cup of the brew he had made.

Proffering the steaming mug to JJ, Bridger told him, "Here. Drink about half of this cup."

Struggling up on one arm, JJ accepted the drink and wrinkling his nose, sniffed at its dark and acrid smelling contents. "What is it?"

"This n' that, mostly. Drink it. We'll put half in you and half on you. Then I'm gonna patch up your leg."

After another sniff and a slight hesitation JJ tentatively sipped at the concoction

"Wagh! Drink it," Bridger growled with impatience.

While the drink was scalding and tasted woody and strong, it was not altogether unpleasant. In fact, JJ found it calming and drank the half cup as he had been told.

Bridger squatted in the dirt and squinted at him through bushy eyebrows. "Pants gotta come off. You doin' it or am I?"

His hand shook as he handed the cup to Bridger. JJ gritted his teeth struggling internally with the frustration of being in this weakened position. Being dependent on a man he intended to kill was not how he pictured this scenario going. His eyelids grew heavy and then snapped open. Where's my gun? The concoction was sapping what little strength he had left.

"I'd appreciate it if you'd do it," JJ muttered weakly.

Bridger removed the pants and the bloody strip of cloth from JJ's leg. Dipping the fresh cloth bandages into the cup of hot broth, he cleaned the wounds. After sponging them off, he made a compress using the herb mixture from the bottom of the boiling kettle. JJ flinched as he wrapped and bound the bandage with a leather thong. Bridger inspected his work and readjusted JJ on the bed.

He smiled at him and said, "You must be ready for some water, ol' coon. Or, maybe something stronger would do. I'm feeling a bit dry myself." With that, the mountain man took a swig of something brown in a mason jar. A dribble of liquid ran down his matted beard as he handed JJ the drink.

Waving off the jar, JJ asked for some water. After taking another swig, Bridger rose to his feet and shook his head. "That's some mighty fine tangle foot."

Trying not to smile, JJ remembered with a brief flash of fondness the archaic expressions and stylized manner of speech Bridger used. Damn it. The flaming anger that had burnt inside him for weeks was being minimized by memories of familiarity and friendship for the man, and he didn't like it. At least, he wanted to question Bridger.

The frustration must have shown in his face and Bridger asked, "Them wounds a-naggin' you? Tell you the truth; I thought you was a gone beaver you was a-bleedin' so bad."

JJ looked at Bridger. "What?"

He continued, "After I brought you back here, you'd lost so much blood I thought you might be near kilt. Y' know? Gone beaver? Dead."

"Oh."

Gingerly, he reached down and felt the warm damp cloth wrapped around his leg. He pulled his hand back and sniffed at his fingers. They smelled piney.

"What did you use on my leg?" he asked.

"It's a poultice made out of mashed tree bark and comfrey leaves. Takes the pain and flammation down. That and this willow bark tea I'm fixing for you should be making you feel right pert in no time."

JJ watched as the mountain man poured the steaming mixture into a cup.

"I'm gonna let it cool a tetch afore you drink it." Bridger told him as he set the cup on a flat rock near the fire. "I'm feeling kinda wolfish myself. I don't s'pect you're ready to put anything in your meat bag jest yet, but I'm gonna fix me some pemmican soup, and we can jaw a bit if you're up to it."

Jackson filled the pot, put it back on the fire and dropped some pemmican cakes into it. The meat, fat and berries in the cakes gave off a pleasant aroma as they simmered.

JJ tried once again to sit up so he could drink the willow bark tea infusion that Bridger brought to him. Leaning on one elbow, he took the cup and brought it to his lips. It tasted sharp and strong, but soothed his pain even as he drank it.

Feeling calmer than he had in a long time, JJ tried to absorb the surreal situation. Weeks of pent-up outrage and single-minded determination had driven him to finding and punishing Jackson. Now that he had found him, he could only feel the warmth and compassion of the man who had been such a strong and positive influence on him as a boy. If it had not been for Bridger, he would have died back on the mountain. The image that he had let himself buy into and the reality of the avuncular man sitting across from him didn't jibe.

"I guess I should thank you for taking care of me."

Stirring his soup, Jackson replied, "Ye're mighty well told you should, ol' hoss. Weren't fer me, you'd have gone under for sure. I reckon I could apologize for my bow trap that put you in this situation. But, I won't. Nothing sours my milk more than people traipsing round up here hunting in the off-season." Jackson peered up at him through his bushy eyebrows at this last sentence, as if waiting for an explanation.

After a brief pause, he continued, "But, I guess you weren't hunting since all you was carrying was that pistola. That pistol shines though, don't it? It's the real beaver. If not hunting, what were you doing up here?"

"Where is my gun?" asked JJ.

"Now, don't get all worked up. She's in a safe place. Safe for me and for you." Bridger arched a bushy eyebrow and leaned forward. "You gonna tell me what you're up to way up here, or are you just paying me a social call?"

JJ said nothing, but lay back on the bed, closed his eyes and tried to think of a plausible answer to the question.

"You know," continued Jackson, "I've been a free trapper on my own hook since I was a pup. I don't bother no flatlanders and all I want is that they don't bother me. I catch my own food and I live by my lonesome except for once a year when I'll go to rendezvous."

"Are you still going to rendezvous?" JJ asked, eager to change the subject.

"Mountain men have been going to rendezvous for over a hunnert year. In the olden times, it was when the trappers and Indians would get together once a year afore the winter to trade furs and re-supply for the upcoming year. It was about the only time the trappers would see another man, which was purty much how they liked it. Although there ain't many true mountain men left, they's still some of us who prefer living the way our paps did and their paps afore them. Now there are more and more people who like to dress up and collect things like real trappers used to carry and wear. They ain't authentic mountain men, but I respect that they are trying to preserve the traditions. We'll all come together once a year at rondyvoo and swap ole yarns and have ourselfs a time."

Jackson halted here and stared into the fire, apparently lost in memories of rendezvous of the past. He started again. "So, like I was saying, I live up here not bothering no one; and all I want is to be left alone to do it. But, people jest can't seem to keep from blaming me for this or that and coming after me, dragging my sorry ass into town. Is that what you're intentions are? I ain't seen you or your pap for many a year. I'll allow as it is good to see you again, JJ, but I have a feeling you're up here on some kinda business. You blaming me for something I didn't do?" He looked JJ in the eye, and this time waited for an answer.

JJ remained silent.

Bridger continued. "You ain't the law, I guess. No lawman would be carrying as fancy a piece of hardware as that pistol of yours. So, what's this all about then, JJ?"

Still at a loss as to what to say, JJ cleared his throat, looked at Jackson, and said, "There was a woman killed not far from here recently."

Jackson held JJ's gaze and waited for him to finish. JJ looked for but didn't see any recognition of the incident in the mountain man's eyes.

"I knew her," he continued. "She was my sister-in-law." JJ paused. Still no clue from Jackson. "They found some things where she was killed, and some people think they belong to you."

Narrowing his eyes without blinking Jackson peered at JJ and replied, "And what do you think, ol' hoss? You figuring it was me killed her and you came up here to exact a little revenge with your fancy gun?"

"Look," said JJ. "I don't know if you did it or not. All's I know is there was a tomahawk and a . . ."

Bridger held up his hand to stop JJ from continuing. "JJ, it warn't me, and that's the plumb truth in it. I know they probably found my hawk and my skinnin' knife down there. And, I'm certain everbody's ready to string me up, but it warn't me and that's all I can tell you. I ain't blaming you for having some doubts, but I'd a hoped you'd a thought better of me than that."

They stared back at each other in silence for some time, each taking the measure of the other. Looking deeply into Jackson's familiar steely grey eyes, JJ felt a grudging certainty that what the mountain man was telling him was true. He lowered his eyes, no longer able to look at the other man directly.

Finally, JJ spoke, "To tell you the truth, I don't know what to think. Why were your things at that cabin?"

Jackson sighed letting out a long breath. "I hole up there at times over the winter. I was staying there before that girl got kilt. I'd gone out to catch me some rabbits and when I got back I found that pore gal chopped up in there. I'm real sorry she was kin to you, JJ."

Not ready to give in yet, JJ continued, "A girl told the sheriff and me she'd seen you running away from the cabin this morning."

Jackson nodded, "I seen her. Yep, I was there, alright. I was collecting my medicine bag and bag of possibles that I'd left. Didn't want to leave them behind. I was also looking for my hawk and knife, but I reckon they're long gone or the sheriff's got 'em."

JJ took another gulp of his tea. "Yup, the sheriff's got them, and they're looking for you. In fact, the sheriff came up here the same time I did, except he headed more over towards Big Timber."

A look of concern came over Bridger's rough visage. He rubbed at his beard and grumbled under his breath, "Wagh! That ain't good news. Law's looking for me once again fer something I didn't do. But, this time it's purty heinous and the track points to me. Bad doins. Bad doins. I can't say as I'd blame anyone for thinking I was the one done her like that. But, I didn't know the woman, and I had no reason to kill her. Whoever did it was one sorry coon. I seen what they done to her, and that was the business of one sick individual. That's not me, JJ. It ain't the way my stick floats, and I hope at least you believe me."

The two men remained silent, each wrapped in his own thoughts. JJ looked Jackson in the eyes for a few seconds before answering. "I do believe you, Bridger. But I'm afraid others aren't going to."

Jackson shrugged, and grunted, "Well, be that as it may, we need to get you back down off this mountain. I reckon your people are looking for you, and I don't need even more search parties scrambling 'round these parts. Maybe once you're down there you can put in a word for me."

"I'll do what I can. But, I can't promise you much. Maybe I can help you get a lawyer. You got a pen? I can write down my address for you if you end up needing to get in touch with me."

"Ain't got no pen. Ain't got no use for one since I can't write a lick."

"Well, if you do end up in town, ask how to get in touch with me and most likely you'll find someone who can reach me."

The strained look on Jackson's face softened. "Much obliged, JJ. I've missed you and your Pa these past years. How's he doing?"

"He doesn't get out hunting anymore. Arthritis keeps him crippled up."

"I'm sorry to hear that. You tell him Bridger was asking after him"

The two men reminisced about their days of hunting together. In spite of his initial bitterness about Jackson, JJ's emotions shifted as they spoke of old times and memories that were close to his heart. The more he listened to Jackson and his uniquely familiar way of speaking, the more relaxed and comfortable he became. Whether it was the sonorous voice of the mountain man, the effects of his special tea or an accumulation of the events of the day JJ's eyelids drooped as Bridger prattled on. Soon he was asleep.

❧ ❧ ❧

JJ AWOKE TO FIND he was alone in the dark cavern. The fire had burned down to some glowing embers. He shivered and pulled the blanket up to his chin. The stiffness in his leg made him wince. Gopher was lying next to him, but when he stirred, the dog stood and licked his face.

"Bridger?" he called. No answer.

It was too chilly to get up and stoke the fire. He did not want to leave the comfort of the heavy blankets. Staring at the roof of the cave, he thought about the events of the morning and his reunion with Bridger. It had been fifteen years since he had last seen him. JJ was fourteen and he and his father were hunting elk with Bridger. Unlike other adults who generally ignored him, Bridger treated him as an equal and patiently taught him the secrets of tracking and hunting. He also instilled in him a deep respect for nature and all living things, be they animals, plants or humans. As the memories flooded back, the notion that Bridger could have savaged Kaitie seemed ludicrous.

Gopher emitted a low growl, breaking his train of thought.

JJ heard bushes rustling at the mouth of the cave and lifted his head to see Bridger shuffling through the low entrance on all fours like a big bear. He turned and dragged in a bundle of wood.

Peering through the hazy half-light of the cavern and his own bushy eyebrows, Bridger said, "Evening, JJ."

"Is it evening?"

"It is. You been sleeping pretty heavy. How's that leg feeling?"

"It's not too bad, actually. Whatever you put on that poultice seems to be working good. I could probably get down the mountain if you can get me to my horse."

"Well, your horse is right outside. After you dropped off asleep, I went outside and heard him whinny down below, so I brought him up for you. But, I don't expect you'll be leaving now. Its past dark and you shouldn't be trying to make your way down the mountain this late. Plus, the temperature's dropped, and it feels like it could snow up here tonight. You stay here this evening and we'll get you headed home in the morning."

JJ thought about Annie who was probably wondering where he was. He folded back the cover and attempted to stand. "I really should try to . . . Ow!" His leg had stiffened while he was sleeping and getting up was not an option. He sat back down and stretched his leg out.

Jackson winced. "Still feeling hinchy, huh? Let me take a look-see at that wound."

JJ watched as Bridger unwrapped the cloth bandage from his leg. His wound was waterlogged, but was already healing well. The mountain man went over to the kettle, ladled out some more of the herbal medicine onto a clean cloth, and brought it over to JJ's bedside. Gopher lifted his head, sniffed at the fragrant mixture of herbs, and watched intently as Jackson re-wrapped JJ's leg.

JJ gritted his teeth and drew in a sharp breath as the hot poultice blanketed his skin. Soothing warmth flowed up from his leg as Bridger tightened the thongs around the cloth.

"There," said Jackson as he finished binding JJ's leg. "How's that feeling?"

"Some better. You got anymore of that tea?"

"I can sure fix you up some." Bridger heated up some water. As he was getting his bag of herbs he paused and said, "I ain't telling you what to do, but I think the wisest thing for you to do is get some rest here tonight, then head out in the morning. Considering the condition of your leg and the possibility it might snow out there tonight, not to mention you don't know your way around up this high, you're better off waiting."

"I reckon you're right. I just hope Annie doesn't worry too much." As he said it, JJ wondered if in fact, Annie really would worry. She didn't even acknowledge his presence when he was home anymore and didn't seem to care when he returned from his rides in the mountains.

Bridger ladled out a cup of tea and handed it to JJ. "Relax, JJ. She'll be all the gladder to see you in the morning."

JJ rested with his hands behind his head, looking up at the crevices in the roof of the cave high above as Bridger rambled on through the evening. He was grateful that he no longer had to suspect Bridger, but now he was back to square one over who had murdered Kaitie and what he was going to do about it. His thoughts mixed with the drone of Bridger's stories and soon JJ drifted off to sleep.

Chapter 22

JJ'S NOSE TWITCHED at the smell of wood smoke and coffee. He rubbed the sleep out of his eyes and sat up. Though his leg was stiff, it felt better and he struggled to his feet to test his ability to walk. Taking each step slowly he limped to a seat near the fire and warmed his hands over the flame.

Bridger greeted him with a steaming cup of coffee, "Morning. Seems you slept alright last night. How's that leg doing?"

"A little tight, but it'll be okay. Thanks for letting me stay last night."

Bridger gave JJ a friendly wink. "It was purely my pleasure. It was nice to catch up with you, even if you did fall asleep while I palavered," he chuckled.

His mood got more serious. "Listen, JJ, I been thinking. You know I know these shining mountains about as good as any ol' coon. Maybe I can help you track down whoever kilt your sister-in-law. I know the sheriff's on the case, but if they're thinking it was me what done it, they're on the wrong scent. Maybe a couple of old trackers like me and you can come at it with fresh noses. What do you think?"

Last night JJ had been comforted to settle in his mind the question of Bridger's innocence, but at the same time was frustrated that he had no further clue as to who was responsible. Nor, apparently, did the sheriff's office. He had faith in Bridger's skills and thought that this might indeed be a chance to ferret out the murderer.

"I'd appreciate that, Bridger, but where would we start?"

"I'll need to think on it. But, today we need to get you back down to your wife so's she ain't frettin' over you. Let me change your dressing and then we can get you back on your horse and headed home. It's gonna hurt some, but I reckon you'll do alright."

Bridger re-wrapped JJ's leg in a fresh poultice and helped him to his feet. With Bridger supporting him, JJ took a tentative step toward the cave entrance. The pain shot up his leg like a cold sharp knife. He reminded himself he had been in worse hurt in his rodeoing days, so he grimaced, gritted his teeth, and kept on going.

The two men hobbled their way out of the cave to where Spot was tethered to a tree. JJ shivered as the cold air needled his skin.

"I'll be right back," Bridger said. He returned to the cave and re-emerged carrying JJ's pistol and a woolen Indian blanket. After adjusting the blanket on the saddle, he hoisted JJ up and covered his leg, tucking the extra material under the saddle

Before stowing JJ's pistol in the saddlebag, Bridger ran his fingers over the lush wooden grips with an admiring smile. "She sure is purty."

Taking the reins of the horse, Bridger turned to JJ and said, "Okay, pard. We're gonna head down the opposite way of which you came up. I'll lead you part way over the rough stuff. Then you can make it the rest of the way on your own."

JJ shifted his weight in the saddle. It wasn't comfortable, but he was relieved to be heading home. Gopher wagged his tail and danced around Spot's legs, apparently relieved as well.

❧   ❧   ❧

BRIDGER LED THE HORSE and rider slowly down the loose rock and narrow trail. The mid-morning sun felt good on JJ's back and the expansive blue sky and fresh mountain air helped brighten his sprits despite the dull pain in his leg.

The path they were taking appeared random rather than well trod, and the going was rough. Much of the ground they traversed was covered with broken rock shards, and Spot slipped more than once on the way down. They had been walking along the bottom of a steep rock face when Bridger abruptly stopped the horse and rider. The leather saddle creaked as JJ leaned forward to see what it was that had made him stop.

It looked like a load of clothes had been dumped onto the trail ahead. As they moved closer JJ saw that the pile in front of them was actually the mangled body of a person. He sat in the saddle and watched as Bridger approached the body. His stomach turned at the grisly sight. The man's neck and back were broken. His jaw dropped as he noticed the uniform.

Bridger bent down, examined the twisted body, and turned it over. JJ nudged Spot closer to where Bridger was kneeling. When he flipped the body on to its back, JJ gasped.

"It's the sheriff! Is he dead?" The question was ludicrous, but JJ could not believe that Colton Stollar was no longer alive.

"Yes. He must have fallen from up there," said Bridger pointing far above their heads at the top of the cliff.

"How could he have fallen? He was riding my horse. If the horse slipped, where is he?" JJ looked around to see if he could see Chief anywhere.

Still kneeling, Bridger laid both hands gently on the sheriff's chest over his heart. He closed his eyes and let his hands rest for several moments. He muttered something in a Native American tongue that JJ assumed was a prayer. Bridger remained kneeling with his hands on the sheriff's chest and his eyes closed reverently. Suddenly he pulled his hands away from the body as if he had received an electrical shock. JJ noticed a quizzical expression come over Bridger's face. He ran his hands slowly over the sheriff, inspecting him for wounds. Finally, he stood.

Bridger cleared his throat and shielding his eyes, surveyed the steep rock face before them. "The way his body's layin', I'd say he fell from up there. Don't know where your horse is. Maybe he spooked and threw the sheriff. I don't have all the answers, hoss. But, I'll come back and look around. Looks like you'll have to pack him down with you. You set there and I'll load him up."

Slumped in the saddle, JJ watched as Bridger moved the twisted body of the great man. Colton had always seemed invincible to JJ. If he hadn't been trying to track down Kaitie's killer this wouldn't have happened. Now another person's life had been lost because of the murderer. JJ set his jaw and ground his fist into the saddle pommel.

Bridger struggled with the sheriff's big body. With some effort, he dragged him to the horse and heaved him up behind JJ's saddle. He spent some time tying Stollar's body securely to Spot with a lariat that had been lashed to JJ's saddle.

After checking his knots, Bridger stepped alongside JJ and said, "A little ways on from here we're going to come to an old game trail. You'll be able to follow it down the mountain and into Clyde Park. And, JJ . . ." Bridger paused, seeming to take the measure of JJ. "You're gonna do what you're gonna do, but I'd be mighty grateful if you didn't lead anyone up to my cave."

JJ shifted in his saddle and looked around to get his bearings. "I'll tell you what, Bridger. I appreciate you taking care of me. And, I believe you when you say you had nothing to do with Kaitie's death. I don't want to see you wrongly convicted, but I can't tell what's going to happen with the law. I'm going to have to show the police where I found Sheriff Stollar's body, and there may be officers climbing all over this mountain. But, I will try to keep them away from your place. That's all I can promise."

Bridger nodded acknowledgement and replied, "That's all I can ask."

They went on together in silence and shortly reached the game trail Bridger had mentioned. They stopped and Bridger looked up at JJ. "Alright, son, follow this trail down the mountain and you'll come out just above Wilsall and Clyde Park. I know you can find your way from there."

JJ reached his hand down. His old friend clasped it and they shook. "Well, thanks, Bridger. I'll try to make it back up tomorrow and we can begin trying to sort this all out."

"Alright, JJ. Take care of that leg now."

JJ and Gopher turned and headed down the trail into the timber as the mountain man watched them go.

ﾠ   ﾠ   ﾠ

THE GAME TRAIL JJ headed down was steep and narrow. Although Spot was sure-footed, each jarring step caused JJ to shift in his saddle and another shot of pain to race up his leg.

To take his mind off his discomfort, JJ focused on Annie. She probably was worried about him. He regretted that he would be the cause of more anguish for her. She didn't need it. Didn't deserve it. A pang of guilt twisted inside him for his indiscretion with Kaitie. At the time, he had meant no harm to his wife. It just happened he had told himself. We were drunk. But, he knew it wasn't right. Annie had always been good to him, even if she lacked the passion of her sister.

Before all this happened, she had been a happy woman. She was in love with him and their scrappy ranch with the dogs, the horses, the chickens and the few head of cattle that his dad had given them when they bought the place.

Sundays and holidays they would have supper at Annie's folks' place over to Willow Creek. Kaitie would come up from Livingston. JJ loved watching the two good-looking sisters laughing and telling each other the latest gossip in their lives.

They were not rich. Hell, no one in Montana was. The saying was the way to get a small fortune in Montana was to come there from somewhere else with a big fortune. Nevertheless, they had a happy life in one of God's prettiest parts of the world. That is, until that world fell apart when Kaitie was murdered.

Both he and Annie were in shock when the police first broke the news to them about the killing. They could not believe that the vibrant woman whom they loved so deeply was no longer alive. Nor was it possible for them to fathom the cruel death she suffered.

Annie never came out of her shock. All JJ could do was stand by as a deep sadness and confusion overcame her. Annie retreated into a dark cave of solitude, rejecting his attempts to cheer her up. Now they rarely spoke to one another.

He wished she were aware of the pain he was feeling. The sense of loss. Not the loss of Kaitie, which was painful, of course, but rather, the loss of connection with her. With Annie. His wife. Maybe it was partially his fault, he thought. He was not one for verbalizing his feelings, but he had tried to let her know that he needed her closeness. His attempts at hugging her, kissing her or even lying close to her at night were met with minor annoyance or outright rejection, never the warm acceptance he hoped for. His grip on the reins tightened into a fist and his jaw clenched. Whoever killed Kaitie had killed his Annie's affection for him as well and he needed to be accounted for.

His thoughts turned to whoever that killer might be. The question still gnawed at him. He had been so positive it was Bridger. Everyone had come to that conclusion. After the past two days, however, he was now certain that Bridger was not the murderer. Who then? What was taking the sheriff's department so long to capture this freak? They were wasting their time trying to locate Bridger and they probably never would. They needed to get on the right track. Maybe he and Bridger together could indeed turn something up that might help capture him. If they were lucky, JJ would get a chance to exact a little revenge on the bastard before he was arrested. The muscles in his jaw twitched and his fist clenched and tightened on the reins in anticipation of the damage he would inflict on the killer.

"Alright, Bridger, it's you and me," JJ thought aloud. His voice caused Spot's right ear to jerk back toward his rider and Gopher to lift his head. Gravel slithered down the mountainside as Spot's step faltered. The horse brought his ear back to attention with the other one. Gopher dropped his head and focused on the rocky trail and JJ drifted back into thoughtful silence.

The brilliant noonday sun heated the day. JJ pulled the brim of his black Stetson down and forward on his head, letting the warmth and the gentle rocking back and forth in the saddle lull him into semi-wakefulness. He rode like this until Gopher's bark startled him awake.

Before he could push his hat back a commanding voice ordered, "Hold it right there!"

With a start, JJ reined Spot to a halt. The officer stood next to his 4-wheeler and was pointing his service revolver directly at JJ. "Get down off your horse."

Chapter 23

GOPHER LOWERED HIS HEAD and growled at the man. JJ winced and swung off Spot lowering himself gingerly to the ground. As JJ dismounted, the blanket fell to the ground. He noticed the look of surprise in the officer's eyes as he stared at his naked leg.

"What the . . . ?" The officer shifted his focus to the body on the horse's back. "Okay," he said. "Get down on the ground! NOW!"

"Officer, . . . "JJ started.

"NOW! DOWN!"

Gopher countered with a sharp bark.

"Quiet, Gopher." JJ struggled to the ground. The cop straddled his prone body and slipped white plasticuffs over his wrists.

"Turn over and sit there. And don't even think about moving."

JJ turned on his back. The officer helped him get into a sitting position, and strode over to inspect the body on the horse.

He muttered, "Jesus! It's Colton!"

He wheeled on JJ and said, "You son of a bitch!"

"I didn't kill him," JJ stammered. "I just . . ."

"You just shut the hell up for now."

Spot stamped his foot, shook his head and huffed noisily. The officer yanked him by the reins and tied him to the back of his ATV. He returned to the body and inspected it. He put his hand gently on Stollar's body and bowed his head for a moment. He cleared his throat and confronted JJ. "What's your name?"

"John Volker. Sir, I . . . "

"Let me see your ID"

"It's in my wallet." JJ twisted his arms around, managed to pull his wallet out of his jeans, and proffered it to the officer.

"Just give me your license."

JJ fished his license out and held it until the officer holstered his pistol, took the license and examined it.

Looking up from the license the deputy sheriff eyed JJ. "Alright, John, what's your story?"

"That is Sheriff Colton Stollar . . . ," he said, nodding toward the body.

"I know that. That's why I'm up here. We've been searching for him for two days. What happened to him?"

"The sheriff and I were both up here hunting for the killer of my sister-in-law."

A quizzical look came over the officer's face. "What are you talking about?"

JJ winced from the pain in his leg and the discomfort of the plasticuffs. "My sister-in-law was Kaitlin Cathcart. She was murdered up here recently. Someone thought they'd seen a suspicious person in these parts and we came up to check it out."

"Your sister-in-law was the Cathcart woman?"

"Yes, sir."

"And you say you and Colton . . . the sheriff . . . were up here together looking for someone?

"That's right. Well, no, sir, Sheriff Stollar didn't actually know I was up here too. He borrowed one of my horses to hunt for the guy and headed up in one direction. I saddled up after he left my place and went off in the opposite direction."

JJ took a moment and explored the face of the officer. The cop looked to be in his 50s, had a weathered but kind, older man's face and was less threatening than at first. His look gave away no reaction. The nameplate on his shirt read R. Gustafson.

"Go on," urged R. Gustafson.

JJ proceeded cautiously, careful not to give away the location of Bridger's cave. Nodding toward the west JJ continued, "The sheriff headed in that direction and I headed off that way." Another nod. "I was out about two hours or so and got turned around and lost up in the high country. Spot, here, my horse, got spooked by a bear and her cubs and reared up causing me to roll downhill into a clump of brush and a sharp branch went through my leg." JJ stopped again to see if R. Gustafson was buying his story.

Gustafson glanced down at JJ's leg.

"A sharp branch." Gustafson repeated.

"Yes, sir. I was bleeding bad, and I wrapped some old rags I had in my saddle bag around it, but I'd lost a lot a blood and I guess I passed out for awhile. When I woke I was in a lot of pain and stiff, so I bedded down and stayed put till I could get back on Spot and head down."

"You didn't find who you were hunting for then?"

"No, sir. Oh, but before Spot threw me, I did hear a gunshot from somewhere west of where I was. It wasn't too close, but close enough so's I could hear it clearly. I thought it was a little strange 'cause it ain't hunting season. But it coulda been anybody just firing their gun for no particular reason."

"A gunshot?"

"Yes, sir."

"What happened to the sheriff? Was he shot?"

"No, sir, I don't think so. After I got back on Spot and headed down, I came across his body at the bottom of a drop off. It looked like he musta fell. I figure he fell about two hundred feet. As you can see, it looks like he broke his neck. I didn't see any other wounds on him."

The two fell silent for a moment. JJ finally spoke, "He was a good man. I've known Sheriff Stollar for a long time. He was a friend of my dad's. I feel really bad about what happened to him. I guess it was just a accident. I lost my horse too. The one he was riding. Chief."

"Can you show me where exactly you found him? We've been looking for him for two days now. We knew he was up here in the Crazies somewhere because he had called in before heading up, but there's no way to get reception on cell phones or walkies up here to reach him. Said he was looking for . . . " Gustafson stopped. "Who exactly were you looking for?"

JJ averted his eyes from the deputy's stare. Choosing his words carefully, JJ answered, "Well, the sheriff was looking for someone they call the Mountain Man. But, I've known Bridger Jackson since I was a boy and I really don't think it was him. So I was going on my own search for any clues that might lead me to who really did it."

"And what did you find?"

"Well, nothing. Once I fell off my horse and headed back down I had given up. For now."

"I think you should give it up for good, before you get hurt any worse. A murder investigation is something best handled by the police. Now, can you show me where you found Sheriff Stollar's body?"

"I probably can, but it's a ways back, and I haven't spoken to my wife since before I got hurt. She's probably worried about me. I should . . . "

"Is your wife's name Ann Volker?"

"Yes, sir. Annie"

"She called us last night. Reported you missing. I should have connected the two when I saw your license. You're right, she is worried about you. Hang on a sec."

Gustafson strolled over to his ATV and pulled a walkie-talkie from a black bag attached to the gear rack. He pushed the button and it crackled on.

"Jim. You there?"

"10-4"

"Jim, I found that MP, John Volker. And, he's got Colton's body with him. Says he found him at the bottom of a cliff. Looks like his neck is broken."

"Colton's dead?"

"10-4. Volker needs to get to a hospital. Got a wounded leg. He also needs to let his wife know we found him. I want to take him back up to where he found the body first. Get down to somewhere where you can call into the station and have them contact his wife and tell her we'll be taking him to Deaconess. Should be there in a couple of hours I guess. After you call in, come back up here. I'm at the end of the logging road I headed up when I left you. After I find out where Colton fell, we should get Rick up here. We need to get Volker down so we can take him to the hospital. You'll see my 4-

wheeler tracks if I'm not back by the time you get up here."

"10-4, Rolf. Hell, I can't believe Colton's dead. You sure it was an accident?"

Gustafson glanced over at JJ who was listening to the conversation. JJ looked down at the ground. "Don't know, Jim. Gonna check it out. Get going and get back here quick. Tell them to send Rick up here too. He might need a horse. And have them send an ambulance for Colton's body."

"OK. I'll catch up with you soon as I can."

Gustafson took a knife out of his pack and walked over to JJ. "I'm going to cut you loose now, son. It's a precaution I had to take. But, I need you to show me where you found the sheriff. I'm going to trust that you're not going to try to run away or anything stupid like that. Right?"

"No, sir. I've got no reason to run, and I can't get anywhere with this bum leg anyway. But, you aren't going to be able to drive that 4-wheeler much farther. It's steep the rest of the way and the game trail is only wide enough for a horse."

Gustafson cut the plasticuffs off JJ. "How far up is it?"

"It's a ways, and I'm gonna have to ride 'cause my leg is in rough shape to be walking."

"Alright, we're going to have to wait for my partner to get back here then."

The two sat and talked until the deputy arrived and JJ led them up to where Stollar had fallen.

They found Chief further up the mountain. After a brief interrogation by an investigator, they took JJ, Gopher, Spot and Chief back to his ranch. A waiting ambulance whisked him off to Deaconess Hospital in Bozeman.

Chapter 24

IT WAS CLOSE TO DUSK when the detective, Rick McConnell of the Montana State Criminal Investigation Bureau, finished his investigation of the accident area and headed back down the mountain. Stollar's death appeared to be a sad accident. According to Mr. Volker, Colton had been hunting for that Jackson fellow and had fallen to his death as he tried to climb down some rocks. It was troublesome that they had not been able to find Stollar's shotgun. It was not in the saddle scabbard nor anywhere near where they had found the sheriff's body.

On the drive back to Bozeman, McConnell reflected on the events of the past week starting with today. It was hard to imagine that Colton Stollar was dead. He was something of a legend in the Gallatin Valley. He had an impressive professional record and law enforcement officers at all levels respected him. Beyond that, though, he was a good man, well-liked by anyone who knew him. Gregarious, an avid sportsman, a mentor and a solid friend when you needed one—he would be sorely missed.

One night after too many beers following a heated MSU Bobcats vs. U. of M. Grizzlies game, McConnell had asked him why he had never been married. Colton had answered that he would have had to divorce the job he loved if he ever married. Plenty of women would have liked to rope the handsome sheriff for a husband, but Colton Stollar was happily attached to his work. Rest in peace, old friend.

Although Stollar's death seemed to be an accident, it would not have happened had he not been trying to find Jackson. The officer's death would spark an intensified effort by all departments to track down the elusive mountain man. Nevertheless, because of his investigations of the past few days, McConnell was not convinced that Jackson was the one who had killed Kaitie Cathcart. The material evidence found at the crime scene— the tomahawk and the knife—pointed at Jackson. However, it was rare in a case like this that the killer would leave such blatant clues. From all that he knew, Jackson was a smart man. Granted, he was eccentric by society's standards, but wanting nothing to do with the modern world and living on your own terms in harmony with the incredible natural world of the Rocky Mountains seemed to McConnell to be more sensible than eccentric. There appeared to be little motivation for the hermit to kill someone like the Cathcart woman or to want to draw attention to himself by leaving obvious clues.

It could additionally be argued that the scalping of the victim had some relevance to Jackson's part Native American background, but that also seemed too obvious, too blatant, too staged. No, Jackson was still a suspect in the case, but McConnell remained unconvinced he was the killer, especially given some of the new information he had uncovered yesterday.

He had driven up to Missoula to investigate the Cathcart woman's studio apartment with one of the CIB lab techs. While the tech dusted for fingerprints, McConnell inspected the items in the room. The victim had kept an exceptionally neat apartment. Everything, even the kitchen, was spotless. The only thing that stood out was a broken statuette on the kitchen table. *Curious*, he thought, *that Miss Neatnik would leave a pile of broken pieces out.* He had the tech dust for fingerprints and bagged the fragments as evidence. He looked through all the cabinets and drawers searching for any clues, but there did not seem to be anything unusual.

Sitting at the desk, he asked the tech, "Have you dusted this keyboard yet?"

"Sure did. Knock yourself out."

The detective turned on the computer. While waiting for it to boot up he opened her desk drawer and saw a thumb drive marked "Journal." His pulse quickened.

"This could be interesting," he said aloud.

Before he plugged in the thumb drive McConnell accessed the email files on the computer. A quick scan of the most recent emails revealed nothing. They were mostly personal correspondences with friends or family as well as some story pitches to various publishers. He decided he would take the computer back to Bozeman and let the specialists in the office comb over the rest of the drive. He was eager to check out the journal disk and plugged it in.

Chapter 25

ANNIE WAS PACING the hospital emergency room when JJ arrived. He flashed a guilty smile at her as he limped into the antiseptic smelling waiting room. Although he felt badly that he had caused her more grief, the concern on her face made him selfishly pleased that her thoughts were about him rather than Kaitie for a change.

"Hi, babe," he greeted her sheepishly. The deputy accompanying him stepped off to the side.

Annie ran and threw her arms around him. She laid her head against his chest and looking up with tears glistening in her eyes she asked, "JJ, what happened to you? Where have you been?"

Stepping back, Annie looked at his leg still bound with the Indian poultice. "Are you okay?"

JJ glanced at the deputy and then put his arm around Annie. "Long story, honey. I'll tell you all about it. First, let me sign in."

Annie slipped her arm into his and around his back helping JJ hobble toward the registration desk.

The officer stepped in front of them. "Alright, Mr. Volker, we won't need any more from you tonight. But, we will want to speak more to you this week. We'll be in touch with you." He nodded at Annie, turned and headed out the exit door.

As the automatic door shushed quietly closed behind the officer's back, JJ turned to Annie. "I'm so sorry about all this. I'm sorry about everything. I didn't mean to upset you."

Annie looked at JJ wide-eyed, "Upset me?! JJ, what were you thinking?! I have been out of my mind worrying about you. When the police called to tell me they had found you I got so scared—afraid of what they would say. I do not need the police calling me with news about anyone in my life ever again. What the hell were you doing up there? And where are Spot and Gopher?"

"When they brought me down the mountain, we dropped off Gopher and Spot at the house before coming to the hospital. You had already left." He gave her a kiss on the forehead and turning, he said, "Let me check in and I'll tell you all about it."

After providing his information to the receiving attendant and being asked to sit down and wait for the doctor, JJ and Annie took a seat on the vinyl couch. A newscaster for CNN on the waiting room television was reporting on the latest political blunder of some congressman as Annie waited silently for her husband to explain himself. By the time the nurse arrived with the wheelchair and took

JJ to an examining room, he had told Annie most of his story. She sat and tried to take in all he had told her as the doctor examined and treated her husband's wounds.

The doctor was young and efficient. After cleaning and patching up JJ's leg, he pointed to the pile of wrappings that he had removed.

"Pretty impressive self-doctoring, John. They ought to take you on here at the hospital. What did you use as a poultice?"

Sneaking a nervous look at Annie, JJ replied, "Oh, this and that. My grandfather taught me some things about using Indian medicine, and I guess it came in handy."

"Well whatever you did, you did a great job, and probably saved your life. I'm sure you lost a lot of blood."

"Yeah, I guess I'm lucky."

"That you are." The doctor handed him some papers. "Here's a prescription for some pain pills. Vicodin. If the pain gets really uncomfortable you can take one of these every four hours. Take this form up to the front desk and you are on your way. You need to keep that leg and foot elevated for a few days."

"OK, Doctor. Thanks."

"You bet."

JJ and Annie dropped the form off at the front desk and headed out to their car.

During the ride home, JJ finished telling Annie what had transpired on the mountain. He described in more detail his discussions with Bridger and his confidence that he was not Kaitie's killer.

"I'd forgotten how much he was a part of my childhood. You'd like him. He talks like he's still living a hundred years ago and he knows the Crazy Mountains backwards and forwards."

Annie looked over at JJ and smiled as she turned up the highway leading to Clyde Park. "It sounds like you really like him, even if he did put an arrow through your leg."

"He didn't put the arrow through my leg. I was trespassing on his 'property' and I tripped his security system. It was my own fault. The Crazies are his home as much as the ranch is ours. I think that he might be able to help figure out some clues to Kaitie's death. I want to talk to him again."

"I think you should tell the police about him."

"I can't do that. I promised him I wouldn't. And, they'd just arrest him anyway. There's too much evidence against him and I don't think they are considering anyone else as a suspect."

"Well, I don't mind you going up to talk with this mountain man if you think you have to, but you can forget about hunting down any suspects with a gun. That's just crazy and stupid. I don't want to lose you, JJ. I know I've been wrapped up in myself since . . . Kaitie. But I love you."

Annie reached across and put her hand on JJ's knee. "I love you, you stupid cowboy," she reiterated squeezing his knee firmly. "When the police called and said your name, my first thought was I can't go on living without you too. I miss my sister terribly, but losing you would be like having my heart ripped out of me. I couldn't bear it. Please promise me you won't do anything crazy like this again."

JJ felt tightness in his throat. Annie's words and her hand on his knee were the reminders of her affection for him that he had been so sorely missing.

"I promise, honey. I love you too. I didn't know what to do. I guess I was being crazy. I've been out of my head lately, and seeing you so miserable and not being able to do anything to help you was making me crazy. I've been so angry and frustrated I couldn't think straight anymore. I'm sorry I scared you."

Annie smiled at him warmly, "Well, you should be, JJ Volker. Now let's get you home. Our bed has been awfully lonely without you."

They rode in silence for awhile, the headlights on the road the only illumination in the moonless night. Both were lost in their own thoughts.

Annie was the first to break the silence.

"What did you mean back at the hospital when you said you were sorry about everything? What is 'everything?' You meant more than just going off to find Kaitie's killer, didn't you?"

JJ caught his breath and stared out the window before answering.

"Yes. While I was up in the mountains, I did a lot of thinking. About us. About me. I haven't been the best husband, and I'm sorry."

"What do you mean?"

"I mean I've been selfish, and I haven't been good at letting you know how much you mean to me."

"I understand. It's been hard on both of us since Kaitie died."

JJ cleared his throat. "I don't mean just since Kaitie died. We've been growing apart for awhile, and I guess it's mostly because we haven't done much together for a long time. I suppose I've resented that you don't like to do things I like to do, so I have to do them by myself."

"Or with Kaitie," Annie said quietly.

JJ looked at his wife for a moment then turned to look out at the dark purple mountain range in the distance. A few stars began to show themselves high in the evening sky.

"Yes. That's true. I admit I never stopped loving her and enjoying doing things with her. But, I've come to realize how important you are to me and how much it means to have you as my wife. And, I'm sorry I haven't made you see that. I want us to get back to where we were when we were first married— when we couldn't get enough of each other, and no one else in the world mattered."

Again, a heavy silence fell over them.

Without taking her eyes off the road Annie said, "You slept with her, didn't you?"

JJ felt a sinking in his stomach and said nothing.

"You don't have to answer. I know the answer. I know you and I know Kaitie. Things were different after that weekend you went skiing with her in Missoula. Something happened with you two, and I could feel it."

"Annie, I . . . ."

"Please don't say anything. It doesn't matter anymore. It was as much my fault as it was yours. I've been selfish too. I've tried to be a good wife by giving you a comfortable home and letting you be who you want to be. But, in the process I focused only on you and forgot about us. I realize I haven't been affectionate with you for a long time. I felt you only cared about yourself and about having a good time without me. And, after you came back from that weekend with my sister, I shut down completely. I should have talked to you about it then. I should have said something to Kaitie. But, I didn't. I kept it to myself and let it eat at me. It seemed easier to stop feeling anything than to deal with my anger."

"Annie . . ."

"Let me finish. I need to say this. I was so angry with you, JJ. But, I was even angrier at Kaitie. All my life I have been in her shadow. She was always the popular one, the one everyone wanted to be friends with or go out with. Do you know I never even dated anyone before you? Then you fell in love with me and I was so happy. I could not believe how lucky I was to have you love me. I dreamed that you and I would have the perfect marriage, have kids, and live happily ever after. Then when we found out we could not have children because of me, I felt more insecure, as if I had failed us. That was when I started shutting down. Over time, we both became more involved in our own things. Me with the house and you with your things. And, Kaitie was a good playmate for you. Just what I couldn't be. I loved her. She was my sister. But, I hated her for being what I couldn't be. I hated her because you still loved her. And, there was a time when I was so angry I wished she'd never been born. I wished . . . "

JJ looked at Annie. Her voice broke.

"I feel so guilty, JJ. It was my fault you went to her. I should have treated you differently and I should never have hated her and wished she . . . wasn't around. Kaitie, I'm so sorry."

Annie pulled to the side of the road and turned off the car. She looked at JJ with tears streaming down her face. He took her in his arms and let her sob against his chest.

JJ stroked Annie's hair and kissed her gently on the top of her head. He held her, feeling her shudder against him, and he looked at the silent night engulfing them and the spray of stars that were lighting the sky above.

"Honey," he said, "you don't have to apologize for anything. I'm the one who messed up. I'm sorry for being weak. I should have been more understanding about what was happening with you. With us. I love you and I knew you loved me, and I guess I took that for granted. Maybe we both did, to the point where we didn't bother to show how we felt for each other anymore. I know you wanted children. I did too. But, I'm okay with not having them and sharing our life as a couple. What's past is in the past. From today on let's be there for each other. I promise I'll be a better husband and never take what we have for granted again."

Annie lifted her face to him and they kissed tenderly at first. Their embrace and kiss turned more passionate and intense as the pent up emotion of years of gradual distancing dissipated into the clear Montana night and the two broken hearts melded into one.

Annie pulled back, looked into JJ's eyes and said, "I do love you deeply, you know."

"I know. I love you too."

She started the engine and headed toward home.

As Annie pulled the car into their driveway, Max and Gopher came bounding out from the front yard barking and frantic with excitement. Even old Petey waddled down from his post on the front steps emitting a deep "whuff!" in greeting.

JJ turned his head away from Annie and wiped away the solo tear of happiness that had risen in the corner of his eye.

Chapter 26

JJ ROSE EARLY THE NEXT MORNING. Annie was still asleep. Her blond hair glistened gold on the pillow in the morning sunlight shining through their bedroom window. The contented look on her face brought a smile to his own as he carefully rolled out of the covers.

Limping into the kitchen, he fixed himself a peanut butter and jelly sandwich for breakfast. He popped a Vicodin in his mouth and washed it down with a mouthful of milk from the plastic jug in the refrigerator. He dashed off a quick note for Annie, telling her where he would be and let himself out the door, sandwich in hand.

His breath frosted in the crisp morning air as he crossed the yard and limped to the barn to saddle Spot. By the time he pulled the cinch tight, the pain pill had done its work and he barely noticed the dull throb in his leg until he swung up into the saddle. Gopher and Max danced around Spot's legs wagging their tails expectantly.

"Get back, Max," commanded JJ. "You're staying here." Max sat obediently, but Gopher followed the horse and rider up into the Crazy Mountains.

∾ ∾ ∾

JJ DISMOUNTED and approached Bridger's cave cautiously. He did not want another trap to surprise him like the first time he was here.

When he was within shouting distance, he called out, "Bridger! Hello? It's me, JJ. I'm coming up. Okay?" He stopped to listen. The only answer was the far off high-pitched piping of a bald eagle. He tied Spot to a pine tree and continued up the slope focusing carefully on each step he took.

"Wagh!" A familiar gravelly voice growled out from the rocks above him. "You by yourself?"

JJ peered up to where the voice was coming from, but saw nothing. "Yup. It's just me. Can I come up?"

"Guess I can't stop you."

Alternately clambering up and slipping back through the loose rock flakes, JJ made his way up the slope to the larger boulders and outcroppings that camouflaged the mountain man's dwelling spot.

He pulled himself onto a crumbly ledge and surveyed his location. Below him, the jagged rocks and boulders stood like sentinels guarding the border of dark green fir trees leading down to the broad valley stretching for miles across to the

Bridger Mountains. Three hundred feet above him was the peak of the mountain. Still no sign of Bridger.

"Ho, pilgrim!"

JJ jumped at the deep voice greeting him from behind. Bridger appeared as if from nowhere an arm's length above him. The mountain man's toothy smile shone out from the depths of his hairy face.

Bridger gestured to JJ's right. "Head on up around there and there's a switchback that will bring you up here."

"Any traps I should be aware of?"

"Nope, ain't ary a one. Well, there's one, but I decommissioned it in your honor."

JJ moved carefully along the flinty shale fearful of slipping and sliding down the apron of loose rock beneath him. The switchback Jackson had referred to was little more than a footstep wide indentation in the rocky path. JJ made his way up with one hand against the mountainside steadying himself so as not to slip. Losing his footing would send him hundreds of feet down a splintering slide. The hot Montana sun, the strenuous climb and his heightened nerves caused sweat to cascade down his face.

Bridger greeted him as he took the last few steps to the cave's well-camouflaged entrance.

"Good to see you again, JJ. I'm surprised you remembered your way up this far."

"Me too. I wasn't sure if I was on the right track there for awhile. I'm glad you called out, or I might never have found you."

"That's the idee, hoss. Don't want people prowling around me. Well, c'mon in and let's jaw."

The two squeezed between large boulders and ducked through a small entranceway. JJ once again found himself in the huge cavern that was Bridger's home. They walked toward the center of the cavern where the ever-present fire burned low and steady. Bridger nodded JJ toward a chair hewed out of a large tree stump while he sat cross-legged on the floor of the smoky cave and waited for JJ to speak.

"I wanted to thank you again for fixing me up. The leg is still a little stiff, but it healed up real quick from whatever you put on it."

"Ain't nothing as good as Indian medicine. I guess you made it back home okay."

"Yes, I did. I got the sheriff's body down too. The police made me take them up to where we found him. Don't worry, I was careful to steer them away from exploring up in this area."

Bridger nodded his appreciation, but knitted his brow as if in thought. After a moment of silence he asked, "Did they find who killed your sister-in-law?"

"No, they didn't. The police don't seem to be getting anywhere in the investigation. If you're still willing, I'd like to take you up on your offer to help me see if we can find anything out about who really did kill Kaitie."

Bridger did not answer, but stared at JJ from across the fire for several moments, his face red and reflecting the heat and the ebbing flame. A small branch popped, shooting a tiny orange ember out toward JJ's feet and breaking the silence. He looked into the fire, scratched his beard and spoke.

"I get feelings sometimes. Feelings and dreams. Visions. Maybe it's the Indian blood in me. I don't know what it is, but I reckon it's that." He paused, still staring into the low burning fire.

"When we found the sheriff's body that day I put my hands on him and said a Cheyenne prayer to send him safely to his father. As I held my hands to his chest, I had a brief vision that he was telling me he had had no accident. But he had been shot."

JJ, who had also been staring into the fire, looked up as Bridger lifted his own head – both of them looking at each other.

"Shot?" JJ said.

"Yep. That's the message I was getting. But, when I looked him over I couldn't find any wounds of any kind, other than his broken neck. But, I tell you, the feeling was strong. And I've learned to trust my feelings."

Bridger unwrapped himself from his sitting position and walked over to a stack of wood, picked out a couple of small pieces and brought them back, dropping them on the fire. Reverse whirlpools of sparks percolated up and disappeared toward the cave's roof.

Sitting back down, his legs folded beneath him, he continued. "After you left I went back to where it appeared the sheriff had fallen. I noticed a small outcropping and climbed up to it. I saw where his boot had taken off part of the outcropping as he fell. There was also a broken piece of a branch hanging above that spot. Looks like he might have been holding on to it and it snapped as he fell. To the left of that branch was a large rock that had a piece freshly broken off from it. A chunk was missing." He paused. "It had been shot away."

"Shot?" asked JJ.

Bridger nodded. "I could tell by the way the rock was chipped. I reckon he was climbing up or down at that spot and someone shot at him, missed and hit the rock he was holding onto and he fell."

JJ pondered this. "Do you think someone was trying to kill him?"

"That's what I'm thinking."

"But why? It doesn't make sense."

"Maybe whoever shot your sister-in-law shot him. I also found the remains of where someone gutted a sheep, and this ain't hunting season. I don't know if whoever shot at the sheriff is connected with your sister-in-law's killing, but I had another vision that night. Or, I should say, a dream. There is something or someone with a negative spirit be-devilin the mountains and my feeling in the dream was powerful that the bad things happening are connected to this one spirit."

JJ absorbed this information with a mixture of skepticism and hope. Skeptical that this wasn't crazy man talk and hope that somehow there was a connection that might lead to Kaitie's killer.

"Do you have anything more to go on than your vision?"

"Mebbe." Bridger offered, but said no more.

Discerning he would get no more out of Bridger on the topic, JJ asked, "When you went up to inspect where we found the sheriff, did you happen to find a shotgun?"

"No. What makes you ask?"

"Colton, the sheriff, had a 12-guage with him when he left my place. But, when we found Chief, the horse he was riding, the gun was not in the scabbard. The police never found one at the site where he fell . . . or was killed, and they looked all over the place."

"No, I surely didn't see any sign of gun, but I did find some track up near there."

"What kind of track?"

"Seen it near where the sheep was killed. Boot prints. And this." Bridger dug into the pocket sewn into his deerskin pants and pulled out a bullet slug. He handed it to JJ. "It's a .270 caliber. Found it in what was left of the sheep cleanings. Guess the coyote or griz or wolf that ate the guts musta spit out the bullet or et around it."

JJ rolled the bullet in his fingers.

"Now, I ain't saying it is or it ain't, but the bullet that took off that piece of rock where the sheriff fell from coulda been a .270 too. Especially if it was fired from the distance of around where that sheep was killed."

The two men stared silently across the fire at each other until another piece of sapwood popped.

"Did you follow the boot tracks?" JJ asked.

"No, I didn't. It was coming on dark and I couldn't have got too far tracking. You want to go back up there with me and see what we can find?"

JJ thought that this might be a job better left to the police. In addition, the Vicodin pill he had taken that morning was wearing off and his leg was still causing him enough pain that stomping around in rough terrain was not something he was looking forward to. But, reporting it to the police would bring them sniffing around this part of the mountains and might expose Bridger, opening him up to a trial where the predominance of evidence pointed at him. JJ was still convinced that the mountain man was innocent, and he wanted to be sure that whoever had killed Kaitie got the punishment he deserved.

"Alright, I'm game. Let's do it. Can I keep this?" he asked holding up the .270 slug.

Bridger shrugged, "I ain't got no use for it. You gonna be able to climb around with that leg?"

"I'll be ok. I made it up this far. If I need to I've got these to keep me going." He pulled the orange plastic bottle of Vicodin from his jacket and rattled it before stuffing it back into his pocket.

Bridger snorted incredulously. "Alright, hoss. Let's go."

∾   ∾   ∾

JJ RODE SPOT while Gopher and Bridger walked alongside leading them to the spot where he had seen the boot tracks and what was left of the gut pile from the sheep. There was little left in the way of track anymore. Wild animals had cleaned up the gut pile even to licking the grass clear of blood. There was, however, some trace of hunting boot tracks leading off to the southwest and Gopher was already sniffing at them.

Bridger smiled. "It's a good thing you've got your dog with you. 'Pears he's picking up some scent."

"Yeah, Gopher's a great tracker. Looks like he took off that way." JJ climbed off Spot and knelt next to the fading boot track. Pointing to the prints for his dog he commanded, "Gopher! Find it!"

The yellow Lab with nose to the ground, zigzagged his way ahead of the two men. JJ remounted and he and Bridger followed after Gopher's wagging tail.

It was only a short hike to the top of the ridge and they headed down the other side. The trail was easy to follow because of the swath the hunter had left dragging the sheep carcass down the slope.

Another hundred yards or so and they entered the timber. The temperature rapidly changed from the warm mid-morning sunshine they had been traveling in to the cool shaded green of the towering fir trees. Patches of pine needle bewhiskered snow mounds clung to the ground on either side of the game trail. A committee of jet-black ravens eyed them from their perches high in the branches cawing loudly to each other as an impudent squirrel taunted Gopher from the safety of a jagged stump.

As they dropped deeper into the thickening trees, Bridger broke his silence. "I reckon I know where we're headed. There's a cabin tucked into a gulley not far from here. I've come acrost it a coupla times in my travels, but ain't never seen a body living there. I reckon it's a hunting cabin. It's well hid. Somebody uses it though. Could be our man. You might want to walk your horse from here. No need to announce our arrival."

JJ nodded and grimaced as he dismounted. He gave a soft whistle and Gopher turned around and trotted back to his side. Taking Spot's reins, he led the horse down the trail. With his first step a bolt of fire shot up his leg and he stumbled against the horse's side grabbing the saddle horn to keep from falling. His leg had stiffened on the long ride. He reached into his pocket and brought out the orange pill bottle.

Bridger eyed him with some concern. "Wagh! Wait a minute, hoss. Try some of this."

He opened a pouch he carried on his belt and withdrew a bottle containing some foggy brown liquid with herbs floating in it.

"Take a pull on this. I brought it along figuring you might need some. She's better hot, but she'll put out the fire in your leg."

JJ took the bottle, opened it and sniffed tentatively at the concoction. It appeared to be some kind of tea.

"Drink her all down and set a spell."

With some trepidation, JJ lifted the bottle in salute to the mountain man. "Here's to you!" He gulped down the contents of the bottle and handed the empty back to Bridger. It tasted slightly bitter, but not unpleasant.

Tucking the bottle back into his pouch, Bridger gave a quick nod and squatted down on the forest floor. "Now, take a load off your feet, and give her a chance to work."

The two sat and swapped hunting stories. JJ found it interesting that for someone who treasured his solitary lifestyle so much, Jackson certainly enjoyed telling tales. The mountain man was in the middle of a story he had heard on the Blackfeet reservation when the unmistakable cry from a bald eagle circling high in the sky stopped him in mid-sentence.

Pointing to the bird, Bridger stood and offered his other hand to JJ. "My friend tells me it's time to go."

JJ smiled and said, "Your friend?"

"The bald eagle is my spirit guide. I have a strong connection to my brother eagle. He is wise and strong and can see many things from a great distance. He is a good guide to have. We should go now."

JJ let himself be pulled up and was surprised to find the pain in his leg was gone. Giving Gopher the tracking command again, JJ led Spot on foot with Bridger following close behind the dog.

Chapter 27

AS BRIDGER HAD JUDGED, it was not long before they halted and he pointed out the barely visible rooftop of a cabin well-protected by a stand of tall trees tucked in a small canyon.

"It might be best to leave your horse up here in case there's anyone down there. You'll also want to keep your dog there close by and quiet," Bridger cautioned quietly.

JJ nodded and tied Spot to a tree. He called Gopher to his side and said, "Heel."

The trio silently worked their way toward the cabin below them. As if in empathetic cooperation, the creatures of the woodland remained silent as snowfall. Even Gopher, his ears perked to attention, treaded carefully over the deadfall and under the closely bunched branches.

JJ was grateful for whatever was in the soothing potion Bridger had given him, as the going was steep, yet his leg gave him no trouble. He adopted Bridger's well-practiced Indian technique of stealth, placing the heel of his foot down first and rolling his foot slowly and gently towards his toes onto the ground. As they neared the cabin both men bent lower at their knees.

While the cabin was well camouflaged by the trees in front and at its sides, a small clearing at its back appeared to be a working area—a cord of split wood, a chopping block with a rusted axe leaning against it, a large midden of bleached bones, skulls, whiskey and beer bottles and various decaying animal pelts with a cloud of black flies circling it.

JJ pointed to a large sheepskin tacked to a board and drying in the sun. Bridger whispered, "I'd wager that's the skin of the ram that got killed up where I was reading sign."

The men sat quietly just inside the edge of the timber observing the lay of the land and the cabin itself. There appeared to be no movement inside as best they could discern.

After a few more moments of reconnaissance Bridger said to JJ, "Hoss, you sit tight right chere. I'll go reconnoiter the sitiation and let you know if the coast is clear." Without waiting for a response, the mountain man slipped whisper quiet like a panther skirting the clearing and covering the ground to the rear of the cabin.

JJ lost sight of Bridger in the tangle of trees. But, then, magically saw him appear for a moment then slip around the side of the cabin. Gopher, too, appeared to be watching intently and gave out little nervous whimpers at JJ's side.

Shortly, Bridger reappeared at the front of the cabin and hailed JJ with a wave of his arm.

JJ and Gopher made their way out of the woods and down to the cabin and Bridger.

The door to the cabin was padlocked from the outside. JJ peered through a small fly-specked window into the dim interior. Various animal skins and skulls were piled around the room and tacked to the walls. He did not want to even think about what it must smell like inside. Leaning against the worktable was a 12-gauge Remington shotgun.

"See anything interesting in there, Pard?" Bridger asked from behind.

"I'd say by the drying sheep skin over there, this looks like a poacher's cabin. Lots of skins and skulls. I also noticed a 12-gauge that looks like the one Sheriff Stollar had taken with him. I wish we could get in there to look around." JJ went back to looking in the window.

Bridger walked around the cabin inspecting the foundation. The structure was built on a slight hill that ran down to the creek below. The creek side was about 3 feet lower than the uphill side. It was a simple construction of logs on stone footings.

Gopher was sniffing at a corner of the foundation. A hole was dug into the soil under one of the logs on the downhill side. Bridger poked around the opening with his moccasined foot and bits of soil and gravel fell away. Following Bridger's lead, Gopher began to dig furiously at the hole, wagging his tail and whining. With an amused look on his face, Bridger stepped back and watched the frantic excavation.

"JJ! Come see what your dog has found."

In the time it took JJ to join them, Gopher had managed to dig enough of the hole to get his head and front paws under the cabin. The Lab pulled himself out of the hole. Black dirt covered his snout. He peered into the hole tipping his head questioningly and whining.

"Must be something in there. Get it, Goph! Get it!"

The dog scratched and scraped with increased vigor widening the opening with surprising speed. At last, he was able to squeeze the front of his body up to his chest under the cabin. A deep and threatening growl came from within the dark interior and Gopher backed out rapidly, whining as he withdrew.

"Skunk bear," Bridger said, his bushy eyebrows arching above his eyes..

"Skunk bear?" JJ asked.

"That's what the Blackfeet call them. That's a wolverine growl. Good thing Gopher got out of there. Them critters are mean and nasty when they're cornered. He musta climbed in there 'cause he smelled the carcasses inside. Let's hollow this hole out some more so I can get in there and see if I can't chase him out."

The skunk bear's warning was enough for Gopher and he sat back and watched the two humans do the rest of the digging. Once the hole was big enough, Bridger wormed his way in. The angry wolverine kept up a continuous low snarl as the mountain man's feet disappeared under the building.

"JJ, get me a big stick. A big one."

JJ ran up to the trees and brought back a good-sized limb. Relieved that it was Bridger challenging the wolverine rather than himself, he pushed the branch through the opening.

Taking the branch, Bridger warned, "Get back from the hole. Don't need anything blocking his exit."

JJ and Gopher obligingly stepped well back and watched.

Although he could not see the animal clearly, Bridger could make out a large shadowy hump backed up against the front wall of the foundation. He snaked the tree limb toward the growling wolverine.

"Got yer bristles up, don't you, you sorry son of a skunk? Git outta here! GIT!" He jabbed at the snarling shadow, forcing it to slink along the ground toward the opening. After making a loud and vicious snap at the offending spear, the wolverine scrambled toward the hole and out into the sunlight. Blinking at the man and his dog, the angry animal turned and bounded up toward the timber with Gopher hot on his trail.

JJ called his dog back. "Gopher! Leave it! Get back here." With a last longing look at the trees and a sniff, the yellow Lab turned and padded back to the cabin.

From inside his burrow Bridger called out, "Wagh! That skunk bear was after the meat inside this place. He scratched and chewed the be-jesus outta this plank. Grab me a good-sized rock, Ol' Coon. I believe I can knock on through this floorboard."

JJ went down to the creek bed and returned with a hefty rock. He handed it through to Bridger.

Lying on his back, the mountain man pounded at the tattered floorboard, which quickly split and gave way. He hammered at the adjacent plank. Each knock caused dirt to fall in his eyes and mouth, but it did not take long for him to pound the next board loose from the old wooden floor.

"I believe we're going to be able to get in here soon, hoss. One more board ought to do her."

A few knocks with the stone hammer and he pounded a third floor plank free, allowing enough room for a small man to squeeze through.

"I'm a-coming out." JJ watched as Bridger slid out from under the cabin. Dust and cobwebs covered his eyebrows and beard.

"I'm too big to squash up in there. But, I reckon you ought to fit up there just fine. Give her a try."

JJ lay on his back and squirmed his way under the cabin. The opening through the floor looked too small to get through, but JJ managed to pull himself up and into the cabin with minimal difficulty.

JJ coughed at the stench of chemicals and dead animals. He took a red bandana out of his pocket and tied it over his nose and mouth to keep from gagging. It took his eyes several moments to adjust to the dark room that was only dimly illuminated by the foggy sunlight allowed in through the dirty window. Skulls, antlers and skins hung from hooks, over chairs, a sofa and a large wooden table in the center of the room. The shotgun JJ had seen through the window was leaning up against the table.

He walked over to the gun and inspected it. It was an older piece, but had been well cared for. The metal parts were worn with age and use, but had been kept well oiled, as had the stock. Initials had been burned or carved into the right hand side of the stock, but JJ could not make them out in the hazy light. He took the shotgun over to the window and saw that the initials were "C.S." Colton Stollar! Maybe not. Maybe the owner of the cabin had the same initials, but something told him this was Colton's gun.

"Find anything?" Bridger called up through the cabin floor.

"Yeah," JJ answered. "Pretty sure this is the sheriff's 12-gauge."

A growly, "Wagh," was Bridger's only response.

JJ walked over to the desk. Nothing much there—a book of some sort, miscellaneous papers, a camera, a hammer, a box of .270 rifle shells and some old Cabela's sporting goods catalogs. JJ read the name C. Tomlinson on the catalog mailing labels. On the floor beside the desk was a dented old five-gallon paint can used as a trash bucket. It was stuffed with torn papers with pictures on them. JJ pulled some of the pages out and took them over to the window. Some of the pictures were of the skins and interior of the cabin. Some were pictures of a logbook or accounting ledger—entries of names and dollar amounts. Odd things to take pictures of. Not exactly picturesque. Apparently, the cabin owner didn't think much of them either since they had all been torn into pieces and tossed into the trash.

JJ crossed the floor and dumped the pictures back into the bucket. He picked up the book off the desk and leafed through it. They were the same pages he had seen in the torn photographs. He looked at the entries, but they held no meaning for him, other than that someone was making a lot of money dealing in wild game. $30,000 for a mountain lion! Shoot, maybe he should go into the hunting outfitting business. Several entries indicated bear gall bladders shipped to Asian countries. A friend of his who was a game warden had recently told him that this was a major felony offense that the Fish, Wildlife and Game people were cracking down on.

He closed the book and dropped it back on the desk. He poked around at the junk on the desktop, not sure what he was looking for, but mostly being curious. Reaching for some of the papers, he noticed the tip of something shiny at the edge of the desk. With everything else being dirty and dingy, the shiny article stood out in the darkened room.

JJ picked it up. It was a silver pen. It looked familiar. As he held it in his hand, his heart started racing. He hurried over to the window again to get a better look. Sure enough, it had the engraving "Good Luck K.C." that he knew would be there. He and Annie had given this pen to Kaitie when she graduated. He ran his fingers gently over the inscription.

From outside he heard Gopher barking followed by voices. He slipped the pen into his pocket and peered out the window.

Chapter 28

CHIP TOMLINSON LIFTED the Winchester semi-automatic off the gun rack in his pickup, slid out of the front seat and headed across the pasture toward his cabin. He had lots to do today—bring in the sheepskin, get it ready for shipping, burn the pictures in his trash and get his gear ready for the moose hunt on Monday.

Checking the paper this morning, there was still no story about them catching the mountain man for that chick's murder. What did the cops need—a map to the guy's house? All the evidence he had planted pointed to that crazy man. Maybe that is who the sheriff he had killed the other day was looking for, not him.

Tomlinson pondered these thoughts as he entered the thick cover of the trees. He neared the clearing where his cabin stood and spotted a dog running around playfully into the creek and back to the shore where it rolled around on its back. A yellow Lab. He stopped short and knelt down behind a tall fir tree. That dog was somebody's pet and was not up here alone. He reached into the pocket of his camo jacket and pulled out a couple of .270 shells, slid them into his rifle and clicked the safety off.

From his vantage point, he saw the door was still padlocked. *Good.* He worked his way stealthily around the trees to get a view behind the cabin. He moved quietly around the perimeter of the clearing just inside the tree line careful not to step on any fallen branches. As he neared the back view of the cabin he was relieved to see his sheepskin untouched.

A few more steps brought the full rear of the cabin in view. It was then he spied a figure at the creekside of the cabin.

"I'll be damned," he whispered under his breath. It was the mountain man, and he was peering under his cabin at something.

A BALD EAGLE SOARING in circles in the blue morning sky called out and Bridger looked up. A feeling of unease crept up his spine and lifted the hairs on the back of his neck. Maybe it was time to go. He scanned the area.

"You see anything more in there, son?" Bridger called softly into the opening under the cabin.

JJ was still riffling through the papers on the desk and didn't hear Bridger's question.

"Maybe we should leave this place." Bridger's lowered voice didn't reach JJ's ears.

❧　❧　❧

IT LOOKED TO TOMLINSON as if the mountain man was speaking to someone, but he could not make out what was being said. Treading carefully, he made his way through the trees toward the cabin, the Winchester trained on the trespasser. The shaggy interloper was on all fours and had his head stuck in the foundation of the cabin. The Lab was still preoccupied by the creek and had not yet picked up his scent.

As he reached the last tree before the clearing, Tomlinson raised the rifle to firing position and stepped out in the open.

"Hey, you!" he yelled.

Bridger pulled his head out from beneath the cabin, spun around and saw the man with a rifle pointed at him. At the same moment, Gopher also turned at the sound of the man. He lowered his head and growled.

As the man approached with the rifle still at his shoulder, Bridger came around from the back of the cabin and walked toward him, his hand held out in a gesture of greeting.

"Ho, there, friend. No need for the gun. I'm just passing through. Didn't mean to be nosy. That's a fine sheepskin you got drying over there."

Tomlinson, gun still pointed, walked slowly towards the mountain man. As he neared Gopher's growl turned to a harsh bark. His hackles were up and his canines were bared.

Tomlinson pointed the gun toward Gopher then back at Bridger. "If that dog of yours comes at me he's dead."

"Gopher! Settle down." Bridger commanded. Nevertheless, the dog raised the threat level in his bark and crouched, ready to attack. As his tone grew more threatening and constant, Tomlinson got more impatient. He swung the rifle toward Gopher and fired. The dog yelped as the bullet grazed his hip. Gopher ran whining through the timber and toward the pasture.

Bridger took some quick steps toward Tomlinson but stopped short as the rifle swung toward him.

"There weren't no need to shoot the dog . . . " he said.

With the rifle still trained on the mountain man Tomlinson sneered, "If I wanted to kill the dog he'd be dead."

At the sound of the gunshot and Gopher's yelp, JJ dropped back down through the floor, hastily replacing the floorboards above him. He scrambled out from under the cabin and rounded the corner. He stopped short when he saw a man with a rifle pointed at Bridger.

Tomlinson shifted and turned the gun on JJ.

"Alright, stay right there."

JJ didn't move.

"Now, you, mountain man, move on over to your buddy there."

Bridger walked back to where JJ was standing.

JJ clenched his jaw. "What the hell did you do to my dog?"

Walking toward JJ and Bridger, Tomlinson said, "He was trespassing. I shoot trespassers. I guess you fellows didn't see the No Trespassing signs posted everywhere around here. What are you doing snooping around my place?"

Bridger gave a quick warning look at JJ. "Wagh! We was jest passing through, hoss. Didn't mean any harm. Didn't cause any. No need for the gun. You want us off your property, we'll be glad to move along."

"What were you doing over by my cabin?"

"Jest being nosy, I guess. To tell the truth, I was feeling kinda wolfish and was hoping there might be something in there to fill my meat bag." Bridger patted his stomach. "But with that big lock on your door I s'pose there ain't nobody getting in there for nothin."

Keeping his rifle pointed at the two men Tomlinson glanced over to reassure himself that the padlock was still secure on the door. He walked toward the rear of the cabin from where he had seen JJ emerge. "Anyone else back here?"

JJ and Bridger glanced nervously at each other as Tomlinson neared the corner of the cabin.

"Nope," Bridger said quickly. "Jest us two and the dog."

Tomlinson rounded the corner carefully and saw the break in the foundation the two men had made. "What the hell? You sons of bitches!"

Chapter 29

"WHEN WILL YOUR HUSBAND BE BACK, Mrs. Volker?" Detective McConnell stood in the doorway with a pen and a black notebook open in his hand.

From the other side of the screen door Annie scrutinized the handsome officer. He looked to be only a few years older than she, maybe mid-thirties, with neatly trimmed short black hair, intense black eyes and the serious face of a professional lawman.

"I'm not sure." Remembering JJ's wish to keep the mountain man's location a secret, she cautiously added, "He went out early this morning before I got up. I guess he's out riding. His horse and our dog, Gopher aren't around either, so I suspect they're somewhere up in the mountains."

McConnell tapped the pen against his notebook. "Do the initials 'CT' mean anything to you? Anyone you or your husband knows with those initials?"

Annie pursed her lips. "Not that I can think of, no. Maybe JJ knows, but it doesn't ring a bell with me. I'm sorry— would you like to come in?" She swung the door open. McConnell smiled, nodded, and stepped into the living room.

Showing him to the sofa, Annie offered, "Can I get you some coffee or water? Anything?"

"No, thank you. Mrs. Volker . . ."

"Annie."

"Annie. I'm sorry about what happened to your sister. Do you mind if I ask you a few questions?"

Annie took a deep breath. She would not let herself tear up in front of this stranger. She shook her head, "No, I don't mind."

McConnell flipped his notebook open and poised his pen over it. "Do you know if your sister knew anyone with the initials 'CT?' Was she seeing anyone who might have those initials or did she mention anyone recently?"

"No, as far as I know, Kaitie wasn't dating anyone and none of her friends have those initials. Why? Who is this 'CT' person anyway?"

The detective paused. "We're not sure who the person is. We were going over some information we collected in your sister's apartment and came across a disk with her journal on it. The entries in the journal are not particularly detailed, but over the last week, someone with those initials was mentioned several times. We think she was working on some story or article pertaining to this person."

Annie's eyes widened as she listened. "Do you think CT could be the one who . . . ?" She still could not speak the word.

"We can't say that at this point. We would like to speak to this person, however. Please think hard,

Mrs. . . . Annie. Anyone at all. We think the person may be an outfitter or a hunter perhaps living in the Big Timber area. Most likely male. Anyone your husband might know. Does he have an address book we can look at?"

Annie bit her lip as she tried to recall the names of everyone JJ knew, but no 'CTs' came to mind. "No, I'm sorry, I can't think of anyone. However, we do have an address book. Let me check that. Excuse me, it is in the office. I'll be right back."

Annie disappeared into the back bedroom. She sorted through the chaotic mess of papers, catalogs and mail ready to avalanche off JJ's desk. Shuffling through the pile, she finally came across the worn leatherette book with "Addresses" gold stamped on the cover. She was about to open it when she noticed the case that held JJ's special pistol was sitting on top of one of the stacks of paper. She remembered him returning the pistol to the gun case last night when she had made him put it away. With a feeling of dread, she opened the box and gasped when she saw it was empty.

"Damn it!" she swore.

McConnell called out from the living room, "Everything okay?"

Slamming the lid down on the empty case she felt a flash of anger that JJ had gone against her specific insistence that he not take a gun up into the mountains. Then again, he never listened to her anyway—why would he start now? Sometimes he made her so mad. With a heavy sigh, she returned to the living room.

"Is something wrong?" McConnell pressed.

Annie began rapidly leafing through the address book. "Yes. I mean, no. Nothing. Just . . .   Never mind. What were those initials again?"

"C T"

Annie's heart was beating hard against her chest. She couldn't concentrate. The names on the pages were a blur. That damn JJ! He thinks he's such a tough cowboy. He's going to hurt someone or get hurt himself in the foul mood he's been in the past few weeks.

McConnell gently took the book from her hands and offered, "Here, let me take a look, if that's alright."

"Yes. Of course," Annie stammered. "I'm sorry, it's just . . . ." Before she finished her sentence, she glanced out the front window and saw Gopher limping into the yard. It looked as if his leg was bleeding.

Chapter 30

TO CONFIRM HIS SUSPICION Tomlinson gave a quick look into the entry hole at the back of his cabin. Judging by the fresh earth scraped from the opening and the streak of dirt down the back of the men's clothes they had entered his workshop from underneath. Furious, he turned and snarled at them, "You bastards broke into my cabin, didn't you? I ought to shoot the two of you for that, and I'd be in my rights."

"Your rights?" the younger one snapped taking a threatening step towards him.

"JJ." The mountain man stayed him with a hand on his arm,

Tomlinson took a step backward and shifted the rifle muzzle directly at JJ. His hands were sweating.

"Your rights?" JJ spat out again, his face red with anger. "What are you doing with Sheriff Stollar's shotgun? What are you doing with my sister-in-law's pen?" Tomlinson was shocked. His sister-in-law?

The mountain man spoke quietly to his friend. "JJ, I think you should keep quiet."

A bead of sweat ran down Tomlinson's face. He looked from one to the other sizing them up. If push came to shove, he outweighed the younger one and could probably take him. The mountain man might be a different story, however. He had heard enough of the legends about the hairy guy to be apprehensive about his capabilities. He had to even the odds.

"No, that's okay, Bridger. That is your name, isn't it? Bridger Jackson, the mountain man of the Crazies? Let him talk."

Bridger did not respond. He turned to JJ "And your name is JJ, right? Well, JJ, it's none of your business where I came across the things in my cabin. This is my property and you're trespassing, and that really pisses me off." He paused.

Jackson kept a firm grip on his friend's arm keeping him at bay. Tomlinson sensed the restrained rage in JJ's posture.

"I'll tell you what, JJ. I need your help. While I decide what I should do about you two, I would like you both to relax. Let's start with Mr. Jackson here. See that piece of rope over there by the porch?"

JJ looked in the direction he gestured with his head.

"Bring that over here for me, will you?"

"Fuck you!" JJ barked.

Tomlinson stepped toward JJ and cracked the butt of his rifle into JJ's cheek knocking him to the ground. Bridger took a step forward with fists clenched, but stopped when Tomlinson pointed the rifle at him.

"Don't move or I'll shoot you both," Tomlinson ordered. "Now, JJ, get up and bring that damn rope over here. Now!"

Rubbing the bleeding welt on his cheek JJ scowled defiantly at Tomlinson and did not move.

"Either you bring that rope here now, or I'll smash your friend's face too." He made a threatening gesture with the rifle butt at Jackson.

Reluctantly, JJ got up and got the rope looped over the porch rail. Poking Bridger in the ribs with his rifle, Tomlinson gestured for him to move over to two trees growing close together that had a bar affixed between them about ten feet from the ground. This was where he hung his game to skin it. As JJ approached with the rope, Tomlinson instructed him as a teacher telling a young child what to do, "Now, JJ, I want you to throw that rope on over that bar up there for me."

JJ did as instructed.

Tomlinson continued in his condescending tone, "Very good, JJ. Now, please tie one end of the rope around this tree." He watched as JJ followed his instructions. To Bridger in the same tone, he said, "Please move over to JJ, Mr. Jackson. And turn toward me with your hands behind your back."

Jackson did as he was told.

"Now, JJ, please bind Mr. Jackson's hands tightly with the other end of the rope. Be sure you do it tightly, because I'm going to check your work."

JJ fired back, "You can go to hell. I ain't . . . ."

Before JJ finished his sentence, Tomlinson fired a loud report from his gun into the air. Both JJ and Bridger jumped at the sudden rifle crack. His tone turning vicious, Tomlinson threatened, "Cut the crap, and tie him up or I'll shoot him where he stands. Then you're next. Trust me, kid, you wouldn't be my first killing and I'm not afraid to do it again."

JJ tied Jackson's hands snugly with the rope.

"I'm sorry about this, Bridger," JJ apologized through clenched teeth.

"It's okay, Hoss. Don't fret about it. It's this no account hide hunter who needs to be sorry." He squinted one eye at Tomlinson and launched a wad of spit at his foot.

Tomlinson stepped closer and inspected JJ's rope work. Satisfied that the mountain man could not get loose, he ordered JJ to pull the other end of the rope up and tie it off so that Bridger's arms pulled back and up forcing him to bend forward.

"That's good enough. I don't think Mr. Jackson will be going anywhere. Now, what are we going to do with you, JJ? Hey, I know just the thing! Let's go get the sheriff's shotgun. It's in my workshop. But you already know that, don't you, 'cause you were snooping where you shouldn't have been." Poking

JJ with his rifle, he pushed him forward toward the cabin.

∾   ∾   ∾

THE PAINFUL THROBBING in JJ's head and the sharp jab in his ribs only fed the outrage that was twisting inside him like a mean bronco with the flank strap pulled tight and desperate to break free from the holding pen. In his soul, he knew Tomlinson was the one he had been looking for. The one who had killed Kaitie. The one who had probably killed Colton. And, the one he had sworn he would kill if he ever found him. He had grown less confident about his ability to take this ultimate revenge on Kaitie's killer, however, given the current circumstances he knew if it came to it, he could and would kill this slimy bastard. He needed to be ready to take whatever action possible whenever an opportunity arose. This was a desperate situation and called for desperate measures. He wished he had not left his pistol in Spot's saddlebag.

They climbed the steps to the cabin. Tomlinson jabbed JJ in the back with the rifle and told him to stop at the door. JJ halted and glanced over at Bridger trussed up like a deer ready to be skinned. The angry bronco inside JJ was kicking and crashing itself against the holding pen gate.

"To answer your question, JJ," Tomlinson said, "Maybe I found the sheriff's shotgun where the mountain man left it after he killed you."

JJ stopped. "What the hell are you talking about?"

"Well, the talk is that Mr. Jackson there murdered your sister . . . ."

"She was my sister-in-law, not my sister. And Bridger wasn't the one that killed her."

"Oh, really? Everyone seems to think it was him, including the sheriff's department. That's why the sheriff was searching around here looking for him. It was his knife and tomahawk that was used to kill her, and . . ."

"How do you know what was used to kill her? That has never been reported."

"Well, let's just say it's a logical assumption. So, as I was saying, maybe Mr. Jackson was responsible for the sheriff's death. Maybe he came across the sheriff who was tailing him. Maybe he pushed him to make it look like an accident, or they got in a fight. Whatever. Then maybe he took the sheriff's shotgun and came across you looking for him too. You confronted him about Kaitie and he ended up shooting you with the sheriff's gun. Make sense? I'll bet it will to the cops who find your body and the shotgun with Jackson's prints on it."

JJ felt his stomach turn. This guy was going to kill him and Bridger and then frame Bridger— which is what he must have done with Kaitie. The bronco inside him kicked even harder. He had to do something and he had to do something soon.

Tomlinson took his keys out of his pants and held them out to JJ. "Here, take these and unlock the padlock. But do NOT open the door, or you'll blow us both to kingdom come."

Realizing this might be his only chance, in one swift move JJ reached for the keys, snatched them in his fist and smashed Tomlinson in the face with all the pent-up fury that had built up inside him. The satisfying crack against the man's jaw was almost as rewarding as the look of astonishment on Tomlinson's face as he fell backward missing the top step and landing on the ground. JJ flung the keys as far as he could. Tomlinson's rifle had fallen a few feet away from his body and JJ leapt toward it. Shaking his head, Tomlinson rose to all fours and scrambled to the rifle at the same time, grabbing it before JJ reached it. Rolling to his right he swung the gun up toward JJ and fired. But, JJ was close enough and fast enough to knock the rifle barrel away from him and the shot missed its mark. His ears rang from the blast and his adrenalin was pumping through the roof. Jerking the rifle out of Tomlinson's grip, he brought it to his shoulder training it on him and pulled the trigger.

Nothing. The gun was empty.

Tomlinson laughed and kicked out at JJ hitting him in the shin. JJ cracked Tomlinson in the side of his head with the butt of the rifle. He crumpled back to the ground and lay there unconscious.

JJ stood over Tomlinson's body shaking and trying to catch his breath when a loud growl erupted behind him.

"WAGH! That was beautiful! Just beautiful!"

JJ had all but forgotten Bridger during the struggle. With a mighty heave, he tossed Tomlinson's rifle into the creek and ran to where Bridger was hanging.

"That was a shining piece of work, JJ!"

Wrestling furiously with the tight knot, JJ said, "That son of a bitch was going to kill us. And I'm damn sure he's the one who murdered Kaitie and framed you. Damn it, this thing is tight." The knot had been snug when he had tied it, but Bridger's struggling as he hung had made it impossible to loosen. The poor old man was sweating and in obvious agony.

"I can't get this damn thing loose. Do you have your knife?"

"No, our friend there took it from me when he checked my riggings. I sure would like to get free from this though."

"I've got a knife up in my saddlebag. My gun's up there too. It'll take me a few minutes, but let me run up there. I don't think that bastard's getting up any time soon. Hang in there, Bridger, I'll be right back." Realizing his poor choice of words, he threw Bridger an apologetic look and broke for the timber.

ﾐ ﾐ ﾐ

SPOT WAS LAZILY FEEDING on some shoots of grass he had found at the base of the tree where he was tied. Grabbing his pistol and knife from the saddlebag, JJ checked to make sure the gun was still loaded. As he snapped the cylinder closed he heard Bridger calling in the distance, but couldn't make out what he was yelling. Pine branches whipped his face as he ran back through the trees toward the cabin. When he reached the clearing, he stopped short. Tomlinson was no longer on the ground, nor was he anywhere to be seen. Bridger, still trussed up between the two trees, was looking up to where JJ had entered the timber. Bridger had been gagged. Fearing that Tomlinson had re-loaded his rifle JJ ducked back behind a lodge pine and pulled his gun out

He peered around the side of the tree and surveyed the area around the cabin. Nothing moved and there was no sign of Tomlinson, though JJ was sure he was down there. The padlock was still on the door, but Tomlinson might have gone through the floor of the cabin as JJ himself had. He could be in there watching him from the darkened window. He wanted to call out to Bridger, but did not dare. He felt sorry for the discomfort the old man was in and was desperate to free him. No way was he going to risk going into the open to reach him, but the area was wooded behind Bridger. He might be able to work his way around there without being discovered and reach the captive mountain man.

Slipping back into the cover of the timber, JJ circled quietly through the trees toward the spot he had picked out to rescue Bridger. His senses were on high alert. The soft carpet of pine needles allowed him to move silently, enabling him to hear the other sounds around him – the soft wind whispering in the treetops, the rapid gurgling of the spring run-off in the creek and from high above came the familiar piping of Bridger's spirit guide, a bald eagle.

He arrived a few feet behind where Bridger was tied, and knelt down next to a tree trunk. It would be impossible to be seen from the cabin's window. Still no sign of Tomlinson outside the cabin. It was now or never.

"Hey, Bridger," he whispered. Jackson turned his head towards JJ. The pain and exhaustion showed in his eyes and from the sweat running in rivulets down his face soaking the gag tied around his mouth. "Where's Tomlinson?"

Bridger shook his head indicating he did not know.

"I'm going to cut you loose. Once I do, drop back here with me and we'll get out of here."

JJ put his gun on the ground and pulled his knife out of his pocket. As he opened the knife blade, a branch cracked from behind him. In one swift move, he dropped the knife, grabbed his pistol and rolled to his side, catching the wide-eyed look of surprise on Bridger's face fixed on something behind him. He knew who it was. Having no time to fix on a target, he pulled the trigger at the blur in his peripheral vision. Like a stop action photograph, the last thing he saw was Tomlinson swinging a two by four broadside toward his face. The last thing he heard was the explosion of his gun going off.

Chapter 31

ANNIE POURED GOPHER ANOTHER BOWLFUL of water, which he lapped slopping water onto the floor. As he drank, she gathered up the cloths she had used to clean the blood from his hind leg. It did not seem to bother Gopher that Detective McConnell was still inspecting his wound.

Annie twisted the rags in her hand. "Are you sure it's a gunshot wound?"

"Pretty sure, yeah. And, he's lucky. One more inch and the bullet would have ripped apart his hind end and he'd be dead." McConnell stood and looked at her.

"Annie, I can see that something is upsetting you. Even before your dog showed up something was wrong. May we talk about that?"

Annie looked at McConnell wondering how much to say, where to start. Her heart was pounding and her head ached. Something was wrong. She felt it. She had promised JJ not to say anything about Jackson, but he had promised her he would not go off with his pistol doing anything stupid. Now Gopher had shown up with a gunshot wound and no JJ. JJ always took Gopher with him when he went riding, and Gopher never left his side.

"Mrs. Volker?" the detective repeated.

With a trembling sigh Annie started, "I'm worried about my husband."

Annie told him about Jackson and JJ's confidence that he was not Kaitie's killer. She also told him that she was afraid that her husband had gone back up to visit Jackson to enlist him in tracking down the real murderer. No, she did not know where Jackson lived; only that it was in a cave not far from where Sheriff Stollar had died. What worried her most was that JJ had taken his pistol with him. While she could not believe JJ would ever shoot anyone, he was so embittered over Kaitie's death she could not be certain what he might do if he did find the murderer. When she had finished unloading everything she knew, she sat silently looking at the detective and picking at the rags in her hands.

McConnell said nothing as he jotted down a few notes in his notebook. He looked up, gave Annie a comforting smile, and said, "Thank you, Annie. I think we need to find your husband. Excuse me for a minute."

McConnell went outside and sat in his car. Annie saw him talking on his police radio. From behind her, Gopher whined. She turned and he was looking up at her wagging his tail. She knelt next to the dog and hugged him. "Poor Gopher. I'm sorry about your leg. Where were you? Where's JJ?"

At the mention of JJ's name, Gopher pulled out of Annie's embrace, perked up his ears and tilted his head. He looked up at her and barked.

The screen door creaked open and Detective McConnell stepped back into the kitchen. "I've called for some backup. One of our other officers will be here in a few minutes and we'll look for JJ."

Gopher barked again at JJ's name, shifting his attention to the detective. Both Annie and McConnell looked down at him. He wagged back at them and headed for the door looking over his shoulder once he reached it.

Annie and McConnell looked at each other in amusement. "Gopher is JJ's hunting dog and his baby," she said. "Sometimes I think he's closer to Gopher than he is to me. He's a great tracker. I think he's trying to show us where JJ is. I really do."

McConnell smiled, "You could well be right. Would it be alright with you if we took Gopher with us to find your husband?"

"I think it would be a good idea. Can I get you some coffee while we wait?"

∾ ∾ ∾

MCCONNELL HEARD THE SHERRIF'S SUV kicking up gravel as it pulled into the Volker's front yard. Standing, he handed Annie his half-empty coffee cup.

"That will be Deputy Gustafson. We'll take Gopher with us and find JJ for you. Thanks again for your information, Annie, and please let us know if you happen to come up with who "CT" might be. Come on, Gopher."

"I will. Please be careful. Here, take his leash."

McConnell and Gopher left the house and crossed the yard. Rolf Gustafson nodded a greeting to McConnell as he was getting out of the truck, but the detective waved him back in.

"Get in, Rolf. We're heading up toward where you found Colton's body. This is Gopher. He's going to help us find his master. Aren't you, boy? I'll put him in the back." Gopher barked an impatient greeting to the deputy and jumped into the backseat of the white Ford Explorer.

Gustafson started the truck. "Where to, Rick?"

"Well, there's only one road heading up the mountain, and that's where Gopher was coming down from, so let's head up that way. I think we can start looking where we found Colton's body."

Leaving a yellow cloud of dust in its trail, the Explorer tore its way up the mountain with Gopher hanging out the rear window, ears and lips flapping. As they bounced across the rutted hardpan, McConnell filled Gustafson in on what he had learned from Annie Volker.

"She says her husband knows Jackson from when he was a kid. Used to hunt together with his old man. At first, he thought the guy was the killer and had gone hunting for him. He was wounded and Jackson took care of him and sent him back down the mountain. That was when you found him. While he was up there Jackson convinced him that he had nothing to do with the Cathcart murder."

Gustafson snorted, "Yeah, and how did Jackson explain the little details of his tomahawk and knife at the scene?"

"Don't know. But I'll tell you Rolf, I've got a suspect with a much more credible motive than that mountain man."

Gustafson turned his head to McConnell with a quizzical look. As a result, he missed seeing a deep pothole and the truck bounced so hard they both hit their heads on the roof of the cab and Gopher lurched to the floor.

Gustafson returned his attention to the road and Gopher jumped back onto the seat. "Wo, sorry about that. So, who is this new suspect?"

"I don't know his name," said McConnell. "All I have right now are his initials – CT. The Cathcart woman kept a journal on a thumb drive I found in her apartment. The entries were sketchy. Just brief notes. But, the entries from the week before her death indicated she was doing some research for an article she was writing or going to write on poaching. She had located someone with the initials

'CT' who had taken her to a workshop somewhere up in the Crazies. The shop was loaded with skins and trophies. According to her journal, this CT was not aware that she was writing an article. She mentioned she had taken photos of pages from his record book and that there were some "biggies," as she called them, listed as clients. We have not been able to locate these photos either in her apartment or on her computer. And, we haven't found a camera so far, so we don't know who the biggies are. From what I could gather from the journal, this CT is a big player. My suspicion is that CT might have discovered what she was up to and killed her before she could expose him. "

"What about the murder weapons? You think Jackson was CT's partner maybe?"

"That's a possibility. But, I don't think he was. From all we know about Bridger Jackson he was a loner. He has never been known to poach or shown any other criminal tendencies. Lots of accusations, but they've all proven false. He smart at being invisible. We've never been able to locate where he lives. If he doesn't want to be found you can't find him. I seriously doubt that he would be careless or stupid enough to murder someone and leave his evidence all over the place."

"What about his fingerprints on the weapons?"

"That's kind of a clue right there. All prints were wiped off the handles of the knife and the hatchet, but not off the blade of the knife or the head of the hatchet. Jackson's prints showed up on the blade and the hatchet head. If he were trying to hide his prints he would have wiped everything down, not just the handles. If someone else used them, he probably would have just wiped down the parts he touched and ignored the rest of the weapons. On the other hand, if he was trying to frame Jackson he might have purposely not wiped down the other parts. And as I said, it's highly unlikely that Jackson would have been so careless as to leave them lying around outside the crime scene, especially if he'd taken the trouble to wipe the prints."

Gustafson chewed his gum thoughtfully. "Hmm. Any other clues?"

"Yeah. Shoe prints. Jackson's moccasin prints were all over the place outside the cabin. Some were fresh and some were older as if he had been coming and going for some time. My guess is he was staying in the cabin over the winter. We took a cast of the moccasin print and determined he had a size twelve shoe. The new kid from Forensics found bloody boot prints where the body was mutilated and on the porch. Size nine. There were no bloody moccasin prints anywhere. No way could Jackson fit into size nine boots."

"Interesting. Any ideas who CT might be?"

"Not so far. That's why I was questioning the Volker woman to see if she knew anyone with those initials. She didn't. We're running a check on known poachers, but so far we haven't turned up any matches."

"Did you find anything else in the girl's apartment?"

"I don't think so. We took her computer and they're checking that out, but I did a quick check and didn't find anything on it. We dusted for prints, and I'm waiting to get those results. But, I'm not hopeful. She kept that place spotless. The only unusual thing was a broken moose statue on a table. It's probably nothing, but it seemed out of place given how spic and span that place was. Other than that, though, the thumb drive journal was the only significant evidence we turned up. Now that I'm thinking of it, I should call in before we're out of signal range and see if they did get any results on the computer or the prints."

"Good idea."

McConnell pulled out his cell phone and called the police lab.

"Hey, John, it's Rick. Any results on the stuff from the Cathcart apartment yet? Nothing on the computer yet, huh? What? I missed that. We're up in the Crazies and I've got a weak signal. I didn't catch that last thing you said. Yeah, I remember – the moose statue. What about it?"

McConnell sat up straight and put his finger in his other ear to make sure he was hearing clearly.

"Whose prints were they? Say that again?" There was excitement in his voice and Gustafson glanced at him.

"Charles Tomlinson? CT! That's our man! He's wanted for what? Nebraska? No shit. Do they have any idea where he is? It's been that long, huh? Well, do they . . . . You what? No kidding. Did you say 'Chip?' In Big Timber? John, my boy, you have earned yourself a steak dinner at the Oasis on me. Get the sheriff's office to look into this guy right away, but don't bring him in. I want to question him myself. Rolf and I are in the middle of something right now, but I should be back by the end of the day. John, you're the best."

McConnell turned to Gustafson with a wide grin on his face. "Looks like we may have identified CT. The prints on that statue I told you I found in the girl's apartment matched those of one Charles Tomlinson who is wanted for an old murder in a tiny town called Sumner, Nebraska. Seems he killed his grandfather and disappeared 14 years ago. The town cops didn't have the manpower to put on a full-scale hunt for him and the case went cold. On a whim, John in Forensics did a name search in Montana and found a Chip Tomlinson living in Big Timber. Guess what our boy Chip does for a living?"

Gustafson shrugged his shoulders.

"He's a hunting guide and taxidermist. I think we're finally on to something here, Rolf. This is turning into a good day. Now, if we can find JJ

Volker and he can lead us to Jackson, this day will be close to excellent."

THE EXPLORER LURCHED from side to side as it ground its way higher into the mountains. The road became rockier and more deeply rutted, causing them to slow to a crawl. McConnell smiled, enjoying the ride and taking in the scenery, nearly forgetting the purpose of their expedition. The news from forensics had put him in a good mood; probably the best mood he had been in since the Cathcart case fell into his lap. He was looking forward to interrogating Tomlinson. Finally, a break!

From the rear seat, Gopher began to whine. McConnell turned and looked at him. With his paws giving him leverage the dog's head and chest were well outside the window as he had been for most of the ride. But, his ears and entire body were more alert. His tail had gone stiff and was no longer wagging as it had been. As they rolled past a pair of tire tracks that broke off from the road and headed to a pasture, Gopher let out a loud bark causing Gustafson to jump in his seat.

McConnell tried to see what had caused the dog's reaction, but saw nothing other than the tire tracks winding off into the distance.

"Hold up, Rolf," he said. "What is it Gopher? What's out there?"

Gopher looked at McConnell, barked and turned back to the window. Gustafson stopped the truck and McConnell opened his door. Gopher leaped out the window bounding to the other side of the road. He crawled under the bars of the gate and began sniffing the ground.

"I think we ought to follow him and see where he's going. Seems like . . ."

A gunshot rang out in the distance and McConnell and Gustafson looked at each other in surprise. McConnell ran to the fence gate and found it locked. He called across the road, "You got a tire iron or a hammer in there, Rolf?"

Gustafson went around the back of the SUV and came out with a fire axe. "This ought to work," he said, handing the tool to McConnell. The detective only had to smash the lock once before it shattered and fell to the ground.

Gustafson called, "Get back in and get Gopher. We'll follow the tracks with the truck."

McConnell called the dog but Gopher was on the scent and zigzagged his way through the field. "Looks like we better follow him. He seems to know where he's headed." He unsnapped his holster strap and climbed back into the Explorer.

They bounced their way through the pasture behind the dog. As they approached the other end of the field, they saw a pickup truck parked against the fence. McConnell took the leash he had brought from Annie's house, called Gopher over to the truck, and hooked it to the dog's collar. "Rolf, call in those plate numbers and have them run a check on the truck."

"I tried, but I can't get reception out here. How about your cell phone?"

McConnell said, "Yeah, right. I can barely get a signal in town. But, I'll try."

The signal meter on his phone indicated it was no use. Gopher strained at the other end of the leash trying to pull him toward the timber. He put the dog in the back seat of the Explorer and returned to the pickup. The door was unlocked. He rifled through the mess of papers stuffed into the glove box and found the truck's registration and broke into a broad smile.

"How about that? Guess who owns this truck?" he asked waving the papers at Gustafson.

"Volker?"

"No. It's registered to a Mr. Chip Tomlinson. Let's go find where that gunshot came from. I think we should leave the dog in the car, though. If we need him for tracking we can always come back, I don't want him giving us away."

The two men left the truck and headed for the woods on the other side of the fence as Gopher, trapped in the truck, barked after them.

Chapter 32

THE SIDE OF TOMLINSON'S FACE and lips were badly swollen from where the rifle butt had smashed him. Despite the jack-hammering pain in his own head, JJ noticed with some satisfaction that four of Tomlinson's teeth had been knocked out. He pronounced his 's's' as 'th' sounding as if he had a triple dose of Novocain from the dentist, Tomlinson pointed JJ's own gun at him and said, "Too bad you missed, asshole." He turned the pistol over in his hand admiringly. "This is a nice piece. I'm glad you brought it. Now I can not only make it look like the mountain man shot you with the sheriff's shotgun, but I can kill him with your pistol making it look like the two of you dueled it out to the death. Now, let's go get that shotgun. Give me the keys to the cabin." He held out his hand.

JJ, sitting on the ground, looked up at him with a sneer, "I don't have them. I pitched them over there somewhere and I don't know where they are."

Tomlinson glared at him. "Well, you're going to find them, partner. My truck keys are on there too, so get up and get hunting."

Without moving JJ said, "Find them yourself."

Tomlinson pushed JJ with his boot. "Get up, or I'll shoot your friend right now." JJ stumbled to his feet and headed toward the tall grass into which he had thrown the keys.

The pain in his head and the fury in his heart whipped around inside him like a nest full of angry hornets. He no longer cared what would happen to him; he only wanted the chance to tear Tomlinson apart.

"You piece of shit. You killed Kaitie, didn't you?"

"She killed herself, friend. She stepped in a bear trap and chopped her foot off. She bled to death. We reap what we sow, JJ. We reap what we sow. She'd be alive today if she minded her own business. Bitch." He spat on the ground.

"You son of a . . . " JJ turned and leapt at Tomlinson before he could react, knocking him off his feet and sending the pistol flying. Rolling on the ground, the two tore and pounded at each other with a vengeance – a flurry of fists, blood, sweat and dirt, thrashing and grappling and ripping the earth beneath them. Evenly matched in strength and size, each blow took a heavy toll. But, JJ had the advantage of youth on his side.

Tomlinson crab-walked backwards, gulping for air. JJ threw himself on top of Tomlinson, grabbed him by the hair and smashed his head into the hard packed ground repeatedly. Each blow felt like glorious retribution for what had been done to Kaitie, to Annie and to himself.

With all his strength, JJ jammed Tomlinson's head one final time into the ground and watched his eyes roll up and his body go limp. Eyes closed and gasping for breath, JJ remained straddled on all fours over Tomlinson, sweat, blood and drool running down his chin. Totally drained, he spat in Tomlinson's face and stood.

A sudden gut rending spasm of intolerable pain ripped up from his groin as Tomlinson drove his knee between JJ's legs. He collapsed in a fetal position clutching his smashed crotch. Tomlinson stumbled to his feet and snatched the pistol from the ground.

Breathing heavily and wiping the sweat and dirt from his eyes Tomlinson said, "Like I told you, JJ, we reap what we friggin sow. Now, reap this." He turned, pointed the gun at Jackson across the yard and fired two shots into the mountain man.

"Gaahh!" JJ cried out in a tormented wail, unable yet to speak, as he watched Bridger's body slump suspended by his arms.

Tomlinson scuffed over and kicked JJ in the stomach. "Now, get up and find those keys."

"You fucking bastard," JJ whispered and struggled to stand.

They shuffled through the spring grass but neither JJ nor Tomlinson could locate the lost keys. In the distance, JJ heard a dog barking. It sounded a lot like Gopher. Tomlinson stopped and looked up listening to the distant insistent barking.

JJ called out, "Gopher! Here boy!"

"Shut up and keep looking for the keys."

"You shot my dog. That's probably him out there and he's probably wounded.

"He doesn't sound wounded to me, and I don't give a damn anyway. Shut the hell up."

"Gopher!"

"Goddamn it!" Tomlinson yelled and fired the gun twice into the air making JJ jump. "I told you to shut the fuck up."

AT THE SOUND OF GUNFIRE and voices, McConnell crouched down behind a tree and drew his service revolver. Wide-eyed, Gustafson dropped next to him with his gun drawn.

"Can you get a signal on that cell phone? It would be nice to call in some backup."

"Rolf, you are my backup. And no, I can't get service out here. At least now, we know where we're going. My guess is that we've got both Volker and Tomlinson. Let's go."

The two officers moved from tree to tree down the game trail. The path wound up to the right. To their left two men, one with a gun, searched the ground for something. McConnell watched them from the cover of the woods. Clutching Gustafson's forearm he pointed to the man hanging between the trees.

"That's got to be Jackson," Gustafson whispered. "Looks like he's dead or wounded. Which one of those guys is Volker and which is Tomlinson?"

"I figure the younger one is Volker and the one with the gun is Tomlinson.

❧   ❧   ❧

TOMLINSON KICKED AT a stone in exasperation. "Screw it. We'll just go in the way you guys went in. I've got extra car keys inside. Come on, move it." He shoved JJ toward the rear of the cabin. "Climb on in there."

JJ dropped to all fours and crawled toward the opening in the foundation.

"Hold it! Sheriff's Department!"

Tomlinson whirled around. Two men stepped out of the timber with guns pointed at him.

"Get out of my way!" He pushed JJ away from the entrance and scrambled in himself. Pushing at the floorboards with his hands, he found the loose ones and climbed into the cabin. Once inside he crawled to the window keeping low to the floor.

One of the men outside yelled, "Down on the ground! Sheriff's Department."

He lifted his head and peered out the window. JJ had made it halfway to the timber. He saw him drop to his knees and lay down with arms and legs spread-eagled on the ground. One of the two cops approached him cautiously but quickly, crouching low to the ground covering both JJ and the cabin with his gun. The other one disappeared out of his line of sight in the direction of the mountain man.

His mind was racing. He pounded his fist against his head. This was it. The final showdown. All these years of successfully hiding out in Montana. All the money. It was all over. That damn bitch had screwed his life. He didn't stand a chance if he was captured. He couldn't let that happen. That's all there was to it. He looked out the window again. JJ was on his feet hands clasped on his head and being hustled back into the timber.

Now or never, Chip, he told himself. Getting to his feet, he smashed the glass out of the window with the gun, took aim and fired.

The deputy lurched forward as if he had tripped over his own feet. JJ turned toward him, then ducked and ran for the trees. The cop tried to lift himself from the ground, but Tomlinson drew a bead on him and dropped him dead. JJ had taken cover behind a large pine and was not moving.

"Rolf!" The other cop yelled.

Tomlinson smiled and spoke aloud to himself, "Too late, man. Rolfie's not getting up, and you're next."

As he expected, the officer ran around from the side toward his partner. He kept low with his gun drawn while looking back toward the cabin. Tomlinson waited for him to reach the downed man and as he was checking him, he stood at the window and took careful aim at the man's chest.

"Bye, bye!" he said. Grinning, he squeezed the trigger.

Nothing happened.

He had already unloaded all six shots. The gun was empty.

"Shit!" he yelled. The cop must have heard him and dropped behind his partner's body to shield himself, firing at the cabin.

Tomlinson ducked back from the window, but saw the officer race around to the side of the house. Tossing the useless pistol aside, he grabbed the sheriff's shotgun and checked to make sure it was loaded. He clicked the safety off and waited, all senses alert.

From below the cabin, he heard some movement. The cop was coming through the back of the cabin. He trained the shotgun at the opening in the floor and fired. The gun blast in the close confines of the cabin deafened him and he could not hear the scream from the man below. All he heard was a loud ringing in his ears. He sidestepped to the hole in the floor, gun at the ready. The shot had shredded the floorboards and ripped the hole even wider. Looking down he saw nothing but dirt. No body.

❧ ❧ ❧

THE PELLETS EMBEDDED IN HIS ARM FELT like a thousand burning coals. Nevertheless, McConnell was grateful he had not been any further under the cabin when that shotgun was fired. Things were not good. His arm was a bloody mess. Rolf was dead. Jackson was either dead or dying, and there was an armed killer in the cabin. He needed help. Charging across the yard, he ran to where JJ was still hiding behind the tree. He slumped down next to him.

"Jesus! Are you ok?" JJ asked staring at his shredded arm.

"Not exactly," McConnell replied. "I take it you're JJ Volker. Right?"

JJ nodded, still staring at his arm.

"I'm Detective McConnell. That's Tomlinson in the cabin, right?"

JJ nodded again. "He killed my sister-in-law and I think he killed my friend over there too. Thanks for untying him. Tomlinson tied . . . ."

McConnell cut him short. "I don't know if he's dead or not, but listen, I need your help. Can you use a gun?"

"Yeah."

"Then, here, take my gun. I'm going to get my partner's gun over there. Can you cover me?" He winced from the pain and the sweat rolling into his eyes.

"Yes, but . . . "

"Do it. Now." McConnell took a quick look around the tree and snaked his way to where Rolf's gun had dropped when he fell. He snatched the pistol and turned expecting any moment to hear a gunshot and feel it rip through his body. Crawling back, he saw JJ ready to fire if needed. The kid had guts. That was good. He was going to need them.

"Thanks, JJ. How are you doing? You alright?"

"Yeah, I am, but how are you?"

"I'll be okay. Here's what I need you to do. I'm going to go in the front door . . ."

"You can't, it's padlocked"

"Yeah, I saw that. But, I'm going to shoot the lock off and take Tomlinson. There's no back door, but there is a hole at the back of the cabin that he might try to escape from. I'm going to need you to get yourself back there. You can use some trees for cover. If you see him pop out the back, I want you to stop him. Can you do that?"

"Stop him? You mean kill him?"

"If you have to. Think you'll be able to do that?" McConnell looked intently into JJ's eyes. He was reassured to see JJ looking back with the same intensity.

"I have no problem with that at all."

"Okay, then. Get going. I'll wait till you're in position."

He watched as JJ circled his way around and behind the cabin. Once he had found a good location, JJ waved back at him.

Here goes nothing, McConnell thought to himself.

ALTHOUGH HIS EARS WERE still ringing, from outside the cabin he heard, "Chip Tomlinson! This is Detective McConnell of the sheriff's department."

He moved to the windowsill and peeked out. All he saw was the dead body of the officer in the yard. Detective McConnell had to be off to the side out of view from the window. But, he was close.

"You need to throw your gun into the yard and come out with your hands on your head. Both entrances are covered. There's nowhere for you to go. No one's going to hurt you, but it's time to give it up."

Tomlinson got as far as possible into the corner of the window to see if he could spot McConnell or any other cops in the yard. There were none that he could see. Hopefully, McConnell and the dead one out in the yard were the only two up here. He could not see JJ, but he was probably halfway down the mountain by now.

McConnell called out, "Either you come out, Chip, or we're coming in. What's it going to be?"

If he could get McConnell out into the yard, he could pick him off. On the other hand, if he could get him to come up around the back through the floor, it would be easy to shoot him as he popped his head up.

Tomlinson yelled out through the open window, "You can't come in the front, Detective. It's locked, and I don't have the key. If you want to come in, you'll have to come up through the back. Or step out into the yard where I can see you and we'll talk."

"That's not happening, Chip. Why don't you come out through the back? We don't need anyone else getting hurt."

Tomlinson positioned himself in the corner next to the window. He eased the shotgun barrel just beyond the sill, angled it to the left toward where the detective's voice was coming from and fired. The kickback of the gun threw his shoulder back into the window frame. There was no response from outside. Tomlinson cautiously stuck his head out of the window to see if his shot had hit its mark. It had not. The cop was moving quickly around to the front and taking aim at the door. Tomlinson realized with horror that he was going to shoot the lock off and charge through the front door any second, and when he did, the trip wire would be released. It would be all over for him and the detective. He had to get out and now. He dropped his gun and made a dash toward the hole at the back of the cabin as the padlock shattered into bits. He was not going to make it. He could hear the cop charging the front door, and then there was a massive explosion.

❧ ❧ ❧

JJ WATCHED FROM HIS SPOT at the rear side of the cabin as McConnell charged up the steps of the cabin and slammed into the door with his shoulder. As he did, the entire front of the cabin exploded outward raining chunks of wood and pieces of Detective McConnell across the yard. The concussion knocked JJ back from where he had been squatting behind the tree. The hideous sight of McConnell's shredded body made him gag.

Turning back, he had to shield himself from a windy blast of heat. A raging fire engulfed the gaping front half of the cabin. Huge curls of orange flames and oily pitch-black smoke swirled into the sky as they hungrily devoured the dry wood and years of built-up animal fat. Chemical bottles and ammunition exploded like a Fourth of July display. The deafening explosion and the roaring blaze temporarily blocked his sense of hearing, but a scream from the back of the cabin attracted his attention and he saw a burning column of rags running toward the stream. It was Tomlinson consumed in flame.

JJ picked up the pistol he had dropped and chased after Tomlinson who had thrown himself into the creek and was thrashing about in the shallow water. Training the service revolver on the writhing bundle of rags and blackened flesh JJ approached the edge of the water. Tomlinson rolled on his back and JJ gasped at the sickening mess. All but a few patches of his clothes were either burned or blown from his body. Every inch of him was charred. His hair was scorched off, and his face looked like a nightmarish skull from a horror movie. He was convulsing from shock and the icy creek water and his teeth chattered like the joke shop wind-up teeth JJ had as a child. His eyes stared up, white orbs bulging out from his hideous blackened head.

He pleaded with JJ. "Shoot me," he croaked. "Shoot me."

JJ pulled the hammer back on the revolver and pointed it at the center of the loathsome skull. He had hoped for this moment. Finally, he would make the killer pay for Kaitie's death. At last, he would keep his promise to Annie to avenge her sister. He would exact retribution for what Tomlinson had done to Bridger, Gopher and the dead officers. JJ's hand began to shake.

"Go ahead," Tomlinson rasped.

JJ's hand stopped shaking. He knelt next to the quivering body and put the gun's muzzle against Tomlinson's head. Tomlinson closed his eyes. "Open your eyes," JJ commanded.

Tomlinson's lashless lids fluttered open looking first at the gun barrel and then at JJ. JJ bent to within inches of his face and said in a whisper, "You go to hell." He pulled back on the pistol's hammer with his thumb, slowly uncocked the revolver and stood. Tomlinson started to cry.

For a few moments, he looked down at the quivering body, then turned and climbed the bank. In the distance, he heard Gopher's insistent bark as he trudged slowly toward the yard. The scene was a vision from hell. The cabin was fully ablaze with columns of flame roaring high into the sky. What was left of McConnell's mangled body lay in the middle of the yard surrounded by pieces of his legs and arms and smoldering chunks of wood. The deputy's dead body was stretched face down on the ground. To his left, Bridger lay in a heap, his hands still bound. JJ was going to need the rope for Tomlinson.

He walked to Bridger's limp body. McConnell had managed to unlash the rope that hung from the tree lowering the mountain man to the ground, but he had not had time to unbind Bridger's hands. JJ worked at the knot. Bridger's wrists were raw and bleeding where he had tried to twist loose while hanging. As the knot came free, Bridger released a quiet moan causing JJ to gasp and fall back.

"Holy shit! I thought you were dead." He rolled Bridger onto his back and saw that he was shot in the shoulder. There was no other bullet wound. Tomlinson must have missed with the second shot.

Bridger opened one eye and looked up with a weak smile. "JJ," he said in a cracked voice. "Glad to see you. Guess I passed out. Where's . . . ."

"Take it easy, Bridger. You're shot. I'll get back to you in a minute. I've got to get Tomlinson." JJ stood and gathered the rope looping it over his arm.

Bridger opened both eyes and looked anxiously around. "Where is he?"

"Don't worry. He's out of commission down by the creek. I'll be right back, and then I'll get you down to the hospital."

"Don't need no hospital. What I need is some water."

"I'll get you some water, but you're also going to a hospital, like it or not. You've got a bullet in one shoulder and I think your other shoulder might be dislocated from where you were hanging."

Bridger grunted and JJ headed down to the creek. Tomlinson was unconscious and panting in short gravelly breaths. JJ tied his hands with the rope and dragged him up the bank and into the yard. Bridger had managed to sit and was leaning against the tree taking in the confusing disaster in the yard.

"Appears I missed the party. What in the good lord's creation happened here?"

JJ threw the other end of the rope over the bar where Bridger had been hung and pulled Tomlinson so that his arms extended skyward. Then he tied the rope securely to the tree next to

Bridger. "It's a long story. I'll tell you on the way into town." Placing the pistol in Bridger's hand he said, "The man's near dead, but in case he does manage to try anything, use the gun on him. I'm going to get Spot and some water for you."

Before he headed up into the trees, JJ checked the deputy's body and located his keys, grateful that he did not have to search McConnell's clothing, and put them in his pocket. He made his way up to where Spot stood tied to the tree. He mounted his horse and rode down to where Bridger sat.

"Here's some water," he said, holding out a bottle from his saddlebag. Bridger tried to reach for it but with one shoulder shattered and the other dislocated he could not move his arms. JJ opened the bottle and held it to his parched lips. Bridger greedily drank the water finishing it off in a few gulps.

Bridger clenched his jaw as he adjusted his position to look at JJ. "I been hearin a dog barking while I was settin here. Is that your Gopher?"

"I think so. It sure sounds like him. Listen, I got the deputy's keys and I'm sure he's got a car not far from here. Do you think you can walk?"

"I reckon I can if you can help me stand. What about our friend here?" Bridger nodded at Tomlinson's unconscious body.

"I'll lash him to Spot and walk him down. The deputy over there is dead, and the other guy . . . well, there's nothing we can do for him, obviously.

I'll have the sheriff's office come up and get the bodies. Meanwhile I need to get you and Tomlinson to the hospital in Bozeman."

After loading Tomlinson's charred body onto the horse and helping Bridger to his feet, JJ and his haggard caravan headed down the game trail in the direction of the repeating dog barks.

Gopher spotted the trio before they saw him and his slow repetitive barking turned to a non-stop frenzy of excitement. When JJ let him out of the Explorer, he jumped all over his master licking him and whining sounds of dog happiness. JJ knelt and hugged Gopher. He inspected his hindquarters where he had been shot.

Tomlinson was gasping and shaking badly. After helping Bridger into the front seat, JJ took a blanket from the back of the SUV and laid it on the ground next to Spot. Untying him from the back of his horse, he let Tomlinson slide down onto the blanket and wrapped him in it. Tomlinson moaned quietly from his unconscious sleep as JJ loaded him into the back of the truck.

After checking that the pasture was fully fenced, JJ unsaddled Spot and turned him loose. "Enjoy yourself," he said rubbing his horse's nose. "I'll be back to get you soon."

He got into the truck and tried the radio, but got no signal. Bridger sat with his eyes closed in the passenger seat and JJ assumed he was already sleeping. Driving slowly to minimize the jarring of the pasture trail he drove through the gate and headed toward home.

Chapter 33

ANNIE POURED THE TWO men each another cup of coffee and cleared their breakfast plates from the table. "You look a lot better this morning, Bridger. How do you feel?"

Bridger grinned and patted his stomach with the hand hanging from the sling. "Annie, I tell you that breakfast was some, now. Except for having to be spoon-fed like a pup, I've got a full meat bag and had a good night's sleep. A coon can't ask for more. I'm obliged to the two of you."

Annie smiled back at him and piled the plates in the sink.

"So, JJ, go ahead. You were starting to tell me what happened with that worthless bone picker, Tomlinson. Start at the beginning after he shot me and I passed out."

JJ held the coffee mug to Bridger's mouth, and then took a sip from his own cup. He described the chaotic events of the other day – how the two officers showed up and the deputy got killed, about the explosion that blew Detective McConnell to bits and set the cabin ablaze and about Tomlinson running from the cabin on fire.

Bridger stopped him. "How come the explosion didn't tear Tomlinson up?"

"I think he must have been heading out the hole at the back of the cabin when it exploded. Only the front of the cabin was blown apart, but the deputy told me that the place was booby trapped at the door with explosives and gasoline. Tomlinson must have been hit with the gasoline when the place exploded. He came flying out the back on fire and jumped into the creek. The detective had me waiting back there to shoot him if he came out."

"So why didn't you? He sure as hell deserved it."

"I was going to. I went over to where he was lying and was ready to shoot. But, looking down at his pathetic burned body, I decided he wasn't worth it. I'd let him die in prison or from his injuries. Whichever came first. But, it wasn't up to me to finish him off. Looked to me like he'd pretty much done that all by himself."

Bridger nodded

"You were passed out in the truck when I drove down from the cabin. I radioed the sheriff's office and told them what had happened and to send someone up to get the bodies out of there. The sheriff and one of his deputies were waiting for us when I got to Deaconess Hospital. While I was helping you into the emergency room, they hauled Tomlinson out of the truck and rushed him into another room. I was waiting to hear how things were going with you and the deputy came out and talked to me. Turns out he and I went to high school together. He told me they were there to arrest Tomlinson for Kaitie's murder."

Bridger's bushy eyebrows lifted in interest.

"That's right. You're off the hook. Turns out, they went to investigate him at his house because of some evidence they had found in her apartment and at the scene of Kaitie's death. He wasn't there, but his wife was. She was real worked up about him. She suspected he was having an affair. She started spilling the beans on him about his poaching and, get this, she told them he killed his grandfather years ago back in Nebraska!"

Bridger's jaw dropped. "You don't say."

"That's right. They told her he might be a suspect in a murder here and she showed them a pile of bloody clothes he wore the day Kaitie was murdered. She thought they were bloody from some animal, but they matched the blood to Kaitie's. They also matched a print left at the murder scene to his hunting boots."

Bridger exhaled and said, "Whew. I'll be damned."

JJ took another gulp of coffee, nodded and continued. "I told the deputy about finding Kaitie's pen and Colton Stollar's shotgun up at Tomlinson's place, and about the .270 bullet slug you found where Stollar fell. I also told him about your theory that he might have been shot. He told me that they had found Tomlinson's rifle at the cabin and it was a .270 Winchester. He said they would do a ballistics test to see if the slug matched the rifle. If it does, that would be another murder they would pin him with."

Bridger shook his head. "I guess they've got him dead to rights."

JJ smiled. "You're right about that. They've got him dead alright. While I was talking to the deputy, they called him back to Tomlinson's room. He was dying. About a half hour later the deputy came out and told me that just before he died he confessed to Kaitie's murder and admitted he'd tried to frame you. Said he said he wanted to get right with God because I hadn't shot him or something. Can you believe that?"

Bridger's body slumped in relief. JJ could not be sure but he thought he saw a tear in the corner of the mountain man's bushy eye and a tremble to his lip.

After a moment of composing himself Bridger said, "JJ, I'm much obliged for all you've done and for getting me down off that mountain. And I'm also obliged for you getting me out of that hospital. That weren't my kind of place. I'll be out of your hair here soon as these sticks of mine get useful again. How about another gulp of that shinin coffee?"

JJ held the cup to Bridger's lips and let him drink.

"We told you, Bridger, you aren't a problem. You are welcome to stay here as long as you want. We enjoy having you. Dad's thrilled you're here. He is even talking about going along with us hunting this fall. He's coming over again tonight to see you."

JJ crossed the kitchen and put his arm around Annie and she slid hers around him. "Annie and I were talking last night. We don't have any kids and it doesn't look like we ever will. We could sure use some help around here. That back room you are sleeping in doesn't get any use, and if you'd be willing, we'd like to have you stay on and help us run this place. We couldn't pay you anything, but you'd have a good bed and a full . . . meat bag every night."

Bridger looked at Annie who smiled and nodded back at him, "JJ's right. We'd like you to stay."

Bridger turned his head and looked out the window into the beautiful blue Montana morning. The orange barked cottonwood trees along the babbling creek were beginning to bloom. Perched atop the corral fence two red-winged blackbirds trilled their melodious songs to each other. Far above the ranch, a bald eagle glided in wide circles. Bridger cleared his throat and croaked out a wobbly, "Wagh!"

E N D

Glossary of Mountain Man Phrases Used in this Book

BONE PICKER—A despised human scavenger who hunted for, and sold, the bones of dead animals, mostly buffalo.

FEAST CAKES—Pancakes

GET YER BRISTLES UP, TO—To get angry.

GONE BEAVER—Said of someone who has been dead some time. He's about to go

GO UNDER (TO): To die or be killed, usually the latter.

HAWK—Short for "Tomahawk

HELLO THE CAMP—A traditional greeting given before entering any strange camp.

HIDE HUNTER—A low breed of man who killed buffalo for the hides only. Usually despised by all who came into contact with him.

JERKY—Dried meat made by cutting meat into strips about one inch wide, 1/4 inch thick, and as long as possible.

MEAT BAG—The human stomach

MEDICINE BAG—The small bag, used to carry the medicine of the Native American.

OL' COON—A friendly nickname used between mountain men. OL' HOSS—See "Ol' Coon".

ON HIS OWN HOOK, HE IS—A free trapper.

PALAVER—Talk

POSSIBLES BAG—The leather bag in which the mountain man carried his possibles— everything from his pipe and tobacco to his patches and balls.

RENDEZVOUS—An annual late summer event that took place during the height of the fur trade where trappers and Native Americans would gather to swap furs and stories over a period of days celebrating the rough but fulfilling life they led. Many enthusiasts stage re-enactments of the mountain man rendezvous around the country each summer.

SHINING—Splendid. To shine means to be extra good at something,

SHINING MOUNTAINS—An early Native American name for the Rocky Mountains.

SOME— Remarkable, admirable. "That Jed was some, now. He had the ha'r of the b'ar in him. Wagh!"

SKUNK BEAR—Blackfeet term for wolverine.

SPIRIT GUIDE—Physical or non-physical entities, often an animal, believed to protect and provide guidance to an individual, particularly prominent in Native American belief systems.

WAGH—An exclamation, used by both Mountain Men and Native Americans, usually denoting admiration or surprise. This grunt-like sound is supposed to resemble that made by a bear when mildly surprised.

THE WAY THE STICK FLOATS—To know which way the stick floats was to know what's up, what's what. The expression came from the use of a float stick attached to a beaver trap to indicate where the trap was if the beaver swam away with it. Its meaning was extended to suggest knowing the ways of the mountain. From this comes the expression, "That's the way my stick floats," meaning, "That's the way I feel about it."

WOLFISH, I'M—I am hungry.

About Jeremy Soldevilla

After a career as a Boston publisher, Jeremy Soldevilla moved to Montana with his wife and dogs. He and his wife owned and operated a bed and breakfast in Bozeman, where between making beds and breakfasts, skiing and fishing, he began writing novels. He also returned to his roots and founded Christopher Matthews Publishing and its sister young adult imprint, Soul Fire Press.

ALSO BY JEREMY SOLDEVILLA

THIEF CREEK

When Ohio newlyweds Doctor Steve and gorgeous, athletic Heather check into the remote Thief Creek B&B in the Rocky Mountains of Montana, they're ready to begin their dream honeymoon of peace, relaxation, romance, and no stress. With the Prestons—rugged-faced, gray pony-tailed Mike and nerves-of-steel nurse Annie — as the perfect hosts coupled with an awe-inspiring backdrop featuring marvelous mountain air and even a bubbling warm outdoor whirlpool bath, that dream seems to have come true. But wait. Something sinister is lurking in the wilderness beyond the inn.

Four escaped convicts, the Toomey brothers, are on the lam, armed, and very dangerous. A shooting and a suspense-filled accident have the three older brothers desperately trying to save the life of their youngest brother, Tommy. Jesse James, the one-eared, heartless, cruel leader of the group bullies his cold-blooded murdering, harelip brother Butch, and his easily manipulated brother JP through a whirlwind journey that finally ends up at the Thief Creek Inn. As the Inn becomes the hideaway for the four brothers, the lives of the innkeepers and their two young guests are changed forever.

From the beginning action involving Ed Loomis at the Lewis and Clark Gas-N-Go, to the final scenes at the Inn, author Soldevilla keeps readers on the edge of their seats and completely involved with the book's twisting-turning plot and well-developed characters — both the good ones and the bad.

"I spent the last two evenings hanging on tight in Thief Creek. *The pace was fast and fantastic, the action non-stop, and the characters were convincing -- likable where they were meant to be and despicable when they weren't. Well done!" —A. Haar*

Thief Creek Sample

At first glance, Ed was glad to see customers. He liked to chat with folks; find out where they were from and what they were doing off the beaten track in Lame Elk. In the Fall it was usually hunters. In the Summer it might be campers or tourists winding their way back to Oregon or Seattle after visiting Glacier Park. Winter was just dead. If it wasn't for his old cronies stopping in to play cards in the long Winter afternoons, they might just as well close up the store. Except then no one would have any place to get gas. This time of year, it would likely be fishermen, which would mean bait sales and maybe fishing licenses. With nothing better to do, he liked to play a game with himself, trying to figure out where people were from and what they were doing in his little town.

The closest of the four men stood with his back to the counter, searching through the bags of snacks on the end cap in front of him. The other three wandered around further up in the store, loading up with various items. *Take your time boys. We could use the sales.*

"Everything on that shelf there is 25% off," he said to the man's back.

The fellow turned his head and grunted, "What?"

Ed raised his voice. "I said everything on that shelf is twenty-five percent off. Nothing wrong with it, we're just trying to move the merchandise."

"Yeah, I can see the sign," the man grumbled, then turned back.

Just trying to help. No need to get snippy. Ed pushed his glasses up on his nose and squinted across the aisle, trying to get a closer look at the man. I'll be damned, that ol' boy's missing an ear. Sure enough, there was a gnarled stump where his left ear should have been. On closer inspection, the side of the man's face that he could see had a nasty scar running the length of his cheek from the ear stub to his chin. Bear attack? Car accident? *Dang, that had to have been a rough one, whatever it was. Wonder what his story is.*

His curiosity aroused, Ed scrunched his face and surveyed the three other men in the store. The fellow coming from the refrigerator section was huge. Maybe six foot four with tattoos covering both his arms. He had picked up two cases of Bud Lite, and balanced them with one hand while he grabbed a family size bag of Doritos and stuck it between his teeth. There was something not right about his face. Squinting for a better look, Ed noticed an odd shape to the man's mouth. His lip was split clear up to his nose, exposing his top three teeth. A harelip. That's what they call that. He recalled that the Fisher boy was born with one of them.

The Doritos bag behind the one the huge guy had chosen fell to the floor. Rather than pick it up, he kicked it out of his way. The old man opened his mouth to tell the big lug to pick it up, but on second thought, said nothing.

A prickly feeling began to crawl up the back of Ed's neck. He didn't like the looks of these two. But, heck, they were buying a lot of stuff, and Lord knows the store could use the money. Still, it paid to be on your toes. Out in the boonies, near as they were to the rez, it wasn't unusual to get some rough trade even at this hour of the morning. After being held up five times in the past two years he tended to be hypersensitive to suspicious looking characters like these. He fingered the butt of the revolver he kept on a shelf under the counter below the register. *They better not mess with me.*

To his right, a third man with a rusty red mullet strolled down the snack aisle. He wore an orange tee shirt, black jeans and scuffed along in unlaced army boots. He loaded up a plastic shopping basket with two boxes of doughnuts, every bag of beef jerky, and two cans of beef stew. "Tommy!" he yelled to the one at the front of the store.

Ed shifted his attention to the boy by the door. The kid leaned against the ATM machine, leafing through a Hustler magazine. He was decidedly younger than the other three. He had freckles, big ears and a shock of unruly red hair with a cowlick poking up from the middle of his head. The boy looked to be about nineteen and reminded the clerk of Alfred E. Neuman from Mad Magazine.

"You want some of them vi-eenna sausages?" the Mullet called across the store. Tommy appeared too engrossed in the magazine to look up. "Tommy, you dumbass. Do you want these?" He held up the little can and wiggled it.

"Hell, yeah," the boy responded. "Grab me some mustard too, JP."

The clerk observed them closely, and stored their descriptions in his head in case he'd need to file a police report later. Probably no need, but he'd learned his lesson in the past. The kid was Tommy. The Mullet was JP. Tommy. JP. Ed repeated the names in his head, burning them into his memory. On closer inspection he determined that the four men were probably brothers. They all had similar red hair, tiny pig eyes, pock-marked faces and a shared ugliness that didn't speak well for their parents.

The earless one strolled to the counter. He was one ugly looking jasper. His face looked like he'd lost an acid fight. Ed judged him to be a boxer who had taken more falls than he'd won. Maybe that explained the missing ear. His blob of a nose had been broken more than once, and he had beady eyes just like the others. Upon closer inspection, Ed was surprised to note that the color of the man's eyes were grey -- like those of a wolf. He'd never seen grey eyes in a human before. They were cold and blank. Lifeless. A bleak chill ran down his spine.

The skin around the man's eyes was puffy, as were his cheeks which were rosy with broken blood vessels. The most shocking thing about him, though, was the gnarled stump on the side of his head where his ear had once been. A six inch scar carved its way from his missing ear to just above his chin. As he approached, a sharp tang stung the clerk's nostrils. It wasn't just the man's pungent body odor. It smelled like evil.

He placed two beefy hands on the counter and gave Ed a broad grin. There was a gap in his smile where two side teeth were missing.

Ed took a step back. He cleared his throat and quickly composed himself. "Good morning. Can I help you?" He noticed a slight squeak in his voice.

"You most certainly can," the man said with false amiability. His voice was deep and gravelly. It reminded the clerk of the low growl of a grizzly bear, protecting her cubs like the one that he had run across while hunting up in the Beartooths last Fall. As frightening as that had been, he somehow felt more threatened by the fellow standing in front of him now. "Gimme a carton of Marlboros and four bottles of Jack Daniels."

The two other men drew up behind the earless one and set their groceries on the counter. The one called JP left the basket on the counter and strolled to the front door where he leaned against the magazine rack, folded his arms, and peered out onto the parking lot as if he was looking for something. Turning his attention back to Earless and Tattoo, Ed saw they both were looking intently at him. Once again, the hair on the back of his neck came to attention.

His hands trembled slightly as he put the cigarettes and the bottles of liquor next to the basket. He punched the prices of each item into the cash register, bagging them as he did. *Might be needing that gun after all,* he thought, and tried to calculate how long it would take him to pull on these boys if he had to.

The younger one, Tommy, pulled a couple of the cheesier girlie magazines from the rack and brought them to the counter. "Get these too, Jesse." He grinned at the earless one. *Jesse. Jesse -- earless.* Ed's brain stored some more data. *Jesse, Tommy, JP and the Harelip.* He repeated the names several times in his head. Leering like that, Tommy was the spitting image of Alfred E. Neuman. The clerk tried unsuccessfully to stifle a nervous chuckle.

"What's so funny? You laughing at me?" The tattooed man with the harelip, squinted at him with one pig eye, speaking with that nasally way harelips talk.

"Nothing," said Ed, shifting his gaze away from the boy and back to the groceries. "I was just thinking with all that beef jerky and the

Jack Daniels and stuff, you boys are going to have an interesting day. You going fishing, or camping or something? We got bait and licenses if you need 'em."

"That's none of your frickin business." The threatening tone of the harelip's statement lost some of its power and came out almost comically due to his garbled speech impediment. Once again Ed found himself stifling a giggle.

The harelip glared at him and one eye twitched. Ed bit his lip.

"Whoa, take it easy, Butch," said Jesse, putting a calming hand on Harelip's shoulder. "The man didn't mean no harm. Did you, old man?"

Butch. Butch—harelip. Tommy, JP, Jesse, Butch. "Course not. Sorry. I was just making an observation, that's all. Around here fishing and hunting is about all there is to do." Ed managed a bit of a smile. "Well, if that's it, I'll ring you up." He looked at the screen on his register and added, "And, looks like you boys filled up at pump number four, right? Let's see..." he tapped the total button and the register drawer popped open with a ding. "The damage comes to one hundred and ninety-three dollars and eighty-seven cents."

From his position by the door JP called, "Blue light just went by."

Tommy and Butch swiveled toward the front, but Jesse kept his gaze on the clerk. Even though he felt a weakness in his old knees, Ed remained focused on Jesse, and once again touched his index finger to the metal handle of his pistol.

Tommy turned with a wild-eyed look to his brother and said, "Shit, Jesse."

Still looking at Jesse, Ed said, "Will that be check or credit card? We still take cash too."

Jesse turned and patted his rear pocket. "I seem to have forgotten my wallet. Butch, you want to pay the man?"

Harelip smirked. "Sure, but I need my change first."

Ed could hear and feel each beat of his heart, pounding in his ear. His fingers inched across the pistol's handle. "Your change? Excuse me?"

With a quick movement, Butch drew a gun out of his waistband. "I'll take what you have in the register, old man."

The clerk's voice remained steady. He'd been here before. He inched his hand away from the pistol and slowly placed both hands palms down on the counter. "Now listen, son. You don't want to do this."

Jesse spoke up. "You're mistaken, old man. We do want to do this. And trust me, my brother is not a man you want to disappoint. Now, empty the till into a bag and hurry up."

Butch pulled back the hammer on his gun and sneered. "Yeah, don't disappoint me."

"Where's that blue light, JP?" Jesse called out.

"Long gone. Probably already at the donut shop pounding down his second chocolate covered." JP chuckled at his own joke so hard he snorted.

"Look, boys," said Ed with a slight quiver in his voice now. "I got less than a hundred bucks in the register. I don't want no trouble and neither do you. So why don't you just leave the groceries, walk out, keep the gas, no charge, and I'll forget you were here."

Jesse reached across the counter and grabbed the clerk by the shirtfront. His breath was as evil as his body odor. "You don't understand. You see, we need these things and we have no money because we have just escaped from Deer Lodge where Butch here was doing life for murdering a family in Livingston and another fellow over in Three Forks. Now, believe me when I tell you, he has no problem killing you right now. I would prefer he didn't, because it might attract the sheriff who just drove by. But," Jesse's voice took on an icy tone and his grey eyes narrowed, "if you don't put the money in that bag right goddam now, I'll kill you myself."

A bead of sweat ran down the clerk's face and his bladder let go, staining the front of his green work pants. His voice shook and his breath came hard. "Alright. Here --." With Jesse's hand still gripping the front of his shirt and his heart pounding, he took the few bills from the register and shoved them in the bag of groceries.

"Tommy. Butch." said Jesse, "Grab the groceries and let's go."

The boy scooped up the two bags. Butch tucked the pistol back in his belt and picked up the cases of beer, and they headed to the door.

Jesse released the clerk and said, "Do you have a cell phone?"

"No, sir."

"Good. We took the liberty of cutting your phone line before we came in. So, don't think about calling the sheriff. But I'm afraid I'm going to have to tie you up so we have enough time to put some space between us. I guess I should have had you charge us for this roll of duct tape too." He shook the roll of grey tape at the clerk and started to come around the counter.

As soon as Jesse moved in front of the fly-specked cabinet displaying greasy hot dogs, taquitos and fried gizzards, Ed drew his pistol and fired at Butch, the one with the gun. The explosion shook the windows of the convenience store and Jesse dropped to his knees. The shot missed Butch and struck the boy, Tommy, in the back. He screamed and lurched forward, dropping the groceries. Vienna Sausage and beef stew cans clattered across the checkerboard linoleum.

Butch let out a hellish roar that turned Ed's blood to ice water. "You son of a bitch," cried Butch. He dropped the cases of beer, and in one move, pulled his gun, turned and fired at Ed. The impact of the bullet knocked the old man back against the display rack behind him. Packs of cigarettes cascaded down on top of his head. *What the hell?* He looked disbelievingly at the opening in his chest. Thick dark blood dribbled down his shirt front. *Dang, look at that hole. I'm shot. But it don't even hurt. Those sonsabitches. Those goddam sonsabitches.*

"Tommy!" called Jesse as he dashed to the boy's side.

Still wondering about his lack of pain, Ed looked up and saw JP take in what was happening, then run to the car and start the engine. He reached across and opened the passenger door, then pushed the seat back forward. "Come on," he yelled. "We gotta get the hell out of here."

Ed reached for the cleaning cloth and pressed it to his wound. The scene playing out before him swam dreamily as if he were watching it on a movie screen. Butch and Jesse caught Tommy by the armpits, dragged him outside and stuffed him into the back seat of the car. Butch got in the rear with him while Jesse jumped in front.

Gotta stop them. Ed's adrenaline pumped through his system like a jackhammer and pushed him from behind the counter. He began to be more aware of a deep pain rising from within him. His breath was harder to draw. With his gun in one hand and the other clasping the bloody cloth to his chest, he zigzagged to the front of the store. It felt as if he moved in hazy slow motion, almost like it wasn't even his body. His eyes stayed focused on the punks, but everything in his peripheral vision was a blur.

He lurched against a shelf and candy bars and packs of donuts tumbled to the floor. His vision went dark and he had to shake his head to get his sight back. He reached the door and stumbled outside as the red Mustang peeled out of the parking lot. *Mustang*, he stored in his brain. The pistol felt as if it weighed a hundred pounds as he tried to raise it and fire. Before he could get a shot off, a sharp hitch stabbed his chest, and he caught a last breath. Ed Loomis tumbled dead against the bundles of firewood for sale and collapsed to the ground. As he hit the sidewalk, the pistol fired and ricocheted off the pavement, striking the bottom of the retreating car.

The dirt and gravel thrown up by the car's rear tires settled over the old clerk's prone body like a dusty shroud.